CRITICAL ACCLAIM FOR
IN THE DRIFT...

"This episodic tale of life, war and survival in post-meltdown Pennsylvania builds a potent new myth from the grim reality of radioactive waste. Swanwick's clean, strong prose makes the story compulsively readable."

— *George R.R. Martin*

"A powerful and affecting novel...chilling, believable and uncomfortably close to home."

— Baltimore *Evening Sun*

"Swanwick paints a persuasive portrait of a people adapting to disaster...a very readable book ...worth your attention."

— *Analog*

"Swanwick's book has depth and realism, excellent characterization, and scientific and sociological credibility...extremely well done, and well worth reading."

— *Fantasy Review*

"Intriguing and well-written."

— *Publishers Weekly*

IN THE DRIFT

MICHAEL SWANWICK

ACE SCIENCE FICTION BOOKS
NEW YORK

"Mummer Kiss" first appeared, in a shorter version, in *Universe 11,* copyright © 1981 by Terry Carr.

"Marrow Death" first appeared in *Isaac Asimov's Science Fiction Magazine,* the Mid-December issue, copyright © 1984 by Davis Publications, Inc.

In the Drift as a completed novel was first published as an Ace Science Fiction original edition. The first printing was an Ace Science Fiction Special, edited by Terry Carr.

IN THE DRIFT

An Ace Science Fiction Book / published by arrangement with
the author

PRINTING HISTORY
Ace Science Fiction edition / February 1985
Second printing / February 1987

ISBN: 0-441-37072-1

Ace Science Fiction Books are published by The Berkley Publishing Group,
200 Madison Avenue, New York, New York 10016.
PRINTED IN THE UNITED STATES OF AMERICA

The author would like to thank Gardner Dozois, without whose help and encouragement this book and more besides would not be, and also Jack Dann, the Philford Phafia, Ellen Datlow, Terry Carr, and (with a certain overemphatic) Virginia Kidd, all of whom gave advice, help and the occasional push, as needed. You are as strange and motley a crew of midwives as this world has ever seen.

for Marianne:
my oceans, my Cat

"There will always be survivors."
— Robert A. Heinlein

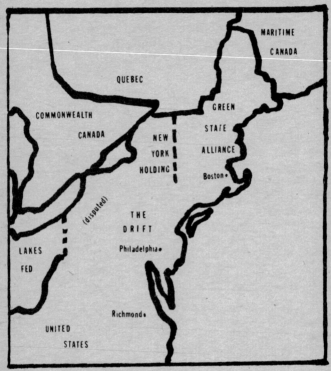

MARITIME
CANADA

QUEBEC

COMMONWEALTH
CANADA

GREEN
STATE
ALLIANCE

NEW
YORK
HOLDING

Boston •

(disputed)

THE
DRIFT

Philadelphia •

LAKES
FED

Richmond •

UNITED
STATES

mcporter

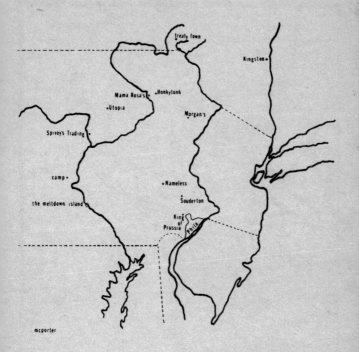

treaty town

Kingston•

Mama Rosa's   •Honkytonk

•Utopia   Morgan's•

Spivey's Trading•

camp•   •Nameless

the meltdown island•   Souderton•

                    King
                    of   Phila
                   Prussia

mcporter

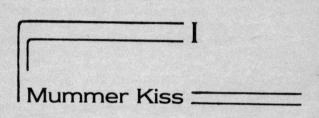

Mummer Kiss

Keith Piotrowicz was in the Italian Market when he saw the Janus monster go by. It was the day before Mummers Eve, and Ninth Street was crammed with shoppers, three jostling streams of people coursing between the four lines of stalls.

The patrol that had bagged the monster was delivering its corpse to Mummer Hall. They had lashed their trophy to two long poles that crossed midway up its back; hoisted more or less upright, it dipped and bobbed just above the heads of the marketers.

Hucksters turned from vegetable stands or from warming their hands at trash-barrel fires to gawk. Children scooped rotted potatoes and blackened lettuce leaves from the filthy street, and flung them at the monster, jeering and whooping. The Mummers responded with grins and swaggering walks. Their white berets set at jaunty angles, they swapped wisecracks with the crowd, jerking the poles to send the monster swooping down at those who flinched away.

There were three small holes in the monster's shirt, where laser fire had fused charred cloth to black, cauterized wounds. A swirl of blisters curved across one cheek, the result of a near-hit. The monster looked to be about seven years old.

Keith stared at the wide head with its doubled face. The two mouths were small and puffy, almost petulant. He wondered what words the creature had spoken out of those mouths, what madness or divine self-contradiction. Then the corpse was yanked away, and he shivered involuntarily.

Beside him, an old woman in black crossed herself, then made the sign of the horns to ward off mutation.

The street buzzed with rumor and speculation. "Somebody said they caught it lurking around the docks," a vender told Keith. He leaned over a pungent tray of onions to be heard. "Living off of garbage and dead fish."

Down the street, the patrol leader broke into a spontaneous Mummer strut, prancing back and forth before the corpse. Somebody hit the thing with a stick and was shoved back.

"Couldn't be," Keith said. "There's all of Philadelphia between the docks and the Drift."

"It's what I heard." The huckster straightened, unwilling to voice their shared suspicion that the monster had been born in Philadelphia and raised in isolation by parents who were willing to circumvent the genetics law. Some things cannot be spoken. He threw back his head and chanted, "Yes, yes, *yes!* Onions and beets! *Fresh—*"

Keith moved on. He edged past shoppers with patchcloth bags filled with loose purchases, and bottles and jugs to be refilled with molasses, vinegar, or wine. Three blocks on, he was pushing past the tanks of aquacultured perch and bass that lined Gambiosi's Meats. They sold cheap but not well, due to the common fear that they might have come out of the Schuylkill or the Delaware.

One of Gambiosi's sons was working the sidewalk, weighing out fish and wrapping them in newspaper. Keith caught his eye. "Your old man around, Tony?"

"He's inside. You see the monster?" Tony grinned, his thin young face openly wistful. "Man, I wish *I'd* been in on the kill." He held up two hands in imitation of a machine pistol, and made ratatat gestures, half crouching.

"Thanks," Keith said. "They used lasers." He pushed into the store.

The shop's interior was dim, with dressed poultry and rabbits laid out on parsimonious layers of ice within display counters that were shoved together like an elaborate and uncompleted puzzle. These were meats that could be raised within city limits, and priced so that most people could afford them at least once a week. From strings on the rafters overhead hung imported Wisconsin cheeses, and meats that only the rich could afford: smoked hams from Virginia, sausages and salamis from Maine in the Greenstate Alliance, the farther away the costlier.

Gambiosi was talking to a customer, holding up a skinned rabbit carcass. It looked preposterously naked and scrawny against his prosperous bulk. "Is it *clean,* you ask?" He hoisted it higher. "This little fellow was raised by my brother-in-law not two blocks from here."

"Mr. Gambiosi?"

"Wait out back, kid." Gambiosi jerked his head to the rear. "Now unless you want something with more meat on it..."

Keith passed through a doorless frame into the dark interior. It was warm and pleasantly smelly there. Crates of live poultry were stacked against the walls, the source of a constant rustling and clucking. There was an occasional pink gleam of frightened rabbit eyes. After a few minutes, Gambiosi joined him.

"Yeah?"

Pulling an envelope from within his jacket, Keith said, "My block organizer sent over the attendance roster for the parade—names and times—for your approval."

Gambiosi leafed through the papers, not really looking at them. "You're Petro-vich, right?" He put the accent on the first syllable, rather than the second, where it belonged. "I seen you around. How old are you, kid?"

Keith shifted uncomfortably, unsure as to what was to come. "Twenty-one."

"Twenty-one." Gambiosi nodded to himself. "And you're still a weekender, right? Now my son Tony—you saw him outside—he's only seventeen, and already he's working patrol, twice a week. He's a dunce, too."

"I wouldn't—"

"A dunce! I'm his father, you think I don't know? But Tony, he's gonna get somewhere. He'll be marching in the parade someday. And you know why? Hah?"

"No, sir," Keith mumbled.

"Because he's got ambition, that's why. I couldn't give him brains, but I *could* give him *that*. What do you think of the monster that just went by?"

The question took Keith by surprise. He blurted out the first thing that came to mind. "I'm surprised it made it all the way to the docks."

Gambiosi grunted. "Easy. It was born in town. Its parents were jerks—thought they could raise it locked in a backroom somewhere. Then, when they finally wised up, they just turned it loose. Now what do you think of people like that, hey? What were they thinking when they didn't turn the baby over to the hospital?"

"I—I guess they just weren't thinking."

"Bingo," Gambiosi said. "They weren't thinking. Year after year, they just weren't thinking. Just like you, Petro-vich."

Small, piglike eyes stared at Keith. He dropped his head, stared at his shoes.

"I see a lot of young people like you, kid. My grandfather woulda called you a day-tripper—you know what that means? That means you do just enough to get along, and no more. With a little bit of hustle, you coulda gotten on the patrols, too. But here you are, still running weekend errands. Acting like if you leave life alone, it'll do the same for you. See that?"

Keith kept his eyes lowered, said nothing. After a minute, Gambiosi said disgustedly, "Beat it. Take the rest of the day off."

"Thanks," Keith muttered. "I'll tell my organizer."

"Don't be a cream puff—just take off. And listen, kid— *think* about our little talk, hey? You ain't no dummy, and the Mummers can use every good man we can get."

Back on the street, Keith found himself angrily running through the arguments he could have made, but hadn't. Arguments he knew better than to voice: Why should I spend my life clawing to the top of a garbage heap? Why should I *want* to kill children? If I have to play your stupid games, at least I don't have to pretend to enjoy them.

But it bothered him that Gambiosi knew that the Janus monster could not have come out of the Drift, that he was so casual about that fact. Keith had always assumed that those in power acted the way they did out of stupidity or ignorance. It was troubling to realize that it was he, himself, who never looked beyond the obvious, never voiced those dangerous truths that everyone knew but never admitted.

That night he dreamed of the two-faced child. It lectured him on the reasons it had had to die, one mouth interrupting the other to clarify a point, sometimes both mouths speaking in unison. The arguments were old and tired, and Keith had heard them all before.

Mummers Eve dawned bright and clear, with a cold north wind blowing out of the Drift. Keith eased the tanker-truck through the blockade, his nucleopore mask hanging loosely around his neck. Jimmy Bowles dozed lightly in the seat beside him, dark face at ease.

The guard waved his clipboard overhead. Keith nodded, fed the engine more alcohol, shifted gears. With a low growl, the truck surged forward. The guard, stationhouse, and red-and-white signs marked DRIFT with radiation logos went bounce, bounce and were gone from the rearview mirror.

"Hey!" Keith jabbed his co-worker's shoulder. "Get out that map and tell me where we're supposed to be going."

Bowles snorted, and his eyes jerked open. He fumbled out a map, unfolded it across two-thirds of the cab, and said: "Out past King of Prussia. You've been that way before, right?" The truck jolted over untended highway.

"Yeah."

"Then don't wake me up again till we get there."

They back-ended the truck to the edge of a short cliff, a drop of perhaps ten feet, and, donning protective garb, climbed out. A glance about showed no way anything larger than a chipmunk could sneak up on them. Bowles slammed the cab's shotgun back into the clips under the dash. Every year or so, a crew was lost to the Drift, but so far neither he nor Keith had ever had occasion to use the gun.

Keith undogged the hose and pulled it loose while Bowles took a wrench and started to mate the connectors. He stood near the lip of the cliff, feet wide, bracing himself. A century-old division of tract houses lay below, silent among small patches of snow. Gently rolling hills slowly rose to the horizon, covered with a black stubble of stunted, sometimes twisted, trees.

Bowles cursed as the cold hindered his efforts to open the master valve.

The hose was thick and filled Keith's gloved hands; together they barely circled it. There was a sharp clank as the valve unfroze under Bowles' wrench. The hose throbbed and moved. Keith staggered and quickly recovered as milky white industrial waste spurted from the nozzle.

The liquid flew out in a long shallow arc to the frozen ground. It flowed sluggishly, covering sere brown grasses in an ever-widening puddle. Yellowish crystals formed, then were partially redissolved as new liquid overran them. They were suppose to find a new site each time out; it was usually easiest to re-use the old dumps.

The land was bleak and dreary. It depressed Keith, left him feeling dull and nihilistic. He remembered stories told of how sometimes the toxic chemical wastes from one dumping would combine with those from previous dumps, and strange alchemical interactions would take place. The ground would burst into flames or weird orange worms crawl out of the earth. There was a site in upper Bucks County he had seen where the ground actually *crawled,* boiling and bubbling year round.

Burst into flames, he thought at the ground. But nothing happened. The last lucid drops of waste fell from the hose. He shook it, then started to reel it back up.

Back in the cab, Bowles had pulled down his cleansuit's orange hood, and slipped off his nucleopore before Keith could get the air-recycler going. Like most oldtimers, Bowles didn't wear his mask much, didn't believe that something he couldn't smell, taste, feel, or see could possibly harm him. Taking his turn at the wheel, Bowles eased the tanker onto the highway.

"Looking forward to the parade, hey boy?" he asked.

"I guess. Hey, watch the road." The cab lurched as they ran full tilt over a mudslide that had obliterated twenty yards of roadway. Bowles cackled.

Bowles was the only black on Quaker City Industrial Disposal's payroll. Only politics could have gotten him the job. But Bowles marched with a second-rate North Philly string band, and even a black man could swing a good job with *that* kind of pull. "Don't start talking like my maiden aunt," he said. "You see any traffic out here?"

"Yeah, well. I'd still feel better if . . ." Bowles swung the truck through a figure S, grazing both sides of the road, and Keith shut up.

They roared past the ruins of a bank. The wind kicked up a white spume of powder from a mound of asbestos tailings that had been dumped in its parking lot.

"There's some nice land out back, away from the dump sites," Bowles said reflectively. "If I was young like you, I'd take over an old farmhouse, do me a little homesteading. You don't really believe it's dangerous out here, do you, son?"

I've heard this rap before, Keith thought. That was the trouble with Philadelphia—it was all Irish and Italian. So of course the Mick dispatcher always puts the nigger and the polack together. Gives you the chance to learn how tired you can get of one man.

"You set up a farm out here, and your balls'll mutate into green fungus," he said, instantly hating himself for the words, for playing down to Bowles' level.

Bowles laughed, revealing a meager scattering of eroded yellow teeth. He swerved to avoid the trunk of a mutated tree that crawled along the ground like a vine, intruding onto the highway. "Then you should be trying to get somewhere with the Mummers. I bet you could, if you showed a little hustle."

"Funny," Keith said. "Gambiosi said almost the same thing."

"*Gambiosi?* No shit. What'd you say to that?"

"There wasn't much I *could* say."

Bowles hit his forehead with a callused palm, stared incredulously. "I can't *believe* you, brother man! That was a signal—a hint. The Man was telling you he had his eye on you. All you had to do was speak up, and he'd have given you a promotion on the spot, son. On the spot."

If Keith pointed out that he didn't want to rise within the Mummers, Bowles would only sneer and lecture him on ambition; it had happened before. Instead, he said, "I don't have the money for costumes, and I don't want to wear feathers. Anyway, I'm not interested in politics."

Keith's father had been in the Mummers, had gotten as far as bottom-rung marcher, and much good it had done him. Kept him poor paying for sequins and ostrich feathers, and all the medical benefits hadn't stopped his wife from dying of leukemia. It had probably killed him in the end, too. The old man had died of *something* funny, anyway, which Keith had always suspected he'd picked up on the job that Mummer influence had gotten him. The job that was all he'd had to leave to his surviving son. . . .

Bowles, swinging wide around a blind corner, turned and said, "I'm talking serious. If you—"

"Jesus, look out!"

Bowles, startled, cut the wheel hard. The front tires hit a patch of ice, and the truck skidded out of control. Keith was slammed against the door, his nucleopore swinging widely.

Something flashed by the windshield, a woman riding a dirt bike. She had been cutting across the road when the truck rounded the corner and its tires lost traction. She leaned over the handlebars, coaxing the last bit of speed from her machine. "Dear God," Keith prayed as the bike slipped past the front fender, barely evading collision.

Before the motorcyclist could clear the road, the tank slewed around, catching the bike a glancing blow on its rear tire. There was a sickeningly loud *crunch*. Keith caught a glimpse of something flying through the air.

Bowles was all elbows and motion, braking the truck and simultaneously fighting to keep it on the road. Tires screeching, he fought it to a halt, still upright, one wheel resting on the shoulder.

Bowles leaped from the truck, his door swinging loosely on its hinges behind him. Keith automatically cut the motor, pulled on his mask, and followed.

The woman's fall had been broken by a tangle of dead brush.

She lay still and crumpled, looking like a bundle of discarded clothing. Some way beyond her lay the dirt bike, bent and twisted, clearly beyond repair.

"It's not a mutie," Bowles said. He straightened from his hasty examination, bent again to count the woman's fingers. "Nope. You know any first aid?"

"A little," Keith said. "Jesus." He stared at a trickle of blood creeping out from one nostril. It was paralyzing, this glistening, liquid red. He shook off the feeling, bent over the woman.

"First we look for any obvious broken bones, um, severe bleeding—it's been a long time since I learned this stuff." She was a lean, muscular woman, somewhere in her late thirties or early forties. Slavic cheekbones, a fierce set to her face, even unconscious. A heavy caftanlike robe had fallen partially open, revealing khaki fatigues, the light green kind that the Northern Liberation Front had worn two decades ago. Her nucleopore was knocked halfway off her face. He checked to see that she was still breathing, reset it. "Well, *I* don't see anything."

"What next?"

"Um, we treat her for shock. Cushion the head, raise the feet." He started to take off his jacket to form a pillow, stopped. "This is no good. We've got to get her into town."

They carried her to the cab, awkwardly distributing her weight across their laps. Keith took the wheel and carefully started the truck rolling.

"What's this tangled around her neck?" Bowles asked. He unstrapped a leather case, looked inside. "Binoculars," he answered himself. He set them carefully on the dashboard, began going through her pockets. "Passport here, stamped in Philadelphia. Occupation: Scholar." He paused. "Didn't know you could make a living at that. Special Drift clearance to visit Souderton."

"Souderton's nowhere near here. It's hardly in the Drift at all."

"Do tell." Bowles replaced the document, continued rummaging. "Hello. She's got two of them." He pulled a second passport from an inner pocket.

"Hey, maybe you shouldn't be going through her things like

that," Keith said uneasily. Bowles ignored him.

"Says Suzette Fletcher on both of them. Same height, same color hair. Age: forty-two. That's the same. Occupation: Reporter. Now isn't that funny? She's a reporter for the Boston *Globe*, up north. And it's not stamped in Philadelphia at all."

"Hey, really, man. I'd feel a lot better if you didn't do that."

"Yeah, okay, okay." Bowles replaced the passport, smoothed the caftan shut again. He studied the woman's face, nested in a mass of dirty blond hair in Keith's lap. "This is one damn handsome woman. How's it feel to have that face in your crotch?"

Keith slowed to negotiate a tricky patch of road, where a careless dumping had let a frozen chemical slick form on the concrete. "Aw, come on," he mumbled, involuntarily embarrassed. "She's old enough to be my mother."

"Looks like she's still got bright eyes, though," Bowles said lightly. "Bet she's got a bushy tail, too. A young man like you could *learn* something from an older woman."

They crossed the denuded strip of land that separated Philadelphia from the Drift, black from repeated burnings-over. The back—outward—side of the barrier fence was bright with hex signs, and beyond this cheery greeting was the city, safe haven from all that lay behind.

Bored guards waved them through the blockades, and the truck cruised through the city fringes. It was largely rubble here, with a few Victorian buildings standing lonely as country tombstones. These were the haunt of self-styled witches and conjur men, who claimed to draw power from their proximity to the poisoned lands.

"Hey. We'll be going by a hospital; maybe we should dump her off there. She might have a concussion."

Keith considered this. The buildings were drawing closer together, and the streets becoming more populous. He braked to avoid hitting a gypsy child, then proceeded more slowly. "Wait a bit and see if she comes to. Let's save the hospitals for a last resort."

Pedestrians scattered and hand-trucks were yanked from their path. A carriage horse shied away, and Bowles snickered, always pleased to see the wealthy inconvenienced. "Shortest way from here's the Spring Garden Street bridge."

Keith nodded. "Okay."

Embalmed monsters hung from each of the old, nonfunctioning lampposts on the bridge, a constant reminder of the horrors that bred Outside. Most had been positioned decades ago, and exposure to the elements had battered them into brown shreds and an occasional exposed bone. Keith found himself glancing up at each pole as it floated by, realized that he was looking for yesterday's Janus monster, and forcibly turned his attention from the grotesques back to the road. He didn't even glance up as they passed Mummer Hall.

The sun was a red smear against the horizon as the truck finally crossed Two Street. It was weakly echoed in the rearview mirror's grimy streaks, and a wide smear on one edge of the windshield. Scattered sweepers were brushing the street clean of any lingering hot particles from the Drift wind, for tomorrow's parade.

The woman groaned and stirred softly. She opened her eyes, painfully drew herself into a sitting position. "Philadelphia," Bowles said. "My name's Jimmy Bowles, and my partner's Keith Piotrowicz."

She bent forward, gingerly touched her forehead. "God, that hurts." She snuffled slightly, accepted a handkerchief from Bowles, held it to her nose.

"Jimmy's the first man ever to create a traffic accident in the Drift," Keith said with a touch of malice. Bowles glared at him wordlessly.

The woman straightened a bit. A corner of her faded blond hair caught the sun, glinted red. "Oh yes, it all comes back to me now." She forced a smile. "S. J. Fletcher. Everybody calls me Fletch."

"Pleased to meet you, Fletch," Keith said. Almost simultaneously, Bowles asked, "What were you doing out in the Drift?"

Fletch watched the worn dockside buildings glide by. Their brick walls were a warm red overhead, shadowed below. "Private genealogy," she said. "I was researching the records in Souderton—they're almost untouched, a real treasure trove—

and I found my grandmother's marriage license. It said she was born in King of Prussia, so..." She shrugged. "I was hoping for the family Bible, but it looks like a lost cause. Hey, you guys *did* pick up my stuff, didn't you?"

"On the ledge," Bowles said. The truck had slowed to a crawl as Keith eased it through the narrow riverfront streets. He made a tight turn into the company lot, nearly scraping two buildings in the process.

"Not that crap! My goddamn saddlebags. They've got all my—supplies and stuff. All my money, my letter of credit."

Keith exchanged glances with Bowles and shrugged. The lot was choked with trucks that had come in earlier; he turned his attention to the clumsy business of parking. They had come in late, and only Slot 23 was vacant.

"Must be with the bike," Bowles said. "We didn't go look at it."

She slammed a fist into her thigh. "Damn, damn, damn." Then, abruptly authoritative: "You'll just have to take me back out there to get them."

"Hey, now," Bowles objected.

Keith cut the engine, yanked the key. "Look around you," he said. The tankers stretched in long, even rows, their white bodies dull in the failing sunset. "The Company isn't going to let us take this thing into the Drift at night."

"I—"

Bowles hopped out of the cab. "Keith, you come out back and read the meters for me," he said. "Then I'll go log us in, and you two can hash this thing out between yourselves."

"All right." He stepped outside and inhaled deeply, savoring the city air. It was dirty, but it was safe. He opened his jacket, letting the cold air hit him, before strolling around back. He vaguely wondered what Bowles wanted to say. There were no meters, of course; either the truck was empty or it was full.

"Listen," Bowles hissed fiercely. "You can do what you want with that woman, tell her anything you like. But you will keep your mouth *shut* about me looking at her papers. You got that? This is Mummer business, boy, and you'd best keep that in mind."

Keith half shrugged, half nodded. Bowles looked at him in

disgust. "Jesus! You wouldn't know an opportunity if it came up and bit you on the ass!" He turned and began the long walk to the dispatcher's shed.

Keith returned to the cab, feeling slightly amused. If Bowles wanted to play secret agent, that was nothing to him.

"I've been thinking," he said to Fletch. "We can take you back out the day after tomorrow, if you don't mind wasting a day in the truck. The dispatcher won't like it, but Jimmy can work it for you. He's got influence."

"Why not tomorrow?"

"It's the first of January—Mummers Day. Everything will be closed."

"And just what the hell am I supposed to do with myself between then and now? Sleep in the gutter?"

He glanced away, to avoid her angry eyes. "Check into a hospital, maybe?"

"I've seen your so-called 'hospitals' and no thank you. Give me someplace I have a fighting chance to walk out of alive."

"I suppose I could put you up," Keith said unhappily. "I've got a spare couch." He wasn't sure he liked this woman, and he had a sick feeling he was going to regret the offer. But for the life of him he couldn't see any alternative.

When Bowles returned, Keith briefed him on the situation. The old man slapped Keith's back. "Behave yourselves," he said, smirking.

It was no far walk to Keith's apartment, a mile or so through the recycling district, what used to be Queen Village. He strolled easily, in no particular hurry to be anywhere.

Fletch studied everything they passed, the piles of bricks from dismantled buildings, rusting steel for resmelting, verdigrised copper tubing that would be melted down and recast to make new bank pennies—everything. She wrinkled her nose at a vat of rotting cloth destined to become paper, jabbed a finger at a bright, kachinalike figure painted on its wooden side. "What's that mean? I've seen it painted all over the place."

"It means that the owner is paid up with the Mummers. Protects him from thieves."

"It does, hey?" Fletch hefted a brick from a nearby pile,

tossed it back on top. It landed with a clink and a sharp puff
of mortar dust. "I could've just walked off with that—if I'd
wanted it."

"But you couldn't have sold it. The Mummers have ears
everywhere. If you tried to get rid of it, they'd find out. They're
all neighborhood people, see?"

Fletch wasn't listening. She was studying another vat, this
one holding mounds of salvaged plastic in a water medium.
Beside the painted Mummer was PLASTECOLI, printed in big
block letters. "You've got tailored bacteria!" She found the
spigot and filter arrangement where alcohol was bled off from
the decaying plastic. "I thought Philadelphia had an embargo
against high-tech."

"Only when it takes money out of the city." They had arrived
at his block. Three gated entryways led to the internal court-
yards, and Keith nodded to one. "This way."

He led Fletch up to his fourth-floor walk up, and opened
the door for her to enter first. He hung his nucleopore on a
hook just inside the front room . "You can take the bedroom,"
he said. "I'll sleep on the couch, I guess."

She surveyed the cluttered rooms. "This place is a dump.
Don't you ever clean up in here?"

"Well . . ." Keith lifted a clutch of dirty clothes from the
floor, dumped them into an already crowded closet. Fletch
examined a framed picture of the Virgin and Child, and smiled
tolerantly. She wandered to the only window that wasn't boarded
over for the winter, jerked the shutters open.

"Nice view of the harbor if you squint between the buildings
on the left," she said wryly. Keith fed a miserly few lumps of
coal into the stove, starting a fire with twists of paper from
last week's *Inquirer*. He did not bother telling her that the
apartment cost him extra because it faced away from the Drift.

Fletch unslung her binoculars, peered through them. Without turning to look, Keith could imagine what she saw: the
sloops and schooners, sails furled, riding in harbor. Mixed in
with them would be a few others, the old retreads.

"It's too dark to make out for sure," Fletch muttered. "But
I could swear that one or two of those ships are coal-burners.
Even—Good Lord! That looks like a converted oil tanker."

"Oh yeah, we got all kinds." He blew gently on the fire, anticipating its warmth. Another few minutes and he'd be able to shed his coat.

"But those things are *old!* Single-hull construction with the bottom rusting out and the rivets popping loose. How can you people allow that garbage in your harbor?"

"What harm could it do?" Keith asked. "Any spill would just wash downriver. The Delaware feeds out of the Drift anyway—nobody's going to be fishing in it for the next few thousand years."

The dinner plates were piled in the sink, waiting for the nighttime water rates, when there was a knock on the door. Fletch, wearing one of Keith's old sweaters over her fatigues, answered it.

Over a dozen of the building's tenants stood in the hallway. "Mummers Gift, Mummers Gift!" they shouted in loose unison. A lone Mummer stood to the fore. He wore a sequined green top hat and baggy blouse and pants that were figured in bright geometric patterns of mirror fragments and embroidery. His cape, which he'd wear in tomorrow's parade, would never have fit through the doorway, and had by necessity not been worn. He stepped inside, sweeping off the hat, and looking like a glittery Hollywood Indian.

"They're here for the Mummers Gift," Keith explained to Fletch. The Mummer held up a muslin sack, and Keith hastily scooped two rolls of silver dollars from a dresser drawer and handed them over.

With a flourish the man broke the rolls open and dribbled the coins into the sack. His lips moved as he quickly counted them. Keith smiled ruefully. The Gift had eaten up most of his savings.

The Mummer was a short man, with a slightly bloated face, and the flush of alcohol accentuated the broken veins in his nose. "Paid in full," he announced. The tenants crowded in, as he waved a benign hand in the air. "The protection of the Mummers is extended to this house for another year. Let the revels continue!"

The tenants cheered and surged through both rooms. Somebody shoveled more coal into the stove, and somebody else waved a jug of grain alcohol in the air. Keith hastened to dig out what was left of last October's cider for mixer. The floating party was an ancient and hallowed custom, and in a city that ran more on tradition than actual intent, it was best to go along with all these things.

Not all the partiers were from Keith's building. Cynthia Doring was among them, and she lived blocks away. She closed in on him with the single-minded intent of a shark, and when she latched onto his arm he imagined white teeth shredding the flesh. "Keith darling," she said. "It's been so long. It has been literally years since I've seen you."

Keith refused to meet her eyes. Her green eyes, with flecks of gold and bottomless pupils. "Yeah, well. These things happen, you know."

"But they shouldn't. They mustn't."

There was a tug on Keith's sleeve. He turned, found himself facing Jerry from the third floor. Jerry was not quite drunk; his eyes were bright with excitement. "You've got to introduce me to your blond friend," he whispered. "Is she yours? Where did you find her?"

"I'll introduce you." Keith was glad for the interruption. "Excuse me, Cynthia." He led Jerry over to Fletch and performed his duties. "We sort of ran into each other in the Drift," he concluded. Knowing it would be a minor bombshell.

"You didn't!"

"Really?"

"What was she doing out there?—the Drift is *dangerous*."

Fletch smiled a polite, almost motherly, smile. "The radiation count is only dangerous if you're right on top of the Meltdown site. For most of the Drift, all you have to contend with is particulate matter. You're perfectly safe as long as you don't eat, drink, or breathe."

There was a slight uneasiness to the group's laughter, but they clustered about her, fascinated. Cynthia seized the opportunity to reclaim Keith. Taking his arm again, she said, "Keith, you worry me. At first I thought it was just me, something I'd said or done. But I keep running into your old friends, and you haven't been seeing *them* either.

"What is it you're hiding from? You could've talked it over

with me. I haven't moved. Hell, I still work the same shift at the hospital; you could've met me there."

Somewhere in the background, Fletch was explaining the rudimentaries of genealogy. "Where were you when Joey died?" Keith asked.

Green eyes widened. "I'm just a nurse, Keith—I empty bedpans. But I looked after your brother, and there was nothing anybody could do for him."

"Nobody dies of rat bites."

"It was *rabies*. Rabies virus 2017B—they were lucky even to identify it correctly." When Keith said nothing, she tightened her grip, pressed her soft young body against him. "I came here with Timothy," she murmured. "But say the word and I'll ditch him. I think we had something going, Keith. Save what's good from the past, and let the rest go."

With a sudden wrenching motion he tore free of her. One hand fisted and rose shoulder-high, and only a deeply ingrained inhibition against hitting a woman kept him from lashing out, striking her in the face.

He stared at the raised hand, forcing it down, hiding it in a pocket. Cynthia's face had gone suddenly white. In the instant that it took her to recover, her expression went from shock to fear, then into the old, familiar cruel lines.

She smiled, feral and businesslike. "I see you've acquired a taste for old meat." A jerk of her head toward Fletch left no doubt as to her meaning.

"It's not like that at all," Keith said. And suddenly he *did* want to confide in her again, for all that memory told him it was a bad idea. He wanted to explain how his brother's death had hurt him, had wiped the life out of almost a year of his existence. But as he thought of it, he realized that there was no explanation, no words, no reasons. Only an emptiness and gnawing pain and residual disgust at the world. "I—" He reached out for her.

"Time to move the party on!" the Mummer bellowed. "Let's get a move on, we can't hang around here all night!"

The partygoers were leaking out the door. "Far be it from me to interfere with your search for Mommy," Cynthia sneered, and left.

The Mummer stood by the doorway, bullying the tenants

into the hall. Keith trailed the laggers, stood to receive the traditional blessing in doggerel.

The Mummer delivered it quickly, and in abbreviated form. "Here we stand outside your door, just like we did the year before. For food and drink our deepest thanks. We've eaten tons and drunk up tanks. We'll return in a year, no more, and if you need our help—just roar." He bowed perfunctorily, and shut the door.

Keith gawked. He listened to the tramp and rumble of feet moving up the stairwell to the next apartment. The Mummer had left off the invitation to join the party, and that was unprecedented. It had never happened to anyone before in his experience.

He turned back to his apartment, empty-seeming now that it held only Fletch and himself.

Fletch looked bemused. "Was it something I said?"

"What did you say?"

"I don't know. Somebody asked where I was searching records, and I explained that I'd started out in Souderton, and suddenly the man in the funny costume was yelling that everyone had to leave."

"Oh Jesus," Keith said. "Souderton."

He tried to explain.

Souderton was the last city within the Drift to die. Its contamination levels were low, and the city had strong and determined leaders. For some twenty years after the Meltdown, Souderton had survived, even thrived after a fashion. They raised their own food, and if they were shunned by the communities beyond the Drift, at least they didn't have to start all over again in the refugee camps.

But their water and foodstuff was still laced with radioactive isotopes. The tumors and birth defects and leukemias piled up. After two decades, they could no longer be ignored. They were too common, too widespread, a constant background to every thought or action.

By popular account the panic started at a mass town assembly to discuss the problems. An alternative version was that it had been triggered by an old woman collapsing from a heart attack. However the hysteria began, it swiftly became a wholesale evacuation of the city, in a frightened mob of thousands that fled like lemmings toward Philadelphia.

They were met at the city limits by a horde of self-appointed vigilantes, citizens who were afraid of mutation, of radiation poisoning, of anything that came out of the Drift.

Masked and hooded men with filters and rebreathers carried rifles into Souderton the next day, and mopped things up.

"See, I go out there all the time so it doesn't bother me. But I guess I tend to forget how everyone else feels about the Drift," Keith said. "And there's a kind of inherited fear of Souderton itself, of what might have happened if the mobs had broken through."

"Sounds more like an inherited guilt." Fletch sat down on the edge of the bed, unlaced her boots, let them drop. "Time for me to hit the sack." She pulled off the sweater.

Her breasts bounced beneath her shirt. They sagged slightly, not much for a woman her age. Keith found himself trying to picture them in his mind. The room was uncomfortably warm, even stuffy. The single drink he had had made him almost dizzy.

"Uh, listen," he said. "The bed's big enough for two."

Fletch smiled scornfully. "Back off, sonny," she said. "You can sleep on the couch for one night without rupturing anything."

Keith awoke at dawn to the sounds of wood on wood and metal on brick and high, childish shrieks. The city's young were in the streets, welcoming in the new year, and delighting in their yearly right to make noise and roust adults from their slumber.

He returned from the toilet down the hall just as Fletch emerged from the bedroom. She was rubbing her arms slowly against the early-morning chill, and looked as rumpled and used as her old fatigues. "Breakfast in a minute," Keith said. "How you doing this morning?" He set about starting a fire in the stove.

Fletch winced as she sat down on the edge of the couch. "Not bad for a woman who's just been run over by a truck."

There was sugar for the oatmeal, and Keith was able to top

off the meal with two large mugs of mixed chicory and coffee. As a bachelor he could afford these small luxuries. Fletch made no reference to his advances the previous night, but chatted lightly and amiably. Before long he found himself almost liking her again.

The meal done, he left to put in a morning's worth of chores for the Mummers. Pausing at the door, he asked Fletch whether she wanted to wander around town while he was gone—he only had one key.

"No," she decided, "I'll stay here and do a few stretching exercises, get my muscles loose again."

"Okay, then. I'll be back before noon."

Keith was put on a work crew tightening bolts on the reviewing stands at City Hall. It was here that the parade would end; after marching up Two Street, the clubs would swing west, then down Broad, to give their final performances beneath the tower of the ornate stone building.

The stands, and the bleachers below them, would hold several hundred privileged viewers: high-ranking city officials, a delegation of Feds up from Atlanta on the weekly train, trade reps from the exporting states in town to hustle up import licenses. A panel of judges was chosen from their number, and the identity of the judges was a zealously guarded secret. There was no easy way to judge a Mummer presentation, to weigh enthusiasm against musical talent, costuming against showmanship, precision against élan. And emotions ran high.

The handful of monetary prizes to be given out would not even cover the expense of costumes for the winners. But the prestige of being the top String Band or Fancy or Comic club was worth more than money to the marchers involved.

Mounted police rode by the stands slowly, their harness cinches and leather jackets creaking ominously. Keith kept to the underside of the bleachers, doing as little as possible. He had checked out the largest wrench available—too large to do any actual work with—knowing that the sight of it made him immune from close scrutiny. For an hour he walked back and forth casually, occasionally stopping to examine an already tightened bolt.

A piercing whistle snagged his attention, and the crew leader gestured him out. "That's enough," he snapped. "Start hauling up the chairs." Keith slung the wrench over his shoulder and complied.

He carried a wooden folding chair under each arm, up the back stairs to the leftmost stand. At the top there was space for a few dozen spectators, a handrail with bunting hanging limply from it, and a grand view down the gray and empty street. A single chair was already in place, a chunky man in a dark and expensive overcoat hunched into it. Keith nodded and started setting up his chairs, moving them first one place, then jostling them to the side.

"Want a sip?"

The man was offering a bottle. "Southern Comfort," he said. "A fine Southern *sippin'* whiskey. Have a seat."

Keith accepted the bottle, pulled up a chair, and took a swig. The alcohol was sugary-sweet, and burned his throat. He gasped.

"Samuelson," the man said. His face was puffy and pale, and it was clear that he had been drinking for quite a while. Keith handed back the bottle.

"Pleased to meet you, Mr. Samuelson. You with the Feds? Atlanta?"

Samuelson shook his head emphatically. "Chief Northern field representative from Southern Manufacturing and Biotech."

There didn't seem to be much he could say to that, so Keith smiled and nodded. Samuelson passed him the bottle again. He sipped more cautiously this time, stopping the lip with his tongue and letting only a few drops dribble in.

"They took my watch."

"Beg pardon?"

Samuelson held up an empty wrist. "My watch. They took it. Made from good homecrafted instrument chips, too. Performs forty-seven different functions *and* tells the time, sweet as anything."

Keith nodded again, waited for Samuelson to go on.

"Now why'd they want to go and do a thing like that?"

Keith didn't know. "Did they say they'd give it back?"

"Oh, sure they said they'd give it back. Right before I leave town. But that's not the point—how'm I going to run up any contracts if I don't have samples? They took all my samples, too, and warned me not to try and sell anything without they okay it first. Now I ask you—how the holy hell am I suppose to sell anything without samples?"

"Well, see," Keith said, "the city is kind of short on jobs. So the authorities don't like any money going out. That's why they ban most of the high-tech stuff, because it doesn't help the job situation." Even as he said them, the words sounded trite and only half true.

"Hell, boy, that's no way to get this country moving again. Free trade, that's the ticket. You cut out all this red tape, and interstate tariffs, and embargoes, and we'd be on our feet in no time. That's how the *old* government handled it. Those were fine times for the businessman, I tell you."

The crew leader appeared at the top of the steps, and bellowed, "Get your ass moving, Piotrowicz! No more of this slacking off!"

Keith shrugged, got to his feet. "Nice talking with you."

"States rights!" the Southerner called after him. "That's what's wrong with this country—you mark my words."

Keith was back at his apartment just before noon. He led Fletch out to Two Street where, because his block organizer had slated him for the twelve-to-two shift, they were able to find standing space not far from the curb. They were in time to see the last several Comic bands.

Fletch watched with fierce interest as men in feathers, in sequins, dressed as clowns, as Indians, as playing cards, strutted by in organized disarray. A female impersonator tagging after one brigade waggled enormous mock breasts at her, turned around, and flipped up frilly petticoats to reveal grossly overstuffed underthings. She threw back her head and laughed.

"Are there any real women in this?" she asked. "I haven't seen any."

"Not any more. They were banned just after the Meltdown."

The Comic group's brass band, bright with mirrors, feathers, and cheap glitter, was playing *The Bummers Reel*. Behind them a ragtag clutch of clowns pulled a wagon float labeled "Christmas with Truceduel." Atop it stood a skinny man in baggy Santa Claus suit, who handed wrapped presents to blind-folded policemen. "What does that mean?" Fletch asked.

"There's a city councilman named Truesdale, and there was an incident last May—um, it's kind of hard to explain if you're not familiar with local politics."

"I get the general picture. I imagine your Mr. Truesdale won't be too amused by this, though."

"No." It was the end of Truesdale's career, in fact, but Keith didn't bother saying that.

The Comics, with their brass bands, floats, and anarchic slapstick, continued to march by, brigade after brigade. Fletch was fascinated by the garish color combinations they chose for their outfits—orange and green and poison blue was one of the quieter mixes. At one point Keith bought two soft pretzels from a vender and introduced Fletch to that old Philadelphia tradition. They were barely warm, and cost three cents for the two, a price the vender could never have gotten away with any other day.

The groups ranged from the bright and gaudy to the bright and gaudy and inventive. Some, obviously, took themselves more seriously than others—their clown outfits with three-tiered umbrellas were stylized and frilled far beyond the point of comedy, and the marchers stepped in perfect unison. By the same token, the more slapdash groups were often more fun to watch.

"Who's next?" Keith asked. The last Comic band was strut-ting away, strewing confusion and firecrackers in its wake.

Fletch lifted her glasses, studied the distant banner that led off the group. "Looks like . . . Center City Club. Would that be right?"

"Yeah. That's the first of the Fancies. After them come the String Bands."

"So tell me. How did all this begin? How did it get orga-nized? What's it all for?"

Keith started to answer, stopped, tried again: "Uh. I don't think anybody can answer those questions. My old man used to talk a lot about the history of the Mummers. You can trace them back for centuries, back to colonial times when they were just random gangs of neighborhood men wandering around on the First, shooting off guns and raising hell. But you can't say when they became *Mummers*. They just kind of evolved."

The Fancy club was less than a block away. A hundred fifty strong, they strutted in neatly ordered rank and file, their ostrich-plume headdresses bobbing, the feathered, mirrored, and be-dangled "capes"—more like false wings than capes, for they towered above the marchers and out to the sides—dipping to the odd cadence of the Mummer's strut. A lone Mummer strutted out front, his costume a larger, fancier version of the others'.

Fletch pointed at some black-clad men slipping through the crowd just ahead of the lead Mummer. "What are *they* supposed to be doing?"

"Don't look! You're supposed to pretend you don't see them."

She turned to face him. "But who *are* they?"

"Men In Black. They're the spotters. They locate certain people and point them out to the King Clown for a tapping-out or—or whatever," he finished lamely. At her questioning glance, he added, "The King Clown is their captain, the one marching in front. King Clown used to be a type of costume, but there's just the one now."

Except for the traditional facepaint, King Clown's costume was nothing like a real clown's. His cape was a full twelve feet high, fringed with white ostrich plumes, and glittering with sequins and mirror fragments and even a bit of diffraction grating, which must have come from somebody's grandmother's trunk. Two guylines led from the tips of the cape to his gloved hands, so he could manage the ungainly costume in the light breezes that sometimes blew up. Like his followers, he wore primarily scarlet and black, though there were a dozen clashing colors admixed. He strutted with great dignity, occasionally bowing slightly to each side in acknowledgment of the crowd's cheers.

Keith indicated the Men In Black with a sideways nod of his head. "Look. They've marked somebody."

Four Men In Black had slipped up on the unsuspecting watcher, quietly easing into position immediately behind him.

Their eyes and mouths were unreadable, framed by the wool of their black ski masks.

The Center City troupe Mummer-stepped briskly down Two Street, banjos, glockenspiels, and horns not playing but at ready, and for an instant looked as if they would pass the man by. Then King Clown raised a hand, and they stopped and wheeled ninety degrees as one man. The Clown strutted around the troupe and into the crowd. They nervously backed away from him.

The Mummer captain strode up to the marked man. The victim flinched away, found himself held firm by the Men In Black. He stiffened. King Clown stretched out his arm and took the man by the shoulders.

One arm rose once, twice, again. It fell on the man's shoulder with an audible crack three times. Then King Clown whirled and returned to his station. The crowd cheered, and the band broke into *Oh Dem Golden Slippers*, turned, and marched on. The man from the crowd joined a motley band of followers in mufti, strutting happily after the troupe.

"What the hell was that all about?" Fletch asked.

"It was a tapping out. The man was a candidate, and the Mummers have accepted him. He's one of the lucky ones."

"I wouldn't mind knowing more about this. Do you think you could swing an introduction to the captain after this is all over?"

"Don't do it. Don't have anything at all to do with the Mummers. Just smile and watch the parade."

"Why?"

"Forget I said anything." Keith stared down the street, ignoring her as best he could. The Fancy club approached, all glitter and flash, advancing, pausing and advancing again in their odd half dance, half march. It *was* odd, Keith realized, and strange that it took an out-of-towner's questions to make him aware of such a simple fact.

King Clown's troupe was parallel to them and marching past, when the gloved hand was again raised. They wheeled to face the crowd. King Clown strode through the spectators, straight at Keith and Fletch. Sweet Jesus, Keith prayed silently. Let it be somebody else.

The crowd parted and King Clown halted before Fletch, placed his hands on her shoulders. He waited a beat. Then he leaned down and kissed her gently on both cheeks. She smiled brightly at him, and dipped a curtsy. He turned as if to move away.

Then he whirled again, and before Keith could react, the gloved hands were on his shoulders, and he stared into the man's bloodshot eyes. Keith tried to jerk away, but several pairs of hands held him firm. He could see the weave of the Clown's costume, could smell the alcohol on his breath. The man's mouth was a thin line within his painted smile.

Slowly, very slowly, King Clown bent over and kissed his cheeks.

In an instant the restraining hands, Men In Black, King Clown, and all were gone. The band was Mummer-strutting away, playing *Funeral March of a Marionette*.

Fletch's eyes sparkled and she started to say something light. Keith grabbed her hand, yanked her into a crowd that shrank away from both of them. Fletch hung back laughingly, and he gave her arm a ferocious tug.

"Come *on!*"

"What's the matter?"

"Shut up and run!"

Away from Two Street the city was practically empty. By law all citizens had to watch at least part of the parade, the hours their block organizers slated them for. In practice, almost everyone stayed to the early evening, to watch it all. This worked to their advantage—there were few about to report the direction of their flight—but it also made them visible a long way off, if anyone was already on their trail. Rounding a corner, Keith came face to face with a large, distraught black man. For an instant he thought he was dead, and then the man turned and fled, another victim like themselves.

"Why are we running?" Fletch gasped.

"Because they're trying to kill us." He would answer no more of her questions. He needed all his attention to escape.

As a boy he played Mummer Hunt, both as victim and assassin, with an intensity rivaled only by the real thing. So he fled from the waterfront because he knew that was the first place the hunters would search. He passed by fire escapes and basement windows that looked like they could be forced for much the same reason. The tall buildings in Rittenhouse Square were tempting, but he knew that the upper, uninhabited floors would be searched room by room several times before the day was over. North and west he fled, toward Mummer Hall, the former art museum.

Only when they'd reached their goal did he realize he'd had a goal in mind at all. It was a pre-Meltdown parking garage, its five levels gaping open to the winds. Panting, he arrived at the stairwell. It was dark and too grittily rubbled to take footprints. Once inside they could ascend slowly, and try to catch their breaths. As they climbed, Keith explained as best he could.

The city government had collapsed after the burnings and panic murders of the Meltdown evacuations. There was no help to be had from the state, which had just lost its capital and most of its land, or from the Feds, who were busy with several million refugees. The self-destruction of New York City in a month-long orgy of riots and fires triggered a worldwide depression almost as a matter of course.

The only organized power remaining in the city was the Mummer clubs. Which was ironic, because they were barely organized at all. The clubs existed for the sole purpose of putting together a troupe to march on New Year's Day, and were independent of one another. They cooperated, but to no great degree; there were no boards of governors, top authorities, or chains of command. Each club was answerable only to itself.

But when governments, fraternal organizations, charities, and organized crime all withered away because there was no way to support their own structures, the Mummers endured. They existed only because they wanted to. They existed without coercion or recompense. The forces that had destroyed their city could not break them.

The clubs were all neighborhood groups, and their members were, by and large, decent men. When the last hospitals were about to go under, several clubs got together to march and collect money to keep them going. When there were no police, they organized volunteers to patrol the neighborhoods.

Before long the Mummers controlled the city, and not long after that they became aware of that fact. The informal planning committees became a little less informal. Club captains took on many of the attributes of feudal lords, though most of them were elected by their memberships.

The Kiss began as a way of flensing mutants and carriers of genetic disease from the population, and the Hunt was initiated only reluctantly, after it became clear that public ostracism was not always enough. It was extended to include those who refused vaccination, when the epidemics began. Finally its potential as a political tool was realized, and no reasons were given.

The rooftop was cold and windy. Keith scuttled to the tool shed standing in its center and beckoned for Fletch to follow.

The door was padlocked shut, with a lock the size of his fist, crusted over with nameless corrosions. "Push on the upper right corner of the doorway there." He grabbed the opposite corner and tugged as she did so. After a heartbreaking instant's hesitation, the door lurched in its frame and tilted askew. There was a gap wide enough to crawl through.

Keith led the way in and, when Fletch crawled after, slammed the door shut with the heel of his palm. "I found a keg of tenpenny nails here when I was a kid," he said. "Rusty, but I sold them for scrap. So probably nobody else has figured out how to get in."

"Very clever. Now that we're trapped in here, what do we do next?"

"Look, I think I've done pretty good so far," Keith said angrily. "At least I've bought us some time to think." He paced the shed—it wasn't large, maybe eight by ten feet—his footing unsure on the rotting burlap sacks that littered the floor. "Why don't *you* come up with something? *You're* the one that got me into this mess, Miss Hot-Shit Reporter."

"So you know about that."

"Bowles looked through your pockets. Jesus Christ!—what kind of monster story were you working on to get the Mummers so upset?" It was cold inside the work shed. Dim light seeped through vacant nailholes in the roof. He could see Fletch watching him calmly, a vague gray figure.

"Could we sneak aboard one of the ships going to Boston?"

"Could we sneak aboard one of the ships going to Boston?" he mimicked bitterly. "No, we could not. There'll be Mummer patrols at every—I can't *believe* how you've fucked up my life! You know, I was doing okay until you came along."

"Keith," Fletch said quietly.

"At least I didn't have half of Philadelphia trying to gun me down!"

"Keith."

He stopped, looked at her. "Yeah?"

"Stop ranting, and tell me how we're going to get out of here alive."

He angrily thrust his hands in his pockets. There was a slight jangle of metal objects, a few copper coins, a salvageable nail or two—and his key ring.

"Holy shit," he whispered. He drew out the ring, triumphantly separated out the key to his tanker truck. "Hey, I may not be dead after all." He laughed softly, ran his fingers caressingly over the piece of metal that could carry him free.

"Let's see." Fletch snapped her fingers twice and extended her hand. He could tell by her expression that she had already deduced his plan.

Keith shoved the keys back in his pocket. "Forget it, dragon lady. I don't trust you. In fact, I'm not even sure I should take you along. You've been dead weight on this little jaunt so far. I might be better off without you entirely."

There was a brief silence. "I see." Something rustled in the gloom. "You want your quid pro quo." With a faint slumping sound, Fletch's caftan fell to the floor.

"I don't—what do you mean?"

Fletch advanced a step, her eyes steady on his, her voice preternaturally calm. "Well, you can take what you want, can't you? I can't exactly yell for help."

"Hey, I—"

"It's understandable. You're a man, and you've got me alone, where I can't back away. Happens all the time."

She was quite close now. Keith flinched back. "You don't understand. You're twisting what I said."

Her expression was scornful. "But you *are* a man, aren't you? I mean—you can still get it up."

Outraged, Keith seized her arms. Cloth bunched up under his angry, clutching fingers. For an instant the tableau held, then he released her, and dropped his head in embarrassment. "Hey, I'm sorry," he said, "I really didn't mean to—"

"Oh, come here." She pulled him back to her.

Their lovemaking was almost tender. Fletch spread out her caftan to protect them from the icy cold burlap sacks, and they undressed kneeling atop it, tugging each other's clothes off item by item, and kicking them away. Some of what they did was new to Keith, but he assumed from her lack of harsh comment, indeed her passionate response, that she could not tell.

When it was over, Fletch tugged and jerked the robe about the two of them, like a thick, heavy blanket. It was warm within the robe, and tangled up in Fletch's arms and legs, Keith felt oddly secure and sure of himself. He stretched a bare arm into the bracing air, and felt a sudden, childish urge to shout or yodel or laugh with glee. It was a urge he dared not give in to.

"I would've taken you along anyway," he said, not knowing whether it was true or not. "You really didn't have to—you know."

Fletch laid a finger on his lips. "It's better this way. Now we can operate as a team."

"A team." Keith spoke the words carefully, listening for their flavor. "Yeah, that's right. A team."

It was hours past midnight before they made their move. They slipped through the streets cautiously, every sense bristling, avoiding the heavily patrolled neighborhoods. It took an effort to walk slowly, to keep from hunching shoulders and darting from shadow to shadow.

Their route was long and circuitous, seemingly endless, because they dared not cut through the unpatrolled areas of the city. Most of the hunters would be concentrated in those parts. They would be young men mostly, eager to hasten their climb to full Mummer status with a confirmed kill.

Keith suggested that Fletch cling to his arm, and that they

proceed slowly and uncertainly. "This is one of the few nights out of the year you can expect to see civilians out this late," he explained. "But they'll all be dead drunk, so we have to act the part."

At Walnut and Twenty-third, they spotted a hunter, his beret a blob of white in the dark. Keith pointed and waved broadly. Fletch let loose a shrill giggle and also waved. For a moment the distant man stared at them, then he raised his rifle overhead in salute and turned away.

"I lust after that beret," Fletch whispered.

"Yeah, well, let's not go fetch it."

They turned west at Bainbridge. Bainbridge was a through street, theoretically capable of handling motor traffic, but in practice far too narrow. Ramshackle sheds and extensions had been built out into the street, making the public access lane an uneven, sometimes twisty path between windowless walls. Exterior doorways were bricked shut. The wooden and iron gateways to courtyard interiors were, by law and by custom, not locked this one night of the year. But they were still and dark. Only rarely could they hear the muted sounds of a late-night party. Still rarer was a glimpse of light from a methane torch or tar-oil lamp.

They continued their drunk pantomime, though no one was present to see them. Leaning heavily on Keith's arm, Fletch whispered, "How much farther?"

"We're almost halfway there. If our luck holds out—"

"Hey—you!"

They turned. A large, heavy-set man strode into the street, swinging a courtyard gate noisily shut behind him. He wore a white beret and carried a thick pole with something curved and talonlike at its end.

Keith grinned and, releasing Fletch so he could stretch out two welcoming arms, cried, "Hey, *paisano!* How goes the hunting?"

The man halted a few feet away. His face was fat and ruddy, and held the belligerent expression of an angry drunk. He held his weapon at ready—up close Keith could see that it was a boat hook lashed to a convenient piece of wood. The lack of sophisticated weaponry was a bad sign. It meant that he wasn't sponsored by one of the clubs, that he had paid to wear the white beret for a night, and would be anxious to get his money's worth.

"Just stand right there while I check you out." The hunter leaned forward, peering at their shadowed faces. Keith was beginning to think they might be able to talk their way out of this one. It was possible the man was to drunk too identify him, that the night shadows might confuse him.

"I hear they caught three over by the Schuylkill," Keith said affably. "You in on any of them, huh?"

The man's face was still with concentration as he mentally ran through the descriptions of victims he had been given. Now he grimaced and angrily barked, "I *said* to—"

Fletch suddenly stepped forward, sweeping the pole to one side with an almost casual motion of one arm. Her free hand moved blindingly fast, smashing into the bridge of the man's nose, just below his brow.

The hunter fell as if he'd been poleaxed, slamming to the ground. His weapon clattered on the pavement.

"Here." Fletch stooped over the body, whisked the beret from its head, and handed it to Keith. "Put this on." She reached for the fallen boat hook. "Don't mind him. He'll be okay in the morning."

Keith looked down at the man. He wasn't breathing. "The hell he will."

Fletch thrust the pole in his hands, adjusted the angle of the beret on his head. "So maybe he won't. What's it to us? Now— are we going to have to pretend that I'm your prisoner, that you're bringing me in alive?"

"No," Keith said slowly. He forced himself to look away from the corpse. "Women can't be hunters, but a lot of hunters bring their girlfriends along. Gives 'em a thrill."

"Then let's get moving. Oh—and that was good work, partner."

"Yeah," he said. "Thanks."

Keith was drenched with sweat by the time they made it to the Company's parking lot. There had been no further close calls, but his nerves were still scraped raw. Row upon row of trucks stretched into the darkness; all was still. He paced off the way to Slot 23, laid the boat hook down, and seized the cold doorhandle.

He grinned and whispered, "You know, there were a couple of times there when I didn't think this would work." With a yank, he threw the door open.

"Stupid," Jimmy Bowles said. "Very stupid, brother man."

Keith jerked back reflexively, froze. Bowles was sitting in the cab, with the truck's shotgun cradled in one arm. It was pointed straight at Keith.

"You've really fucked it," Bowles marveled. A corked bottle, half full of some dark fluid, lay in his lap. Its label was nearly rubbed away from endless handling and refilling.

Behind Keith, Fletch shifted her weight ever so subtly. The gun flicked in her direction.

"Don't you move, bitch!" The veins in Bowles' forehead stood out. He passed a hand over his brow, wiping away sweat. Keith suddenly realized that the man was deeply, dangerously drunk.

Bowles' eyes glared at Keith for an instant, then dropped. His face underwent a strange alteration of expression, becoming almost maudlin. "Listen, buddy, I didn't know they would bang on you. I thought I was doing you a *favor*. When I passed the word about the lady's papers, I threw in a plug for you." He groped about for the bottle and uncorked it one-handed. "And then a few hours later they called me up to Mummer Hall— in a *car*, man, can you believe that?—to tell the whole thing over again for the bigcats." He took a long swig from the bottle, holding his head sideways and watching them from the corners of his eyes. "I did my best, man. Told them you didn't know from shit, but nobody listened. They said it was suspicious that you two were shacking up. Man, I kept *telling* them— but Gambiosi, he said you weren't needed. So the word was to bang you both."

As he talked, Bowles had let the shotgun sink slowly to rest on his knees. His eyes were unfocused, half lost in introspection. Keith mentally took a deep breath. He dove for the gun.

There was time enough to take in an incredible amount of detail. The clumsy way his body moved, not at all smoothly, not at all responsive to his will, so that he more fell than leaped upon Bowles. The way Bowles' hand jerked up involuntarily, the shotgun's muzzle wobbling in a jagged S through the air. The way his hands connected with Bowles' wrist, pushing past cold steel, gripping aged sinew. Contact made, the hand flew up and to the side, and the gun slammed harshly into the dashboard.

Keith found himself stomach down on the seat, gun clutched maniacally in both hands. He choked it by the barrel, by the back of the stock. The silence filled his ears. His palms tingled.

Jimmy Bowles stared stupidly at him. "Aw, man, you didn't have to do that," he mumbled.

Fletch touched Keith's shoulder, put a hand beneath the shotgun. He straightened his fingers slowly, letting the thing drop. She snapped it up and broke it open. After a cursory examination, she tossed it aside.

"You jammed a warped shell in there. That thing would've blown up in your face if you'd fired it."

Bowles ignored her. "Didn't think I could go through with it," he said almost to himself. Then: "Take the truck, man."

He opened the door and unsteadily climbed out. With a glance at Fletch, Keith straightened, slid behind the wheel, and put the key in the ignition.

As they eased out of the lot, Bowles was standing alone in Slot 23, crying drunkenly.

They crashed the barrier at top speed, almost 70 kph, leaving splinters of wood flying behind them. The Mummer guards, caught unprepared, fired after them. Three bullets went through the body of the tanker, making hollow gonging noises. Fortunately the tanker body was empty, and its last cargo apparently not flammable. Something ricocheted about the underside of the truck, as the guards tried to shoot out the tires. Keith kept going.

Just beyond the cleared area some joker had put up a sign reading: RADIOACTIVE CONTAMINATION. DRIVE FAST. Fletch pointed at it and laughed. Keith threw a horrified glance her way; they were barely out of rifle range.

"Don't mind me," Fletch said. "I always get a little giddy after a close one like this." She chuckled softly to herself.

"Well, I hope you're not planning on any more close ones. Hey—what say we circle around Philly and head south? I don't like the idea of heading straight into the Drift."

"You can think of a better way to lose pursuit? Take an old combat reporter's advice, son. Move fast and don't look back. Hey, isn't this where you hit me?"

"No, it's a ways on." The truck crested a hill, and he pointed into the darkness off to their left. "See that blue glow just below the horizon?"

"Yeah." It was a light, eerie smear in the distant black land. No trees obscured it, and it had a curious liquid quality.

"Cherenkov radiation. During the Meltdown, there were five trucks loaded with fuel rods they tried to get out. The state police turned them back somewhere north of here, so they drove them into the swamps. It makes a good landmark. Your bike's somewhere beyond there."

"Well, keep a sharp eye out for the spot. I want my saddlebags back."

Keith discovered the hole in the fuel tank when they stopped for the bags. A dribble of alcohol was leaking out, one slow, steady drop at a time. The bullet along the underside of the truck had apparently sent a sliver of metal through the tank, and in the process screwed up the fuel gauge. Neither Keith nor Fletch could think of any way to fix it. "We should head east," Keith suggested. "Get as far out of the Drift as we can before it dies."

"Will the Mummers follow us into the Drift?"

Keith thought it over. "Yes."

"Then New Jersey's not good enough. We go north."

The engine breathed its last at dawn. Keith let the truck glide to a halt in a stand of stunted pines just off the road.

They were both wearing their masks; they had switched off the recycler back at the saddlebag stop, in order to conserve fuel. Fletch hopped out, slid her rifle from its sheath in the saddlebags, and snapped, "Let's get moving. You take the bags and I'll lead. Don't step in any patches of snow—we can't afford to leave a trail."

Keith shouldered the saddlebags and followed her down the

road the way they had come for perhaps a quarter kilometer, and then up a slope on the opposite side from the abandoned truck. In places the ground crunched beneath his feet, and climbing the slope was hard work.

Keith's muscles ached from the tension of driving. "I could use a week or two in bed," he said. Not so much complaining as making an observation.

"We'll rest at the top of the hill. Right now we're exposed."

The sun had climbed three fingers above the horizon and shone weakly through the clouds by the time they could rest. The sky was white and gray, almost colorless. The endless hills beneath were no more definite. The two fugitives huddled behind a tangle of thorny bushes, near a cluster of spruce trees whose needles had a distinctly brownish tinge. Half an hour passed.

"Here they come," Fletch said. "Following our trail." She peered through her binoculars, careful to keep them in shadow.

With a low growl, three four-wheel-drive vehicles swung into view. They sped down the roadway in close formation, coming to a halt by the abandoned tanker. Six dark figures leaped out and swarmed over the site. They moved quickly, alertly, keeping each other covered at all times. After ten minutes they returned to their vehicles and moved down the road at a much slower pace.

Fletch stood. "They go that way and we go this way," she said with satisfaction. "Let's go, kid. Miles to go before we sleep, you know."

They were trudging up an endless country road, detouring around the scattered patches of snow. The sun was failing. Keith stepped on a cancerous-looking growth, painfully bent to scoop it up and throw it into the lifeless woods to the side. "...snow," Fletch said. Her voice was muffled by the nucleopore and Keith couldn't make out her words.

"What did you say?"

"I said it's like snow!" Then, seeing his difficulty, she fell back a step. "The steam explosions went up like a geyser. They sent the hot stuff up where the winds could catch it, and it filtered down like snow. Then it got blown around, so you'll have bare spots and hot spots throughout the Drift. The big concentrations are still too slight to see, but you can gauge them by their effects."

She stopped near an old stone farmhouse nestled within an almost healthy looking stand of trees, and did a quick scan of their limited horizons through her binoculars. Save for a collapsed front porch, the house was virtually intact. "Not bad. We'll stay here tonight."

They forced the lock on the kitchen door, and chocked it shut with an old dresser. The interior was untouched from the time of the evacuations. Cigars moldered in a humidor atop the refrigerator. A child's drawing taped to a cupboard crumbled when Keith touched it.

There was a woodstove in the living room. Reluctantly they left it alone, eating unheated tins of beef from Fletch's saddlebags. They had to lift their nucleopores for each bite, replacing them immediately after.

When they were done, Fletch carried the empty tins outside. She paused on the stoop and cocked her head. "Listen."

Keith joined her, strained his ears. After a moment he caught it—a long, almost musical howl. A pause, and there was another, equally faint howl in reply. "Some kind of mutated dogs," Keith said. "I've seen them. Big, shaggy animals, like wolves."

"Actually, they're a hybrid—a perfectly natural cross between dogs and wolves. They migrated down from Maine a few years back, and now they're expanding through the Drift. Good luck to them, say I."

Keith peered into the night, but trees blocked his vision, and there was no chance of his seeing the animal. "Hybrid, mutant, what's the difference?"

Fletch gawked at him. "They really do keep you poor sods ignorant, don't they?" She threw the tins away from the house. They fell with a clatter. "The only mutations you have to worry about coming out of the Drift are the new diseases that pop up every year. Now be quiet, and let's see what goes after the trash."

Shivering slightly, Keith complied. The minutes crept by, each one a small leaden eternity, and only a continually repeated resolve not to be outlasted by a woman kept Keith from giving up and going inside.

Finally there was a rustling in the bushes.

Something burst out of the darkness in a thundering, headlong rush. It nabbed the tins smoothly in passing and was gone, leaving behind an impression of small bright eyes and a squat, shaggy body.

"Feral pig," Fletch said. "Now *there's* a mutant for you. I've cut a few of them open. The appendix is malformed, the stomach is—well, let's just say their digestive systems are remarkably inefficient. So they have to eat a lot more than their domesticated ancestors did. They're always foraging, always hungry, and I'd hate to come up against one without a good weapon." She closed the door. "I saw a red skunk once, but I don't see much of a future for that either."

Keith slid the dresser back against the door.

"Well, it looks safe—the pig is able to live around here, anyway. Beddy-bye time for me."

Keith turned. Fletch had dropped her robe, and was shedding her shirt. Her breasts were freckled, and they swayed gracefully as she moved. Keith watched them, fascinated, wondering whether he really wanted to make love to this woman again. The passion of the previous night had a strong hold on his imagination, and yet it was tinged with shame, as if he had done something shameful and unclean.

Fletch pulled blankets about herself and gestured for him to sleep beside her so they could share body warmth. Yet when he reached out a questioning hand, she turned away and mumbled, "Not tonight, boyo. You'll be stiff enough in the morning as it is."

Keith awoke feeling half crippled. Fletch had him out on the road before he was awake enough to protest. Bleak hours passed on tedious roads that Fletch puzzled out from a pre-Meltdown service station map.

Once they had to flee the road and hide when a distant growl warned them of an approaching four-wheeler. They watched it go past, two Mummer assassins in its seat. Still later they were attacked by a feral cat, a small orange-and-white animal descended from house pets. It ran at them yowling when they had paused for lunch, and launched itself at Fletch's face. She had to club it to death with the stock of her rifle.

She turned the small carcass over with her boot. "See right there?" she said. "That big sore on its side? It must've made its lair in a hot spot. It came down with radiation sickness, and the pain made it crazy enough to attack us."

Keith sat down under a flowering apple tree. It leaned over the road, covered with small white flowers—a perversion of its biological programming, for frost would kill the flowers long before they could be pollinated. He picked up his can of beans, spooned out a cold lump, and looked at it. "Fletch," he said wearily, "when are we going to be *out* of this hellish place?"

She gathered him into her arms, gave him a hug. "There, there. I've got friends not far from here. There's a small community of Drifters I know of. They're all outcasts and vagabonds, but reliable in their own way. When we get there we can rest—maybe tonight, if we're lucky."

Two days passed. A noontime sun was shining when they reached the mouth of a small, shallow valley. A cluster of nineteenth-century buildings were huddled below, two or three from the mid-twentieth anomalously mingled in. "There it is," Fletch said. She began loading needlelike projectiles into her rifle.

"What's its name?"

"Nameless."

Keith couldn't tell from her answer whether the community was called Nameless or simply lacked a name. But he was weary and short-tempered from three days of forced marches and sexless nights, and he was damned if he was going to ask. "Not much to look at."

Fletch grunted, and flicked the safety on her rifle.

It was a short thing, the rifle, about the length of a sawed-off shotgun. The stock was carved to fit her forearm, the trigger was far up along its length, and its barrel, though of normal thickness, had a surprisingly small muzzle. Keith thought, not for the first time, how handy it would have been back in Philadelphia.

After a perfunctory scan of the valley through her glasses,

Fletch removed her mask and stowed it in a caftan pocket. "The valley's one of the clean spots I told you about, but you should keep your mask on anyway. Just in case. When we go inside, though, take it off. These people are touchy. Say as little as possible. Don't criticize anything. Don't start any fights."

Keith was staring at a small weathered shed at the end of a short path off of the roadway. One wall was missing, and there was a kneeling-bar just inside it. It looked like a shrine. Where a crucifix should have been, there was a bright, crudely painted radiation logo. "Some friends."

Fletch raised the rifle so that its barrel rested against her shoulder and its muzzle pointed skyward. She led the way down.

The cluster of buildings had once been the industrial core of a small mill town. Over the years the outlying houses had been torn down, bit by bit, for building supplies, for firewood, sometimes just for the sake of doing something. Now all that remained was a miscellany of old factory buildings bordering a small, swift-running river. Sheds and stone additions choked the narrow streets, making the whole a combination windbreak and maze.

There were flickers of movement in the higher windows as they walked past, pale bloated faces that appeared and were gone, like goldfish coming to the fore of their bowls and whisking away. A one-legged old man, his single crutch hung with feathers and oddly marked small mammal skulls, lurched around a corner. He saw them and glared. His lips moved, and an indistinct mixture of obscenities and nonsense words poured forth. They hurried past.

"There must be a hundred people in this warren," Keith said, awed. "What do they all *do?*"

"Whatever they have to. Now shut up!"

The alleyway twisted and turned, and brought them face to face with an ancient gasoline station. Its windows had been boarded over, and towers of old tires almost obscured it from view. Keith wondered what possible use anyone could have for them, did not ask. A bell over the door jangled as they went in.

The interior was a packrat's fantasy. Dimly lit by alcohol lamps were clutters and tangles and piles of furniture, fishing gear, musical instruments, woodstoves—a thousand items, all battered and old, all obviously looted from homes abandoned during the Meltdown. A pale, pockmarked face appeared in the shadows to the rear. "You after girls?" it asked.

"Hell no," Fletch said. She slid the rifle into its sheath. Keith was almost unbalanced by its weight. He staggered, recovered. The face advanced, became a tall, vacant-eyed man with a slouch belly.

"Bringers?" he asked.

Fletch threw him a silver nickel, and he automatically snagged it out of the air. "I want two beers and whatever slop you're serving today."

The man stared at them silently, as if puzzling out the meaning of her words. Finally he said, "Tables in back," and vanished back into the gloom.

While Fletch strode to the tables, Keith remained standing, poking through the mounds of objects. He came across a mirror, wiped the grime from it. His reflection was grim. Mean lines around the mouth, a scowl creasing his forehead. He blinked, trying to erase the wildness in his eyes. No good. A smile was gobbled up by his mask. He pushed it down. A red triangle of chafe-marks remained. He touched them lightly with a finger-tip, pushed the uncombed hair back from his forehead. Still he retained the look of a hunted animal.

Keith took a deep breath of air that rushed into his lungs so readily he felt momentarily dizzy. The hell with it, he was not going to put his mask back on until they left.

"Susie!" A gigantic, black-bearded man exploded from the dim recesses of the back. He rushed forward, flung his arms around Fletch, and lifted her into the air.

Keith had instinctively grabbed for Fletch's rifle, but drew back when he heard her laugh happily. "Bear, you old *pirate!*" She hugged him and thumped his back vigorously.

They drew up chairs to a table, and Keith quietly joined them. "But what are you doing here?" Fletch asked. "Didn't you have business"—she lowered her voice—"along the coast?"

"Haw! I was being set up. They've got a new administration

that's cracking down on smuggling, much good it'll do them. But I've got friends, yes, and they warned me away." He shifted his head toward Keith. "He's okay, right?"

Fletch shrugged, performed introductions. Bear was about Fletch's age, perhaps a bit older, and he had a paunch that bulged over the table whenever he leaned forward. "We met when I was covering the Northern Liberation Front," Fletch said. "The guerrillas set up their camps in the Drift, where the government troops wouldn't go after them."

The pale man brought their beers and two bowls of watery-looking stew. Looking up, Keith noticed a dwarf enter the front, see strangers, and turn to leave. Wary, intelligent eyes met his, and Keith realized with a start that the dwarf was young, perhaps twelve, and had likely been born within this Drift community. An instant later, both he and the waiter were gone, out their respective exits.

Bear had stopped talking in the presence of the pale man. Now he added quietly, "Listen, Susan. I can see you're planning on resting here a day or so, but I think maybe you and your young friend here should come stay with me in my cabin instead." A stray beam of light glinted on a single gold earring in his matted hair.

Fletch was all serious attentiveness. "Why?"

"I was here two days ago, visiting the . . ." He looked embarrassed. "The girls in back. And some men came in, asking questions about you. Most of this crew thought they were Bringers, and wouldn't talk to them, but—"

"What are Bringers?" Keith interrupted.

"Aw, these pissants will believe anything. Bringers are supposed to have the evil eye or something, they bring death with them."

"Never mind that," Fletch snapped. "Go on with your story."

Bear seemed relieved to return to it. "Anyway, I decided to hang around, in case you showed up and might need some help maybe. But they looked like killers to me. Six or eight of them. Southern accents."

"Philadelphia accents?"

"Yeah. I think."

"Shit." Her fingertips tapped the table. "Finish your beer,

Keith. Bear, have you still got your buggy?"

"Out back. I've got my own fuelstill, too. I'm a *rich* man!"

The buggy was an open-pit four-wheel drive, and Bear drove it like a madman. Huddled between Bear and Fletch, Keith concentrated on keeping warm and for the first time actually worried about frostbite. The other two chattered happily over his head, ignoring both him and his misery.

They passed another roadside shrine on the way out of the valley, and later a site where a deer had been butchered on the roadway. Cabalistic signs had been drawn in its blood on the concrete. Bear scowled at them. "Superstitious louts!"

At last Bear roared, "We're here!" He drove the buggy up an almost nonexistent road, across a stretch of meadow, and under a stand of gnarled elms. While Bear was covering the vehicle with a tarp, Keith looked about for the cabin. He couldn't see it.

"Back this way." Bear led them up through the trees, and gestured with a mittened hand. "How do you like it? Not much, but it's home, hey?"

The cabin was built into the slope of a steep hillside. A log wall with one window and door, and a stretch of wood-shingled roof were all that showed.

Bear scooped an armful of wood from a stack beside the door, and led them inside. He talked rapidly, as if trying to make a good appearance for a cabin whose virtues were far from obvious. "Built it myself," he said. "Dug it into the hill, so the earth kinda evens out the temperature. I scavenged a lot of styrofoam, packed it between the walls and the earth. Doesn't need much heating-wood. Leave it alone and it stays about thirteen degrees C constant. Summer and winter."

"Very nice," Keith said politely, not meaning it.

Fletch studied the cabin judiciously, thumping the walls with her fist. She came to an inside door, raised an eyebrow. "Root cellar," Bear explained. Fletch smiled.

"So this is your fabled cabin. I never thought I'd actually be here." She examined the shelves, crammed with boxes and sacks, that covered the free space on every wall, while Bear pulled out prodigious amounts of bedding from several trunks.

He spilled a final armful onto the floor, then stopped and looked ruefully at the mound he'd created, as if seeing it for the first time. "That may be a bit much," he muttered in an embarrassed tone.

"Do you really think so?" Fletch asked innocently. Their eyes met and they both laughed in a warm and comfortable way. Their laughter died down, but they remained staring into one another's eyes.

"Keith," Fletch said. "Maybe you should run outside."

"I—"

"That's a good idea," Bear said. He thrust Fletch's binocular case into Keith's hands. "Play with these for a while." He winked in a friendly, conspiratorial fashion, gently pushed Keith toward the door.

Keith stumbled outside. Someone kicked the door shut behind him. He heard the beginning of an intimate chuckle, and hastened away.

It was *cold* outside. A wisp of smoke rose from the cabin's flue and disappeared a few feet up into the gray sky. Keith wandered off to one side, and came up against a bramble-choked ravine. It was unpassable; he chunked a rock down it, but didn't hear the splash of water.

He slammed a fist against a gnarled tree trunk. Wood crumbled away, leaving a bite-shaped gap in the tree. He felt sick and confused. Could he really be jealous of a man twice his age? He had only made love to Fletch once, and then under special conditions, with death nipping at their heels.

And that was it, he decided. They had only made love once; Fletch had shown no interest since. He had told himself repeatedly that she was too weary, or that she had a low sex drive and required the spice of immediate danger to arouse her. But the tryst with Bear disproved both theories.

Take away the excuses, and there was only one answer. Fletch had used him. He held no sexual interest for her; she'd needed a way out of Philadelphia, and she had bought it.

Well grow up, kid, he told himself. Welcome to the real world. But unbidden memories arose in his mind, of her flesh, of their vigorous coupling, images that were at once compelling and newly repulsive.

Keith moved away from the ravine, trying to control his thoughts. In an effort to distract himself, he raised the binoculars to his eyes and scanned the horizon. Beneath the amplified image of dead and winter-barren trees, something moved. A needle. Set inside the binoculars was a graduated scale, with a small red pointer that sprang up when the glasses were raised to the horizontal.

The needle pointed to a position barely on the scale. Keith shifted the binoculars and the reading held steady. Raise the glasses to the sky, or lower them to the ground, and the needle sank below the scale. Hold them steady and the position was constant, wherever they were pointed, at rocks or hillside, at darkness or light.

The view through the binoculars misted over and was replaced by an involuntary inner vision of Fletch and Bear pleasuring each other on the cabin floor. Keith blinked angrily, then snorted in self-derision. He shoved the glasses back into their case and stalked on down the slope a way. His feet were growing numb. He stamped them against the ground, wishing the two would hurry up and get done.

Some time later, Fletch appeared in the doorway and waved him in. He went straight to the woodstove and hunched over it, holding his hands to its warmth and rubbing them together. From the corner of his eye he could not avoid seeing Bear pulling his trousers up. The man's pubic hair was stark black against his pale skin, and Keith had to admit ruefully that Bear was better endowed than himself. There was no moral he could draw from this.

For the rest of the afternoon and on through the evening, Bear and Fletch avidly discussed politics in the Greenstate Alliance up north, and goings-on within the Drift. Keith listened quietly, having nothing to contribute. He learned a little, but for the most part the dialogue relied on knowledge of previous events that he lacked, and was absolutely meaningless to him. He fell asleep to their bright, relaxed talk.

Something roared at the foot of the hill, a great gravelly noise that peaked and fell and slowly grew less as it became more distant. Keith's eyes opened. It was late night, and the

cabin was flooded with gray shadow. "Fletch?" he said. "Bear?"
The cabin was empty.

Keith went to the door, stood shivering in the cold. Down-slope there was no shadow where Bear's buggy had been. The distant noise dwindled, faded away. He had been deserted.

Stunned, he went back inside, built up the fire, lit an alcohol lamp. What did he do now? He was somewhere within the Drift, with not the foggiest notion of what roads led out, and an unknown number of Mummer assassins scouring the countryside looking for him. His eye was suddenly caught by a square of something white.

It was a sheet of paper. Fletch had left her saddlebags behind, open and partially emptied, with a note atop them. The inner seam of one bag had been ripped open and something—it must have been thin and flat and slightly flexible to be hidden there—removed. The rifle was gone too. Keith picked up the note. It began without preamble.

> Heading for coast—Bear thinks he can get me on a ship for Boston. Suggest you keep heading north. Am leaving you most of my supplies & a pistol, courtesy of Bear. Binocs contain ionization meter—don't sleep anywhere that registers over half-way mark. I put a checkmark on map where Nameless is. If you can't figure it out, Bear should be back in a day or two & can help.

Angrily, he crumpled the note and threw it to the floor. "Nice going, partner," he said aloud. The words seemed foolish and childishly spiteful even as he said them. He took a deep breath and tried to calm himself.

To his surprise, it was not all that difficult. There was a certain grim satisfaction in knowing the worst: that he *had* been used, and then discarded, that Fletch felt no more than a passing affection for him at best, of the sort one might bestow on a stray dog without the least intention of bringing it home. In a way, the knowledge was easier to handle than the suspicion of it had been. He knelt to take inventory of the saddlebags.

He worked briskly, shoving back inside those items he might

need and tossing aside those he saw no use for. He lacked a knife and plundered Bear's possessions until he found one—an Arkansas toothpick with a leather sheath—and clipped it to his belt. The ionization counter would come in handy. He set the binoculars carefully beside the pistol, and began studying the map.

Keith had about decided he could make his way out of the Drift if only he could retrace his way back to Nameless, when he heard another noise. Dousing the lamp, he picked up the pistol and went outside.

There was a deep growling beyond the hills, a changing chord of four bass lines that rose and fell independent of each other, one growl significantly louder than the rest. Crouching in the cold, Keith tried to place its direction. East? West? It echoed and rebounded, rose and fell, so that there was no hope of getting a fix on it. A pale moon floated high in the sky, visible at rare intervals through gaps in the clouds. The noise grew.

Below and to his left a stretch of road was visible through a break in the trees. A shadow slid across it. Keith shifted position, moving behind an outcropping boulder, and waited.

A buggy careened to a halt below, and two figures leaped out. They ran up the slope, one with long graceful strides, and the other lumbering after.

Three gray shadows slipped across the distant roadway. The roar of engines peaked briefly, treble notes coming together in a high, angry whine.

Keith drew a bead on the leader of the two coming up the hill, and wondered whether he'd actually have the nerve to shoot, to kill a human being in cold blood.

"You'd better have some damn fine weapons up there," the lead figure called over her shoulder. Fletch. Keith lowered his pistol.

"Weapons I got," Bear shouted back. "Miracles I'm fresh out of."

"We'll make our own."

They ran past him, Fletch sparing a single cool glance in passing, and into the cabin. Shoving the gun into his belt, Keith followed.

Bear was wrestling a large chest from one of the shelves.

"I'm pretty sure I nailed that fink from back in town," he grunted. "You can bet they wouldn't've been waiting for us without his help. Bastard! If he got away, I'll go back and finish him."

Keith smiled sardonically. "Welcome back, partner."

"Later. What've you got?"

Bear rummaged through the chest, yanking things out and tossing them across the floor. "Incendiary grenades. Bandoliers. One of those Israeli machine guns from—what was that war again?"

"Before my time."

"It's a museum piece for sure. But it's in perfect working order, so maybe I'll use it."

"Got into a little trouble, did you?"

"Give me that." Fletch reached for a new weapon Bear had uncovered. "I'm pretty good with those."

Keith's coolness faded as the others armed themselves, steadfastly paying him no attention. He was not at all sure that he was on Bear's and Fletch's side, but he knew that the Mummers would consider him so. He opened his mouth to volunteer to take a weapon.

At that instant the growl of approaching vehicles died. Bear grabbed his weaponry and bolted for the door.

"I'll take the left," he threw over his shoulder. "Tell the kid how to cover us, then you take the right."

"Gotcha." Fletch took her rifle and thrust it into Keith's hands. It felt odd. He realized that he didn't even know how to fire it. She flipped something on the side of the stock. "Okay, now the safety's off. The rifle's ready. I want you to lie down flat in the back of the cabin—they're shooting uphill, so they'll probably fire over you. Shoot at the sky, understand? Don't try to take any of them out when I'm somewhere in front of you—just provide us with some distraction."

"Don't baby me, damn it! I can fight, too!"

"Like hell. Now this thing's a compression launcher. It fires small rockets; they ignite about halfway up the barrel, so the thing has a hell of a kick, remember that. The projectiles hit at supersonic velocities, and the shock wave ruptures every internal organ in the body. So if you have to, don't shoot fancy, aim at the middle of the body. Anywhere you hit is lethal. You've got a hundred shots, and don't forget to save the last for yourself. You stick the muzzle in your mouth and aim *up*. Got all that?"

"Yeah, sure," he mumbled.

"Sure you do." She tousled his hair, ran for the door, paused just behind it.

A needle of red light, so brief it almost wasn't there, lanced through the cabin, leaving a small charred hole in the front wall, and another at an angle to it in the back.

"Laser pistols," Fletch snorted. "Kiddie weapons!" She was gone.

Three more needles of light laced the cabin. Keith threw himself to the floor at the rear, as directed. Whatever weird weapon Fletch was handling made high, almost whistling shrieks. There was a small explosion, followed by the chatter of Bear's machine gun.

Keith suddenly remembered the rifle, lifted it, pointing its muzzle up through the window. He squeezed the trigger and the window exploded outward in a fountain of glass and casement splinters. There was a deafening boom as the projectile went supersonic, and the stock slammed into Keith's shoulder, numbing it, half rolling him over. He fired again, sending a shot through the roof. Another world-splitting roar.

Plaster, earth, bits of wood showered down. There was a hole the size of a giant's fist in the ceiling.

Four threads of laser light winked in and out of existence, one after the other. Keith crawfished back a foot, pushing his back against the rear wall. Bear and Fletch had been right to leave him behind, he realized. He was confused, almost panicked, of no use at all in a battle that required cool wits.

Somewhere both Fletch and Bear were running, shouting. Their weapons clattered high and low. An incendiary grenade went off, turning night to day for an instant, and there was a hideous, garbled scream.

Blindly Keith fired another shot, just barely remembering to aim high over the horizon. A laser burst struck the hanging alcohol lamp, exploding it, spilling a gout of alcohol over the woodstove.

With a *whoomp*, the alcohol was ignited by the hot iron stove. Flames reached up toward the ceiling, licked against the wall. A dribble of fuel running across the wooden floor went up and Keith futilely tried to beat it out with slaps of his jacketed arm. The flames grew and spread.

Time and again laser bursts pierced the walls but, as promised, they were always too high. The cabin was heating up now, and smoke gathering below the ceiling. Some of it slipped out the hole in the roof, but more was generated than dispersed. The cabin was filling with smoke. Keith gasped and choked. Assassins or no, he had to get out.

He crawled to the door, peeked out at floor level. He could see nothing. There was a short burst of weapons fire, then silence. He caught a glint of red that might have been a laser shot. Sweat beaded up on his forehead. He drew himself into a crouch, and prepared to run.

The front wall was burning now. As the heat scorched him, Keith was involuntarily reminded of the last time he had taken his kid brother ratting. A bunch of neighborhood kids had torched a house in the abandoned outskirts of Philadelphia. They'd ringed the building, standing with sticks and old baseball bats, waiting for the rats to come out. Then, when the rats were forced to flee, maddened with pain, their fur ablaze, they'd methodically clubbed the animals to death.

One rat, however, a piebald mutant, had run straight at Joey, and scrambled up his jacket. Squealing in frenzied terror it had clawed and bit, and Joey had fallen back shouting in fear. Keith had smashed the burning rat off his kid brother's chest with a savage blow of his stick, and then mashed it to a pulpy smear. Not that that had done Joey any good.

Keith ran. He dashed into a sudden madness of noise and flying bullets, flashes of light and screams of rage. He darted to the side and flung himself to the ground, panicked. Little circles swam before his eyes as he tried to spot the combatants, his pupils not yet adjusted to the night.

The darkness coalesced into discrete shadows. He thought he detected motion *there* and down there.

He snapped the rifle toward a sudden bulking of shadow downslope, and almost fired before he recognized Bear's silhouette. Bear wheeled suddenly, and a sliver of light passed neatly through his chest. He fell.

At the same instant, an incendiary grenade went off, briefly illuminating the slope. Keith could see two of the assassins. The nearer one was running downslope, and he twisted in surprise at its sudden glare. Awkwardly he fell on his gun hand, the laser pistol skittering into the night.

Keith was charging toward the second assassin, midway down the slope and facing Bear's body. He had no memory of getting to his feet, but he was running, squeezing off shot after shot that made a hell of a noise but probably hit nothing. The nearer Mummer was crawling on the ground, blindly groping for his weapon.

Running past the unarmed assassin, Keith fired several shots at the place he had last seen the other. When he arrived at the spot, it was empty. He stopped, unsure of what to do next.

There was a sudden, choking cry to his side. "Kid!"

He whirled, his finger tightening around the trigger. The moon broke free of the clouds, briefly flooding the hillside with dim light. He saw two dark figures locked in hand-to-hand combat, the larger slowly, inexorably forcing his laser pistol toward Fletch's head. Keith's rifle went off.

As soon as he squeezed the trigger, Keith knew that the gun was pointed at the wrong one of the pair. That it was pointed at Fletch. With a shattering crash, the projectile went supersonic.

Fletch's mouth opened and her neck arched back, as if in the throes of sexual agony. Her blond hair flew forward, back, lashed her face. Her arms thrashed like a rag doll's, impossibly fluid, broken in several places each one. She toppled over backward, dead before her body hit the ground.

Keith took a questioning step forward, and the Mummer assassin backed away, reminding Keith of his presence. The man's arms seemed to be numbed by the shock transmitted from Fletch's body. They hung uselessly at his sides.

Keith lifted his rifle and almost absently blew the man away. He knelt beside Fletch's body.

Groping fingers touched her face. They came away warm and slippery with blood. Fletch had had another—final—nosebleed. Keith squeezed his eyes shut, let them fall open again. He felt vacant, disbelieving—totally without emotion.

Fletch was dead.

One pocket of her caftan bulged, the corner of a leather case sticking out of it. For no reason at all he picked up the case, leaving bloody fingerprints across its surface, and opened it. Her binoculars. They affected him in a way that her corpse could not. They had been *hers*. She had touched them and used them, and left them briefly to his care. Her spirit was in them.

There was the faintest of noises nearby. Keith snapped out of his introspective daze, feeling a sudden twinge of fear. At least one, possibly several, of the Mummer assassins was still alive. Gingerly he edged toward the sound's source.

Not twenty yards away he came across Bear, still alive. Dark blood covered his wide chest, and his skin was ghastly white. His eyes met Keith's; they were fierce embers of light in a dying face.

"Son of a bitch Bringer. You—killed her." The words were so faint that an instant after they were spoken Keith could not have sworn he'd heard them at all. Perhaps he'd made them up. The fire went out in Bear's eyes, and he was finally, irrevocably dead.

Keith felt tears forming, great salty drops of warm fluid that ran down his cheeks and along the seal of his nucleopore. Whether it was the binoculars, or Bear's accusation, he did not know, but Fletch's death had finally reached him. The tears filled him, choked him, and he pushed down his mask to gulp in fresh air. He threw back his head and cried.

The tears came in an unstoppable gust, and when he fought them down he was empty again, cold and dry inside. *You* killed her, he told himself harshly. Out of spite. Because you felt rejected and jealous. You shot her down knowingly and deliberately. But he couldn't gauge the emotional truth of the thought. It might have been pure reflex, nerves drawn to the breaking point, and no more than that. Honesty forced him to admit that he did not know.

Downslope, at the bottom of the hill, a starting engine screeched. It coughed and choked, time and again, as somebody too anxious to start up one of the buggies flooded the engine. A brief hesitation, and Keith began running down the hillside, in long, rapid strides, heedless of the risk of falling. Branches whipped across his face, leaving raw welts, and he did not notice.

Keith burst out of the trees and was among the buggies just as the engine caught. A short sprint brought him beside the correct vehicle, and he was shoving his rifle into the frightened face of a Mummer assassin.

"Cut it off," he said quietly.

The Mummer obeyed, and the night filled with silence. Up close Keith could see that the assassin was just a kid, even younger than Keith himself. For an instant he didn't recognize the face—his subconscious demanded a gargoyle, an ogre, a monster that reality refused to provide. Yet it was a familiar face, one he had seen before.

"Surprised to see me, Tony?"

The kid squinted at his face, puzzled. Then a wide grin split his thin features, and he relaxed visibly. "Keith! Hey, man—" Keith cut off his words by jabbing the cold rifle muzzle into his face, just below one eye. The smile collapsed into surprise, then fear.

"How many of you are left?" Keith asked. He watched scared eyes try to focus on the rifle.

"None, Keith, just me. I'm the only one." Keith said nothing. Tony tried again. "You killed them all—I can show you the bodies. You killed the captain. . . ." He broke off when Keith moved the rifle gently, massaging the boy's cheek in a small circular motion.

"Good." He spoke quietly, a part of his mind occupied with pushing away the memory of Fletch's death. It was like shoveling back the ocean. "Any of your brothers among the dead?"

"No." Tony would have added more, but Keith silenced him again, by lightly brushing his eyelashes with the rifle tip.

"Okay. Now we come to the good question." Keith paused. "Why?"

Tony blinked. His forehead was slick with sweat. "Why?" he echoed weakly.

"Yes, why?" Keith's voice was calm, controlled. "Why did you and your friends track us out here? Why were you sent to kill us?"

"I don't know."

An instant's rage possessed Keith, an urge to finish this horror by killing the kid where he sat. He controlled the impulse, but something of it must of shown in his face, for Tony shut his eyes and looked as if he were bracing himself to die. "You don't kill people just for the hell of it," Keith said. "You have a reason—a fucking *good* reason. And when the nice man asks you why, you smile polite and answer sweet. Understand?"

The kid began to cry quietly, slow tears squeezing out of the corners of his eyes and sliding down his cheeks. "Honest, Keith, I don't know. The captain knew, but he didn't tell us. He just said we had to bang the woman. He said that anyone with her bought it too, but that the woman was the dangerous one, and we had to bang her."

"Kill her," Keith said. "The word is 'kill.' Let's hear you say it."

"K-kill." Tony almost choked on the word, struggled on. "But that was all we were told, honest, that was all I ever knew."

Keith drew back the rifle, and smiled an insincere smile. "Tell you what. I'm going to let you live. I want you to go back to Philly and give your old man a message. Can you do that?"

The kid nodded.

"I thought you could. Tell Gambiosi that I'm sending him back his son—alive. Tell him that I had you cold, but I sent you back as a gift. You got that so far?"

Another nod. The kid's cheeks were wet.

"And tell him that you didn't kill the woman." Tony looked at him. "I did."

Keith still held Fletch's binoculars, jammed up under one armpit. He dropped them in Tony's lap. "Tell that to your owners. Tell Gambiosi that I did your dirty work for you, and there's the proof."

He backed off a few paces, said, "Well? What are you waiting for?"

The kid's hands fumbled with the ignition. The motor caught and he pulled out onto the road wildly. Keith stood watching him leave.

By dawn he had dragged both Bear's and Fletch's bodies up to the smoldering remains of the cabin. He laid them side by side, then hesitated. It seemed like a violation of the dead. But he had to have an answer.

Keith opened Fletch's robe, and deftly undid the buttons of her shirt. The flesh underneath was an ugly black, massive bruising that had followed her death. Tucked into her belt, protruding over her stomach, was a leather portfolio. He lifted it out, flipped her robe shut.

Standing away from the corpses, his back not quite turned to them, he examined the portfolio's contents. They were hand-written manuscripts, clearly stories Fletch had been working on, cluttered with marginal notes and corrections. They were wrinkled from being carried under her belt and sewn into the lining of her saddlebags before that, but readable nonetheless.

Keith riffled through thin bundles of paper labeled "Drift Communities," "Mutations/Disease," "Mutagenic Offspr." and the like. Halfway through, he hit pay dirt: a bundle labeled "Phila/Drift." He returned the other papers to their sheath, and began reading.

It's the best kept secret in Philadelphia. The infant mortality rate is not a matter of public re-cord. People disappear into the hospitals and the word filters out that they died of "pneumonia" or "flu" or "superflu." Not one person in a thousand suspects that Philadelphia lies within the Drift.

Keith stopped reading. He had his answer. Here were the words that had sealed Fletch's fate, the words that by them-selves could destroy Philadelphia.

A single thicker piece of paper was enclosed in the bundle. Keith thumbed it out from the rest. It was a copy of the map of the Drift that had been drawn up almost a century ago for the first official reports on the Meltdown. Long curving oblongs had been drawn around the reactor site, the outermost just barely grazing Philadelphia. Fletch had jotted a dozen radiation counts onto the map, and redrawn the outermost line. There was no doubt that she had done her homework, no chance of her being mistaken.

Keith tried to imagine the damage the article could do, if published. There were over a million people in Philadelphia, all in mortal dread of the Drift, all superstitiously clinging to their city as a safe haven, clean and free of radiation. He tried to picture these million people, most of them on foot, streaming out of Philadelphia in a panic, clogging the bridges to New Jersey, swooping on the lands beyond like a plague of locusts. The United States was no longer a rich nation; all its fat had been lost in the turbulent post-Meltdown years. There would be no refugee camps for the new fugitives, only guns to mow down this sudden threat to a precarious economy.

It was literally unimaginable. And the only thing that held back this nightmare was the Mummers, with its embargo on high-tech artifacts such as ionization counters, its spies, and its quiet terrorism.

Keith checked his rifle, paced thirty yards downhill, and raised it to his shoulder. He squinted at the hillside just above the ruins of the cabin. Something crippled flew by.

One after the other he shot the projectiles into the earth, until the clip was emptied, and the hillside—whether from the projectiles themselves or from their thundering reverberations—collapsed over the bodies of his former companions.

There were no words worth saying. His duty done, Keith dropped the papers on the ground, and started to trudge down past the corpses of the fallen Mummer assassins. He hadn't gone far before a thought occurred to him, and he returned to scoop up the stories again.

He weighed them in his hand. There was power here, if he knew how to use them. He didn't kid himself. Politics and the acquisition of power were total unknowns to him. But he could learn.

As he started the buggy, Keith became aware again of the irritation his nucleopore caused. He pulled it off and dropped it on the seat beside him. It hardly mattered now.

He shifted gears, and began the long trip home to Philadelphia.

•   •   •

Mummers Day was sunny and blue-skied. Keith stood in the crowd, slapping his arms against his jacket from time to time to keep warm. He was not surprised when the Center City Fancy Club stopped in front of him, not at all anxious when King Clown strode straight at him.

The Clown's gloved hands rested on his shoulders, and Keith looked into the man's bloodshot eyes. He could smell the liquor on the captain's breath. There was a still instant, and then whapwhap*whap!* he had been tapped out, and King Clown was striding away. Keith ran to join the ragtag band in mufti that was strutting happily after the troupe. The crowd cheered.

He was a Mummer now.

II

Nigger Night

The night Jimmy Bowles died, Keith Piotrowicz had to work late in his taproom. A sign on the door read "Closed for Inventory," and half the basement had been dragged out onto the floor. A methane lamp spattered blue light over the countertop, fading to gloom before reaching the walls.

It was a hole-in-the-wall bar, big enough to have a ladies' entrance, but too small for a name or a ladies' parlor. The women shared three tables to the rear of the room. "A regular little gold mine," its previous owner had sarcastically called it, and then had it taken away from him when he shaved the Mummers' share too thin.

"There's a ten-gallon jug of caramel missing since last March," Keith said. The caramel was mixed with alcohol and water, to make the booze for the hard liquor drinkers. That and the beer—which he bought from whom he was told—were all he had to serve customers.

His night man, Jay, flashed a gap-toothed grin. "Yeah, I been wondering when you'd notice that one."

"Well?"

"Well what? It's missing. Maybe somebody walked in the

59

back room one night and lifted it from the shelf. It's gone."

"Oh sure," Keith said. "Somebody walked in the back room and ignored the white entirely and lifted a jug of caramel. Right."

Somebody rattled the door. "Closed!" Jay said. "So I musta ate it, right? You can take it out of my pay."

"Damn it, it's not a question of money, it's a question of trust. You—"

The door-rattler tried again. He began hammering loudly on the door. "*Closed*, damn it!" Jay picked up a length of broom handle that had been drilled out at one end and poured full of molten lead. But Keith waved him down, saying, "I'll do it."

He unlocked the door, peered out. "Hello, Smiley," he said.

The man came in and sat down at the bar. He slid off his hat and laid it down beside his elbow. "Beer," he told Jay. Then, "Big night tonight, eh?"

"You know how these Council meetings are," Keith replied. "Lots of sound and fury, but everything's always decided in advance."

"Well, what I hear is that Gambiosi is going to take it in the ear." He drank down half his beer in a single long draught. "Ouch," he said, placing a hand against his side.

"You planning on paying for that beer?"

Smiley's eyes took on the mournful, betrayed look of a favored dog who has just been kicked by his master. "Now, Keith, I thought we were friends."

"All I'm saying is—you don't pay for the beer, you don't complain about it either."

Smiley cheered right up. "That's just the old kidneys speaking. They act up real bad in this weather."

Keith jabbed a finger at the ledger. "Is this a six or an eight?"

"A nine."

"I couldn't tell."

"How's your nigger doing?" Smiley asked suddenly. "Still in Jefferson, is he?" He took a gingerly sip of his remaining beer.

"The doctors say he's doing just fine for a man in his condition. His age. But you know how these things go." Keith shrugged. "Who can say?"

"You and him was pretty close, huh?"

"I guess." Keith ran a pencil down a column of figures, checked off twenty items in rapid succession, turned the page.

"How'd you and him get together in the first place?" Smiley was like that. He gathered information continuously, even obsessively, in the firm belief that it would do him some good someday. Only he didn't have the faintest idea how to use it, so that he amassed an enormous clutter of fact and speculation, to no purpose whatsoever. But people tolerated him because it was always possible to shake that same information out of him later, and sometimes it was useful. So maybe it did do him some good after all.

Keith corrected a figure and said without looking up, "Well, he took an interest in me when I was just starting out—tried to help me, gave me a lot of advice. None of it any good. So when I started making good, I had to give him a hand, right?"

Smiley nodded. He could understand *that;* it was the way his world ran, on favor and friendship and shared opportunity. "They say that old man practically worships you. I hear he got drunk last month and went around crying and talking how you were his son." He laughed.

"Yeah, well, Jimmy can be a sentimental slob."

Someone else began rattling the door and hammering on its panels. The sound echoed and reverberated in the dark room. Smiley looked puzzled. "Now what kind of asshole—can't he see that we're closed?"

"Just . . . drink your beer, Smiley." Keith got up and went to the door again.

A black man stood there, a skinny, proud-looking creature in a chauffeur's uniform with a cluster of feathers on the breast pocket. In the alley behind him was an American flag. There were only twenty such cars in all of Philadelphia, and they all belonged to the Mummers. "Compliments of Mr. Gambiosi." The chauffeur touched his cap lightly. "He was concerned that you arrive at the Council meeting on time."

Smiley looked on with considerable interest. Keith could practically see the wheels spinning. The Council meeting was not for another two hours. It was possible to walk to Mummer Hall twice over in that time. "Gambiosi must be getting pretty nervous," Smiley said, "if he's—"

Jay rolled his eyes upward. "Smiley," Keith said, "did you ever stop to think that being a fool might not protect you *all* your life?"

"I—"

"Just shut up," Keith advised. He turned to leave.

Mummer Hall was almost empty. Calder's mobile *Ghost* hung motionless over the great stairs. Slowly Keith climbed between the twin rows of mannequins in the costumes of Mummers Clubs of years gone by. These were the great bands, from before the corrupting touch of politics: Ferko, Fralinger, Liberty Clowns, Trilby, Hog Island, Golden Sunrise, Aqua, Strutters, Ukrainian-American, Top Hat, Fancy Dans, Downtowners . . . all in feathers and glitter, instruments in hand, frozen into silence for all eternity.

Keith's office was small, little more than a cubby. It held a desk and two chairs, one for visitors. But it had a painting and electric lighting. The electricity came from the low-head generator at the old Waterworks dam on the Schuylkill, just above Mummer Hall. The painting was by Chagall; Keith did not have the status for a Monet or a Rembrandt. It was called "The Trough," and it showed a woman and a pig both drinking from the same coffinlike trough of blood. The blood was purplered, with bubbles of light rising from its depths. The pig had a knowing look on its face.

Keith unlocked his desk, removed a thick file from one drawer, and began to leaf through it. He was buried in a list of Southern Manufacturing and Biotech products being shipped to the Drift, when two pudgy black hands laid themselves on his desk. Fat gold rings dug into the flesh, and diamonds shone from them.

"Captain Moore," Keith said, rising. But Jason Moore waved him down, with a wide, self-deprecating gesture. He reversed the visitor's chair and sat astraddle it, leaning over the back. At that, he was uncomfortably close, halfway over the desk.

Moore was captain of the North Philadelphia String Band.

There were more powerful men than he, but no one could afford to ignore the head of the largest black Mummers Club in the city.

"I've been to Jefferson, visiting your man, Bowles." Moore shook his head heavily. "I fear that he is not long for this world."

"He's old, Jimmy is," Keith agreed. "But he's led a long, productive life."

"Praise Jesus." Moore folded his two great hands, one into the other. "I wanted you to know that it has not gone unnoticed in the black community, the care—yes, and even love—you have shown one of our own."

Keith bowed his head. "Jimmy's a good man," he said, feeling a twinge of disgust at himself. "A very good man."

"Amen to that, brother! Amen to that! But what I came here to tell you was that I've arranged for there to be a runner waiting at Jefferson around the clock, to let you know if there's any change in Mr. Bowles' condition."

"Well, that's very generous of you," Keith said carefully.

"No, no, not at all." Those pudgy hands moved forward, leeched onto Keith's shoulders, squeezed, and were gone. Moore rocked back, and then heaved himself up out of his chair. "I do it because I'd like to think of myself as your friend."

Keith stood. He recognized the gambit. "Thank you, sir. I'd like to think of myself as your friend too."

Moore's shoe-button eyes gleamed. He nodded and turned to leave, and almost collided in the doorway with Gambiosi.

The two men drew back from each other, like serpents recoiling before striking. They studied each other's eyes, and circled slightly, in the manner of boxers.

Moore was the first to disengage. "Good to see you, Joe," he said. "I expect we'll meet again in Council."

"Yeah, I'm looking forward to it," Gambiosi replied.

But when Moore was gone, he collapsed heavily into the chair. "Jesus." He took out a large, white handkerchief, mopped his brow. "That son of a bitch. He's going to throw me to the fucking wolves tonight."

"Look," Keith said. "I've been over this with you. It's in the bag. We've got answers for anything they might bring up.

You're going to come out of this smelling like roses."

"Yeah, well, I don't think so." Gambiosi carefully folded his handkerchief and tucked it away. "What's the story on your nigger?"

"He's on a respirator. Nobody expects much."

"Well, he's old," Gambiosi said. He stared at the Chagall in silence for a while, finally shook his head and looked away. "Ugly damn thing."

"We could go over the biomass projections again."

Slowly, Gambiosi's head tilted forward, until he was staring directly at his knees. He placed his hands on his upper legs, pushed slightly, as if to keep knees and face apart. "What's the use? I bit off more than I could chew and now I'm gonna choke on it. Another couple of hours and the whole thing goes to you."

"I don't understand."

Gambiosi looked up angrily. "Can the crap, willya? I know how you've taken over on me. It's been a long time since I been running the resettlement program. Hell, even back at the beginning the decisions were all yours. When they ask me questions tonight, I'm not going to have any answers. 'Cause I don't really know what's going on any more."

Keith said nothing.

"I mean, there's no hard feelings or nothing. It ain't like you done it deliberately. Just—I don't want you to think I don't know."

"Captain Gambiosi?"

Gambiosi swiveled to face the two officers of the court standing in the doorway. "You guys mind if I have a couple last words with my assistant?"

The officers looked at each other. "Ten minutes," one said, and they stepped back into the hallway, closing the door behind them.

"I only need two," Gambiosi said. Then, to Keith, "Look, I can take you down with me."

Keith started. Gambiosi looked steadily at him, through eyes that were infinitely weary. "There's no benefit to me in shooting you down, kid, but I swear to God I can do it. Just try me, if you don't believe I can."

"What do you want?" Keith said quietly.

"My boy Tony. I got a good job lined up for him, collecting the cut from a string of tappies down South Philly. It doesn't take much; he ought to do okay."

"All right."

"Yeah, and one of these days he's gonna dip his hand into the till, more than he oughta, and he's going to get caught, you know that?"

"I'll do what I can," Keith said. "But you oughta know, stuff like that—one time's the limit. I can pull him out the first time, but after that, I dunno."

"One time's all he needs. He pulls a dumb stunt like that twice, he deserves what he gets. I wouldn't ask you for nothing you couldn't handle."

"Okay," Keith said. "Sure, I can do that. You got my word on it."

Gambiosi sighed, and shook his head. Slowly he rose, as if by taking his time, he could hold off the future. "If you see Jimmy, tell him I hope he gets well real soon."

The Council had been in session over an hour before Keith was called in. He sat in the antechamber, idly flipping through his folders as he waited. It seemed forever before the officers of the court came for him.

They escorted him through an archway and into the Council hall, with its ancient stone pillars and canopy. The room had originally been part of an Indian temple, dismantled and stolen during the nineteenth century, and shipped to Philadelphia. It had been reassembled there as part of the Oriental wing of the Art Museum. Bodhisattvas and other heathen deities leered down from the roof and colonnade.

Gambiosi was already lost.

The big man was pale and sweating. He did not look up at Keith's entrance, but kept his eyes steadily fixed on the wood between his hands. The other members of Council, captains of the most powerful Mummers Clubs in the city, sat about the vast table, calm and bored and disapproving by turns. Someone coughed, and the sound echoed boomingly.

For the first time it occurred to Keith that he might not

emerge from this unscathed. Fleetingly, he was sorry to have set the machinery in motion.

"Mr. Piotrowicz," Captain Moore said sternly. In the dim light, his dark skin seemed ominous, his massive fat imposing. "Your superior has informed us that there exists some intricate, clever plan for extricating order from the mess that has been made of the resettlement program."

It sounded like an attack, but in fact Moore had given him the best opening he could have hoped for. "Yes, sir," he said. "I believe there is."

The Council sent Keith away, to make their deliberations in secret. But he already knew which way they would jump. He had won them over, all of them. The power that had been concentrated in Gambiosi's hands was now in his.

It had been a long night, and Keith was tired. He returned to his desk, to lock the papers away. Then, since he had to wait on the Council's final judgment, he took out the SM&B requisitions list again, and began crossing off items that could be done without. He lost himself in the work, and so had no idea of how much time had passed when there was a small tentative cough at his open door.

He looked up. There was a black kid, about ten years old, in the doorway. A runner.

"Jesus, what is this—nigger night?" Keith said. The kid trembled but otherwise stood frozen. "Well come on, out with it."

Taking a quick breath, the boy said, "Captain Moore's compliments, sir, and Mister Bowles died at Jefferson this evening at seventeen minutes past ten."

The hallway was empty; Keith could hear footsteps down at its far end, then silence. After a minute, he said, "Okay, you can go."

For the longest time, Keith stared at the shut door, waiting for the tears to come. But there was nothing there.

He bent over his work.

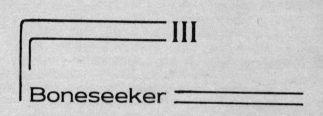

III

Boneseeker

The young vampire awoke at dawn. She was dreaming of her father when the sun squeezed between the boxcar doors and hit her right in the eye. She winced and nuzzled into her battered leather suitcase, trying for a minute's more sleep. Then the woman beside her shifted and dug an elbow into her stomach and she woke up.

The train had stopped. Up ahead the methane-burning locomotive was being yanked and replaced by an alcohol-burner. Samantha could smell the mingled scents over the stink of urine and sour sweat, of human waste and menstrual blood. Only a few women were up, and these sat silent and unmoving among the shadowy sleepers. The sick one in the corner still shivered in the grip of some unnamed fever.

Sam was hungry. Her belly ached so hard it seemed to throb. She clutched the grip to her and opened it warily, jealously. Some of these women would as soon steal your food as look at you. Reaching in, she removed a canteen, a tin of vitamin capsules, and the last newspaper-wrapped egg.

The idiot girl was trying to get out again. She had stretched

one long, anorexic arm through the crack between the far doors
and was struggling to cram her shoulder through. It was hope-
less, but she didn't realize that. She gasped and panted in a
frenzy to be free that was almost sexual in its unreasoning
intensity.

Sam looked away, disgusted, and stared out through the
gap in her own door at the gray, misty morning. She carefully
unwrapped the egg. It was cracked but not broken. She shook
a vitamin capsule into her hand, pulled it open, and smeared
its contents across her tongue. Then she broke open the egg,
separating out the yolk and swallowing the white raw. Surreptitiously, she chucked the yolk and shells out the door and
licked her fingers clean.

Lifting the canteen to her ear, Sam gave it a small shake.
It was almost empty—only a swallow left. She uncapped it,
sniffed to see that the contents hadn't gone bad, then tipped it
back and let the good rich blood fill her mouth. She washed
it about, savoring the taste, before swallowing. Closing her
eyes, she concentrated on the feel of it flowing down her throat.

Gone. With a sigh, Sam recapped the canteen.

From her door she could only see the cinder footing for the
tracks and a few scrub trees. The white uniform of a NIGH
guard loomed up, and the chains holding the doors locked were
rattled and the doors themselves slammed with an iron baton,
to make sure all fingers were clear.

The idiot girl suddenly wailed in pain and fear. She jerked
back from her door and clutched her arm to her body, rocking
back and forth, crying. Women started from their sleep, with
startled demands to know what was happening.

A long hoot sounded from the alky locomotive ahead. With
a sudden lurch and tug, the train began to move. Sam glimpsed
the guard as he trotted alongside, snagged a grab bar, and swung
up to the side of the car. A moment later, she heard him stomp
by overhead.

He was whistling, as if he had not a care in the world.

Baltimore was a sea of gray slum buildings; the train
took hours to wind through it. Ragged children were scattered
along the tracks the entire way, gleaning whatever spillage was
to be found from the freights that passed through. When they

saw the NIGH train, they stood back and jeered and threw rocks.

At noon they stopped at a set of holding pens at the far outskirts of the city. The train jerked and shuddered forward haltingly as the colonists were processed, a car at a time. The morning chill had died away—it was hot now. The process seemed to go on forever.

Then one set of doors slammed open, and a guard bawled, "Awright, you cunts—*out!*" They stumbled down the chute, blinking in the sunlight.

They had all, of course, been processed in the Richmond Detention Camps, and were identically clad in electric purple trousers and blouse—to facilitate identification, they had been told. And they all had the same bruise on their foreheads, where they'd been shot with the tattoo gun, though some few—fast healers—showed only the shapeless blue blob of ink there. But worst of all was how their heads had been shorn in De-Lousing, almost to the skin, leaving them all looking scrawny and awful and horribly vulnerable.

My God, they look barely human, Sam thought.

Guards with electric prods herded them through a maze of "people-mover" gates and fences. Sam could see the local slum-dwellers hanging on the chain link fences, watching, vacant and hostile. She remembered their brethren down in Richmond, when she had been run through the open-air chemical showers, and squeezed her eyes shut tight.

She was jostled forward. A NIGH flunky thrust a bucket of water at her. The water was warm, and not overly clean, but she drank as deep as she could before it was wrenched from her and passed to the next in line.

Someone shoved a package into her arms, and she stared down at it in blank incomprehension. Then a guard goosed the woman ahead of her between the legs with his prod, for not hurrying. He laughed as she leaped spasmodically and fell. Samantha clutched her package tight and scuttled by, and was rotated back into the car.

The doors were chained and tested, and a guard slammed the side of the car with his truncheon. The train lurched forward.

The packages contained food, the food they had been prom-

ised a day and a half ago in Richmond. All had been permitted
to bring what supplies they could, but these were mostly gone,
and the packages were unwrapped with small cries of joy, and
very few of disappointment.

Sam stared at her food. There was a large chunk of wheat
bread, a lopsided slab of unidentifiable cheese, and a lump of
beet sugar. Enough to keep a normal woman going for at least
another day, if she didn't mind hunger. She put a morsel of
bread in her mouth. It tasted good and it would kill the hunger,
but it held no nourishment for her. There was nothing here she
could digest.

She could eat, but it would not keep her alive.

"Is this *all?*" a woman shouted hysterically. Everyone turned
to look. She was grossly fat, and the melanin in her face had
broken down, leaving white patches everywhere and a large
pink blotch under her lip that gave her an indignant look, like
a goldfish with fungus. "I can't *live* on this! I got *glandular*
problems—I need more *food!*" She was waving the empty
paper wrapper in the air, like a banner, her food already eaten.

Somebody snickered. A second joined her, and then more.
Faces took on expressions of scorn. Soon the car all but rocked
with laughter. It was cruel, ghoulish humor, but it was con-
tagious, and they all joined in.

The piebald woman shouted indignantly. She threw the paper from her and the veins on her forehead stood out, but she
could not make herself heard over the laughter. Finally she
turned her broad back on them all and crouched down, facing
into the corner.

When the laughter had died away, Sam eased her way to
the woman's side, and sat. She waited a while, then touched
her sleeve. The woman drew her arm away.

"Missus," Sam said, and when the woman looked up angrily, she held up her rewrapped package. "Would you like
mine? I can't eat it—honest."

The woman stared at her for the longest time, stern and
unblinking. Sam proffered the bundle again, then placed it in
the woman's lap.

Finally the woman looked down. "Well, bless you child,"
she said. And then, after a pause, "That's right gracious of
you."

She broke the cheese in half, put one chunk in her mouth and chewed. "I wouldn't take this if I didn't need it," she said. "I wasn't lying. What's your name, child?"

"Samantha Laing."

"Name's Celeste. I got short bowel syndrome—you ever heard of that?" Occupied with her food, she didn't notice Samantha shiver and draw herself back. "My intestines are too short, see. I ain't got it *bad,* but it takes me twice as much food as anybody else to get any nourishment. 'Cause it passes through so quick, you see. And I got this glandular thing on top of it." She forced the bread into her mouth, mawed it down with great, muscular chewings. "But it ain't none of it genetic. They made a bad mistake about that. I got it from being so sick when I was a child, all burnt up with fever."

Samantha, who knew better, nodded anyway. And when Celeste asked what *her* problem was, she quickly said, "Vitamin deficiency. I can only eat a special diet."

"Well don't you worry," Celeste said. "They be sure to have what you need ready when we reach the Drift." The lie hung between them for a long, silent minute, and then she said, "Where you from?"

"Seven Pines," Sam said. "That's just outside of Richmond. I was living at Miss Levering's Boarding School."

"You like it there?"

"It was okay. I got to ride horses on Sundays, for an hour."

"You got lots of friends there?"

Sam thought of how the other girls looked at her at table, where she had to eat foods she'd eliminate an hour later, the jokes they made, and the stories they spread about her. "No," she said. To change the subject, she asked, "Do you know anything about where we're going?" She meant the resettlement camps, but Celeste misunderstood her.

"I hear tell there's worse places than the Drift," she said. "I mean, it be poisoned up all bad for sure, but you can *live* there. So maybe you pick up a sick cancer ten, twenty years down the line—so what? If the choice is dying now. . . ." She let her voice trail off. "Listen, lemme tell you a story my uncle told me when I was a little girl. He came out of the Drift with my daddy when he was young—had the bad lungs to show for it too. And *he* said . . ."

Off and on for the rest of that day and into the night, Celeste retold her childhood tales of the Drift. They were full of cannibals and radioactive monsters that came out from the swamps and glowing green mutants who returned from the dead, but they helped to pass the time, and keep Sam's mind off of her hunger.

But she began to grow weaker through the day and night that followed and the morning after that, for the lack of food.

Sam's stomach was a knot of solid pain by the time the train reached Philadelphia. It hurt so much she could no longer identify it as pain, and was left feeling numb down there, without sensation. Her cheeks burned like two coals, and her eyes felt dry when she blinked.

The doors slammed open. Celeste helped her to her feet and put the grip into her hands. She was herded out with the others, feeling light and dreamlike. The train went away, and the guards with it; for the authority of the National Institute for Genetic Health ended here, and that of the City of Philadelphia picked up.

They were left standing in a large pen, separated only by a single fence from a similarly large holding of men. A few of the more energetic women were trying to locate their husbands, and they were thrust back from the fence by black-uniformed guards. Mummers, these guards were called, reflecting some weird local power structure.

Sam saw everything lucid and bright, as if the world had been polished and then drenched in a perfectly clear liquid—it all seemed to sparkle. There were a number of battered wooden buildings nearby, warehouses and such, and she compulsively stared at each in turn, as if committing them to memory. It served no purpose, and she stopped when she saw the slaughterhouse.

They were slaughtering cattle. Sam could hear them faintly, lowing somewhere within the building. These same pens must be used for cattle, she thought. A glance downward confirmed it—they were walking through a mud made of churned-up dirt and cattle leavings. There was some little straw ground in.

The usual idlers were by the fence, and Sam singled out

one, a boy of about ten, as most likely. Feverishly she rummaged through her bag, and came up with the canteen and one of the ten silver dollars she had managed to save from the NIGH officials.

She went as close to the outer fence as the guards would allow, and threw the dollar over it. It landed in a puff of dust by the boy. Like a flash, he snagged it from the dirt, and held it two-handed, staring at the thing as if he couldn't believe his good fortune.

"You like that, kid?" Sam called to him. "You want to earn another one just like it?" It was a Bank of Atlanta dollar, probably the first the kid had ever seen. But silver was silver the world over.

The kid nodded. His eyes were big.

Sam threw her canteen after the dollar. It flew wide, but the kid sprinted after it and, puzzled, retrieved it. "Go into the slaughterhouse," she told him. "They bleed the cattle there. Tell them to fill the canteen with blood—it doesn't cost much, a nickel at most. Then throw it back to me and I'll toss you another dollar. Got that?"

The kid stared at her. She might as well have been speaking a foreign language for all the understanding he showed. Sam hurt bad, and she wanted the blood so much she could taste it. "For God's sake," she ranted, "it's easy money! Dammit, do you want me to *starve* to—"

There was silence all around her. Abruptly, Sam realized that she had an audience. All the women and the nearby idlers were staring at her. For a long minute the stillness held.

Then the kid threw the canteen back over the fence at her, turned and ran. The moment broke. The Philadelphians began picking up rubble to throw at her. The colonists edged away, leaving her isolated and alone.

Sam felt fear. "Celeste," she said. But the big woman had backed away with the rest. She saw Celeste stoop to pick up a clod of earth.

Then a stone grazed her cheek, and another struck her knee, and everyone was shouting and the world rose up in a babble of voices.

She would have died then if the black-uniformed guards

hadn't plunged into the crowd, riot staffs flashing. A rough hand closed around her arm and jerked her away. She stumbled after, unresisting.

A leathery face thrust itself almost into hers. "You deaf or something?" the man demanded. "What did you do to start this?"

"I don't know, I just came here and . . ."

"You got a name?" The guard shook her. It was hard to stay awake. "What do they call you, hah?"

"Sam."

"What are you doing in with the ladies, Sam? You got a girlfriend or something?" He began hauling her away, quick-marching her before him. "Don't let me catch you jumping that fence again." He thrust her into the men's pen.

When they divided up the men and led her away with one group, Sam didn't even object.

Sam remembered very little of her ride into the Drift. Only that she was loaded into a truck—one of a convoy— with a lot of men who smelled bad and that it bounced and rumbled on almost forever. There was the smell of burned alcohol in the air, and she remembered thinking how extravagant it was to use an internal combustion engine to transport a corpse, and no more.

Sam was lying on a cot, under a window. Outside, somebody was talking loudly. She kept her eyes closed, listening, trying to make sense of his words.

". . . back to America and even longer if you wanta go north to the Greenstate Alliance. So you just try it, if you want. Nobody's gonna stop you." The voice was faint and had a sarcastic twang, like that of a drill instructor for the Virginia militia she'd once heard. "'Course you got an awful lot of *hot* land to pass through to get anywhichwhere. I do not advise you try. But—"

Someone put a hand to her mouth, removed a thermometer she had not known was there. He muttered to himself and lifted an arm to take her pulse.

Sam opened her eyes. There was a dwarf standing on a stool

beside the cot, calmly studying her. His head was enormous, almost half again the size of a normal person's, and he had alert, intelligent eyes. "Do you feel up to eating something?" he asked.

Because Sam knew she was going to die, the room took on special interest for her. She could see three other cots crammed between ancient cabinets and desks, obviously salvaged from abandoned houses and in bad repair. The mahogany bookshelves were so badly warped that only half could hold books at all, and the floor might have been a funhouse mirror distortion. But every spot was clean, painstakingly scrubbed down.

Two of the cots were unoccupied; the third held a young man, comatose.

"I'm not really a doctor," the dwarf said. He hopped off the stool, carried it to the far side of the room, and climbed up it again. There, atop a rickety table, was a tin bowl resting on a tripod over a small alcohol lamp. Belatedly, Sam caught the scent of broth. "Mostly I just set bones and such. But I've got all these books, and they help. They're over a hundred years old, but medicine hasn't really changed much since the Meltdown."

He fetched the broth to her side. "I'm Robert Esterhaszy," he said. "Bob. Pleased to meet you." He paused, giving her a chance to reply, then began spoon-feeding her broth. It was warm and tasty, and it filled her stomach.

"I'll have you up and around in no time," Esterhaszy said. "I guess I know malnutrition when I see it." When the bowl was empty, he went across the room to check on his other patient.

An hour later Sam's system cleansed itself. She lay groggily passive as Esterhaszy cleaned her up and moved her to a new cot. He frowned. "I think you've got something strange." Sam let her eyes fall closed.

She opened her eyes and it was night. Esterhaszy must have been waiting, for he was at her side immediately. He held her internal passport in his hand. "It says here you've got SBS," he said. "What is that, some kind of disease? What does it mean?"

Sam looked at him steadily, without emotion. She found

that while she could understand his every word, what he said meant nothing to her.

Finally the dwarf went away. Sam thought she was asleep again, but then she heard him sigh and shift in his chair. Pages turned quietly.

A wooden match flared as Esterhaszy lit up a cigar. The harsh, rough-edged odor of northern marijuana filled the room. Half asleep and attenuated as she was, Sam felt herself floating off the instant the light fumes hit her. She looked down and saw her body lying discarded on the cot, pale and thin, and as lifeless as an old rag doll.

Her awareness paused, hovering, near the ceiling. Then it passed through a wall and out of the building. She was in a city of ruins, a nineteenth-century mill town by the look of it, abandoned after the Meltdown in the twentieth. The buildings were mostly brick shells, with collapsed roofs and floors, though some few had been partially restored, with timbers laid across the tops and thatching tied over them.

The streets were overgrown with twisted, stunted vegetation—predominantly scrub sumac and mutant thistle—with paths worn down their centers. Heaps of lumbered wood lay everywhere; entire roofless buildings served as holding pens for the stackwood. In a former park or Little League field, huge distillation tanks had been erected, and the slow fires beneath them were tended by a few ragged, dirty men.

The moon was full, and she could see the stubble on their chins, the way the fingers of one's left hand curled back in an unnatural, broken fashion.

The stench of woodsmoke was everywhere. The building fronts were all black with it. Sam peered into an old brick storefront, and saw that the inside had been refitted as a dormitory, one huge room with line upon line of crudely made cots. Not everyone had blankets, and some of the men she could see belonged in the infirmary with her.

Something went tap-tap. Sam ignored it. She looked beyond the town, past the joyhouse, into the lumbered-over areas, and saw that a wide swath had been burned down to ashes and bare earth. There were soldiers patrolling there, men in black uniforms with small feather clusters on their chests. They held their weapons combat-ready, and they faced outward, toward the Drift, rather than inward, toward the town. Something went tap-tap again.

Someone was gently striking her cheek. "Stop that," Sam mumbled, and opened her eyes and was back in the infirmary again. Bob the dwarf stood at her side, trying to wake her. At the sight of her eyes, weakly reflecting the blue flame of the single alcohol lamp, he gently pried a spoon between her lips, and let dribble a few drops of liquid. Automatically, she swallowed.

Blood.

Her face must have reflected her shock, for Esterhaszy smiled. "Ah," he said. "The patient responds. Old Dogmeat will be glad to learn his sacrifice has not been in vain." He brought the spoon to her lips again. "We'll start you off with just a few tablespoons."

Eventually, she slept.

When she awoke, it was day again. The sun pouring in through the window membrane lit up the blond hair of the man leaning over her, turning it into a blazing halo, and the man himself into an angel. He was beautiful, with deep care lines around his mouth, and clear, sad eyes. He smiled and said, "Good morning."

Sam stared at him wonderingly. But she was wrapped in ice, cool and clear as air, and could not answer. Esterhaszy dragged a chair to her side and began to spoon-feed her a few more mouthfuls of blood. The stranger ran a hand over her short, almost nonexistent hair. It felt strange and prickly.

"Samantha," the stranger said, "my name is Keith Piotrowicz. I hold a high position in the Philadelphia Mummers organization, and it's the Mummers who are administering the resettlement program in the Drift. I have the power to have you returned to your family. But you have to cooperate. You have to tell me your full name."

The ice filled the room, one great lump, and while it did not hinder motion, its cold froze out the pain, numbed it into silence. "Can't she speak?" Keith asked the dwarf.

"I don't know," Esterhaszy said. The dwarf spread his arms

wide in a gesture of helplessness. "My guess is that she can but that she doesn't want to. She's probably had some bad experiences on the way up here."

"Hmmm." Hands behind back, Keith wandered away, to look at a large, hand-drawn map of the Drift the dwarf had hung on one wall. It had been copied from some older chart with meticulous care, with later emendations made in the same color ink. Wobbly circles radiated out from the ancient Meltdown site, and there were little balls of red and green wax stuck to the map at various points. The green wax clustered to the north, near the Greenstate, growing sparser toward the center of the territory—what used to be midstate Pennsylvania—and the red similarly dwindled from the south, by Philadelphia. It looked like a game of Chinese checkers just starting to unfold. "Will it help if I talk to her?"

Again Esterhaszy shrugged. "I'm not a psychiatrist. Hell, I'm not even a doctor."

Keith stared at the map for a time, silent. At last he said, "Your information is out of date," and removed a red glob of wax, replacing it with green. "We lost another resettlement camp four days ago." He went to Samantha's cot and knelt by her side.

"You *are* Samantha Laing, aren't you?" He was silent, waiting for an answer. The ice sparkled about him, cold and peaceful. "Because if you are, I can return you to your family. To your father."

He took something from the dwarf—there was a flash of silver as the object changed hands. He held it up in the air, the antique cigarette case she had kept her passports in. That's mine, she thought, but the ice closed in around her so that she could hardly breathe. It sank deep into her flesh, stilling and calming her.

Keith turned the case over in his hands, opened it. He removed a cracked glass plate from within—an old holograph—and held it up to the sunlight.

A rainbow danced on the bright dustmotes and, as Keith rotated his wrist, coalesced into a fuzzy, doubled image in the air. Seizing the plate by two edges, he lightly bent it until the cracked surface was flat. The images joined, merged, sharpened.

A stern man with angular, hawklike features and a dark mustache floated in the air above her. Her father.

Samantha opened her mouth, and the ice rushed in to fill it, freezing her lungs into silence. A tear formed at the corner of her eye.

"Is this your father, Samantha?"

Something shifted within her, something moved. With a great internal tumult, like icebergs freeing themselves of a glacier to settle into the Arctic water with great steaming splash, she could think again, could feel, could experience pain.

"Yes!" she cried, and her voice was so harsh the word was unintelligible. Tears flooded her eyes. She swallowed and her throat hurt. "Yes," the picture was of her father, and "Yes," she would speak, and "Yes," she was going to live.

Keith cradled her head, and hugged her to him, as she cried and cried.

Sam was too weak to be moved right away. She was bedridden for most of a week, and when she finally got up to hobble about on a cane, she collapsed almost at once. But she improved rapidly, and soon Esterhaszy took to turning her outside during infirmary hours, where previously he had simply placed a screen before her cot.

She was sitting on the infirmary stoop, the evening after the comatose patient's burial, when a work gang was marched by, back—to judge by their tools—from the outlying communal fields. The dozen men were accompanied by a Mummer guard, but she knew enough about the resettlement camp by now to know that the guard was not there to keep the men from escaping, but to report them if they tried to shirk their labor. The guard trudged along as tiredly and dispiritedly as any of the others.

But as they threaded the path between weed-overgrown heaps of rust that had once been automobiles, one of them glanced up at her. His eyes were hard and glittery in his dead face. And in those eyes Sam could see herself as he saw her: young, with no particular face, a purple blotch on her forehead below dirty, crew-cut hair, a face half hidden by a soiled nucleopore mask and still pudgy with baby fat.

And she *felt* his tired, disinterested lust, his cold, impersonal

hostility. He would just as soon throw her down to the ground
and rape her as not, and if he broke a few bones, cracked her
spine, snapped her neck in the process . . . well, it didn't matter
to *him*. He didn't need a lot of life in his meat.

Then he was gone, along with the rest of the work crew,
down the road and around a collapsed duplex. The flood of
images from his brain cut off, and within her own, Sam felt
some newly opened gate shut with convulsive finality. Whatever it was that had happened, she would not be receptive to
it again.

Sam could feel the blood draining from her face, her clenched
teeth threatening to bite through her tongue. Her flesh crawled
with the memory of his cold, reptilian lust. But she controlled
herself; she felt sure her expression mirrored none of what she
felt.

The door clattered open behind her, and she shifted to the
side of the stoop so the last of Esterhaszy's patients could go
by. He didn't glance her way, but stared straight out before
him, a young man with skin as pale as his nucleopore, and
reeking of despair.

Esterhaszy followed him out, more slowly, and with a sigh
settled down beside her on the step. He glanced curiously at
her pale skin. "What's happened to you?"

Sam didn't think she could answer. To deflect the question,
she said, "The big, spongy thing inside your body that goes
from *here* to *here*"—she indicated with gestures—"kind of
like two big wings—is that the lungs?"

"Yes," Esterhaszy said.

"The guy that just left—what's he got in his lungs?"

"Well, I'm not really sure. But the two best candidates are
uranium-233 and plutonium-239, one or both."

"They're in his bones too, aren't they?"

"Yeah, they're both boneseekers. And they've got half lives
of one hundred sixty-two thousand and twenty-four thousand
years respectively. So they stay hot for a long time."

"What's a boneseeker?"

"A boneseeker is the reason we have to wear these damned
masks." He shifted a bit, getting more comfortable. "It sure
would be nice to be able to smoke a cigar on the stoop at the

end of the day, eh?" There was a fine, rich sunset spreading itself over the ruins; he gazed off into it. "A boneseeker is a radioisotope that because of its chemical properties tends to collect in the bones. Most of them are alpha-emitters, and would be harmless enough if they were anywhere else because even a piece of paper will stop alpha radiation. But sitting inside the body, the radiation breaks up the cells, causes lung cancer, leukemia, bone marrow cancer—depends on where it lodges."

"We're talking about that bright glittery stuff, like inside that guy's lungs and bones, right?"

"Yeah, I guess—hey, what do you think you're doing?"

Sam finished untying her nucleopore, and took her first long, clean breath in days. "It's okay," she said. "There's a little dusting of that stuff way down the street there—see? But there's none of it near to us."

Esterhaszy stared down the street, then back at Sam, at a loss for words. Sam stood up.

"I'm awful tired. I guess I'll go in to sleep now."

That night Sam dreamed she hung high over the ruined town and could see it all laid out beneath her. She could see how the long fingers of radioactive dust, glittering blue and pink and white, reached out of the Drift and into the town. One stretched across the communal fields to the north of town. The ruins served as windbreaks, and the drift patterns piled up on the east side, away from the prevailing westerly winds. The entire camp should be moved west a quarter length, Sam realized, and a bit south.

Nestled within the town were the camp buildings, the common barracks to the center, and the privately restored buildings of the trustees in a loose ring about them. Off by itself was a lone house in which lived four or five women, haggard and hard-looking.

She looked away from the town, into the woods that glittered in places like Fairyland and elsewhere were as moonless dark as the pits of Hell. Where the glitter was most pronounced, the trees were scant and malformed, some of them dwarfish and twisted. Just above the trees, to the west, there was still a scattering of light, residual radiation from the sun. To the south—

To the south, the horizon line *glowed*. The glow rose and grew into a great, bulging blue dome, and thrusting up from the center of the dome was a thin, bright spike of light, so unbearably intense that Sam had to flinch away. It was huge, miles high, and felt unspeakably dangerous.

The night pulsed.

Hanging motionless above the town, Sam felt the sky tilt. Slowly, she began to slide into the cold burning light of the thing beyond the horizon. She felt its dark, uncaring glee as it reached to swallow her up. Frantically, she grabbed for support. But the air provided no handholds. She began slipping faster.

The night pulsed.

Desperately, she willed herself downward, toward the safety of the town. And slowly she *did* descend, but still the thing pulled her toward itself, its huge gravities reaching out to crush her in their embrace. The thing was located somewhere far over the horizon, in the direction of the Meltdown site—indeed, Sam realized, the correlation of place was so exact that it must be at the Meltdown site, must in fact *be* the Meltdown site.

The night pulsed.

A wind rose around her. It tore at her with cold, insubstantial claws. Whatever lay beyond the horizon must be *alive* in some sense. She could feel it beating slowly, like a gigantic heart with each pulse so slow that minutes separated it from the last. And it wanted her. Sam struggled like a starling caught in a hurricane, thrashing helplessly and fighting for the ground, but carried helplessly along.

She was swept far past the town, dark trees tumbling below her, mixing in her vision with dark clouds above. The thing was dragging her along more quickly now, thrusting her toward its unseen maw, and Sam cried aloud in frustration. She yearned to leave the sky, the wind, for the dark, comforting earth.

The sky filled with tentacles, and they closed about her, choking off her air.

Then one of her feet brushed the ground, ever so slightly, and she woke up.

· · ·

Keith had returned. Sam had wandered outside (the wind was up and glittery, and she wore her nucleopore) and around the back of the infirmary, and there he was. He and Bob were standing talking in front of an old Fiat dealership that Esterhaszy had converted to a holding pen for the camp's mules.

Esterhaszy was showing Keith the cannulae he'd implanted in several of the mules' throats. They were of tissue-inert plastic with teflon valves, and the incisions were almost perfectly healed. Sam watched the dwarf bleed off a pint of blood from Priscilla, letting it drain into a glass jar.

"Let's see the oxylate," Esterhaszy said. Among the row of saddlebags waiting to be loaded were two aluminum suitcases with Southern Manufacturing and Biotech logos on their fronts. Keith opened one, and Sam was dazzled by a tightly organized array of glass ampules and gleaming surgical tools. He removed a small pill from a chromed half-liter bottle, and Esterhaszy dropped the anticoagulant into the jar of blood. He shook the jar until the blood foamed and the pill was dissolved. "We'll see how long this keeps the blood," he said.

Still full of her dreamtime vision, Sam found it hard to respond when Keith looked up and said, "Well, there! Up and about, I see." She simply ducked her head and smiled.

The man was still beautiful, with golden hair and trim flanks, and eyes that were deep and full of sad wisdom. Sam hated herself for being unable to answer when he said, "We'll be starting off today, to take you to your father. How do you like that?" He waited a second, then ruffled her hair cheerily.

The problem was that her dream would not entirely go away. She could still feel the distant presence of the Meltdown reactors, tugging weakly at her. She could still feel their slow, ponderous heartbeat.

Already Esterhaszy was packing away medical supplies in one set of rough sewn saddlebags. "Made 'em out of a dead mule," he said proudly. "Skinned and tanned it myself." He laughed. "Alive or dead, these critters are going to carry freight."

It was then that the first shot was fired.

The shot was loud and it frightened the mules. They bucked and reared, and Keith almost lost his teeth to one when he plunged in to help Estherhaszy control them. Sam darted forward, and then back as she realized that she had not the slightest idea of what to do.

The firing was steady now, attack and response, all from the west side of town. Esterhaszy led Priscilla away from the others, calmed the beast somewhat, and strapped on a set of packbags. "Not a lot of time," he commented to Keith. "Unless you think your people can hold 'em."

"Not a God damned chance!" Keith struggled with a mule, trying to pull its head down by the reins and not having a lot of success. Esterhaszy joined him, established control. "Laing's troops will have us outmanned and outgunned—he always makes sure of that."

Two mules out. Keith lifted Sam by her waist, and set her atop the second animal's saddle. "Stay there," he ordered. "And see if you can keep this animal calm."

Sam reached out gingerly to pat the mule's neck. It twisted around to snap at her fingers. She drew them back hastily.

Soon enough they had a coffle of five mules. "Leave the rest," Keith ordered.

There was a surreal feeling to their escape, because it was so slow. At a leisurely pace—a mule's walk—they rode out the east side of town, skirting the fields, and up into the surrounding hills. Here they followed an ancient roadway, unused for over a century and overgrown with brush for the first hundred yards or so. Then they passed within the deep woods, where the road was clear and smooth and covered with a foot-deep blanketing of pine needles.

The gunshots faded behind them. There was the whistle of a rocket flare as it arched over the town, and then the trees cut off the noises of warfare. They plodded on, through the cool, eerie silence.

Half an hour passed. "They won't try to hold the camp," Keith said. He was riding lead. The others looked at him. "They'll march off the colonists, snatch up what supplies they can, and torch the distillery tanks."

Whoomp-whomp! Far away behind them, the tanks went up in a double explosion. Keith nodded. He looked as pleased at being proved right as he would have been to win the battle.

They camped that night in a meadow that had once been a service station's parking lot, building their fire against the building's sole surviving wall. Esterhaszy pitched tents nearby, brightly colored things made of an ultralight material that folded up to next to nothing, and which he said predated the Meltdown. "Miracle stuff," he said. "I wish we had a lot more of it."

Sam stared deep into the campfire. It was a warm enough night, but she stretched her hands toward the flames anyway, feeling them tingle with heat. Her back felt slightly cool. "Keith?" she said casually. "Back there—at the camp. You mentioned my father just before we left." It was the first time she had addressed Keith by name.

"Did I?" Keith chucked a stick of wood into the fire. Sparks flew. "I don't remember."

"You said the soldiers attacking the camp were his."

"Well, in a sense they are. Ultimately." Sam turned to look directly at Keith. The firelight made his face ruddy, softly contemplative. "How much do you know about your father?"

Though she was sure that it did not show, that not so much as an eyelid flickered in reaction, this question hit her hard. For she knew next to nothing—*remembered* next to nothing— about her father. There was a very clear picture of him swooping her up in the air while she laughed hysterically, and that was probably real. But there were also memories of him comforting and advising her when she was mistreated at Miss Levering's, and these she was pretty sure she had made up herself, pretend-talking to her father late at night, when the other girls were asleep.

"Well, he's a very important man," Keith said. And to Esterhaszy, "Go get your map case—I'll need it to explain."

When the map—the same one that had hung on the infirmary wall—was unrolled on a flat section of ground, Keith pointed out the chief landmarks. "Here's Philadelphia—from here south and west is the United States. Up here is midstate New York, and the Greenstate Alliance runs from there up to Canada and the Great Lakes. See? Leaving all this nebulously defined area in between as the Drift.

"Now for a number of political reasons I won't go into, the Drift is claimed as a protectorate of both the United States and the Greenstate. The question has been left unsettled because neither country could effectively occupy the Drift."

"It already has occupants," Esterhaszy threw in unexpectedly.

Keith looked at him. "Yes, a few thousand scattered here and there. But with no effective political power among them."

Esterhaszy shrugged, a trifle sullenly, and Keith continued. "Now, until just recently it hardly mattered who owned the Drift since nobody wanted it. But then the United States government began the resettlement program, as a means of getting rid of the—how shall I put this?"

"The term is 'genetically unfit,'" Sam said, with a touch of asperity.

"Who told you *that*?" Keith asked. "The term is 'politically troublesome.' Or maybe 'potentially threatening.' But there were millions of refugees during the Meltdown years, and most of them had children, and great-grandchildren. There are simply not the facilities to move enough people to make any kind of difference at all to the gene pool."

"Hey, but I—" She stood, jabbed a thumb at her chest. "They told me—they dragged me out here because I—"

"I'm sure a number of people shipped up here have genetic problems," Keith said. "Enough to make the project look good. But are you really one of them? Let's ask ourselves—who profits by getting rid of you?"

"As far as I know, nobody."

"Your records say you were at a boarding school. Who paid for that?"

"My father did. He set up a trust fund."

"Which was administered by—?"

"Miss Leveri—" Sam stopped and thought for a moment. Then she kicked one of the rocks ringing the fire. It budged only slightly. "God damn!" She picked up an old brick. It crumbled in her hand, and she flung the handful of powder as far and as hard as she could. "You mean she...that skanky old bitch!"

She picked up another rock and, too disgusted to throw it, flung it back to the ground. Angrily, she stalked off into the woods. Behind her, she heard one of the men say, "No, let her go," and she was so angry she couldn't even tell which one it was.

Once off from the others, and—she hoped—out of earshot, she leaned against a tree to cry. The tears came slowly at first, unwillingly, and they seemed false and forced. But gradually they came faster and harder, until all her face not covered by the nucleopore was wet, and she hugged the tree with both arms and hit her forehead against the bark. She cried until there were no more tears, and then sat slumped on the ground, feeling weak and miserable, and cried again. Twice she had to remove her mask, to suck in enough air to breathe.

And finally she felt calm enough to return.

They greeted her casually when she returned to the campfire, as though she had left on a routine chore and had been gone only shortly. But in her absence, they had cooked and eaten their dinners, and Esterhaszy was cleaning their pots with handfuls of dry sand.

Sam looked at one pot and said, "You'd better do this over; there's a smidgen of boneseekers there on the bottom."

Esterhaszy looked at her oddly again, but he complied, and when he held up the pot, the bottom was clean and dark and she nodded. She went back to the map, squatted down by it. "So there's the resettlement program."

Clearing his throat, Keith said, "There's this big, expensive-to-run resettlement program. Which I, incidentally, have spent the past five years trying to make self-sufficient. Meanwhile, to the other side of the Drift"—he pointed to upstate Pennsylvania, near the New York border—"your father had already created Honkeytonk."

"What's that?"

Keith chuckled. "It's about the prettiest little interlocking set of enterprises you've ever seen in your life. Honkeytonk is a small company town, owned and operated by the Greenstate Alliance. It's a mining town, because it's sitting up on top of the last big reserve of coal on the east coast. It's a farming community—enough to feed the miners. It's a distillery; they crack the coal there and make coal oil, which they ship to Boston. Honkeytonk produces its own cloth, its own shoes, and half the tools for its own industry. They're restoring one of the old railway lines. What's shipped out is almost pure profit, and it was all created by one man—your father. He's been my model for everything I've tried to accomplish in the Drift."

"Mine too," Esterhaszy mumbled. When the other two looked at him, he said, "I wish you could see what he's accomplished there. There are huge greenhouses—all the food is grown inside them, *free of the boneseekers*. He's broken free of the radiation cycle. Do you have any idea what that means to someone born in the Drift? All the buildings have airlocks, all the windows have filters. Little bit by little bit, the contaminated soil is separated from the good, and it's stored down at the bottom of the played-out mine shafts. It's not much to begin with—I mean there's centuries of work to go, but my God, it's hope. Someday people will be able to walk in the open there, without masks. Someday—" He stopped suddenly, reddened, stared down at his feet.

"Meanwhile," Keith said, after an awkward pause, "your father has a small profit-making operation which the government in Boston very badly wants him to expand. But the Greenstate doesn't have the surplus population to draw from that the United States has. His workers are all recruited from the hill people—" He waved a vague hand at the darkness. "The Drifters. He can't hire the numbers he needs as fast as he wants. And then this war heats up. A few brush actions at first, and suddenly the Greenstate has prisoners it doesn't have the facilities to lock away, and your father has mines he doesn't have the people to run. You can see where I'm leading."

Sam nodded.

"So now we're providing your father with his work force. Which endangers the entire resettlement program. If we can't show some signs of profitability pretty damn soon, the whole thing is going to shut down. Probably that's exactly what your daddy wants, but . . . well. There are some in the Mummers Clubs who believe that there is a military solution to this mess, but I am not among them. I believe the whole thing can be cleared up if I have a private little chat with your father."

"Well then, why haven't you?" Sam asked.

Keith cocked an eyebrow. "We're at war, remember? I can't

just walk into Honkeytonk, smiling and holding out my hand. And diplomatic channels have been cut off. Still, I would very much like to talk with your father. So I sat back and asked myself what could I bring the man that he'd be so grateful for that he'd give me a half hour of his time? What thing could he possibly feel that strongly about? Or what . . . person?"

It took a second to penetrate. "You're using me!" she cried, shocked and indignant.

"Be honest now," Keith said gently. "Considering where you were when I found you . . . do you really mind?"

The next day they continued northward into the Drift. They paused frequently to argue over Esterhaszy's map. Bob and Keith would trace short curves on it with their fingertips and argue over roads that were marked and could not be found and others that did exist but were not marked. Sam had never realized how difficult it could be to follow a map without the aid of road signs.

They crossed over a midtwentieth-century bridge, an enormous tall thing with concrete pylons a mile high and almost no side wall. Parts of the roadbed were eroded entirely away, and through these gaps could be seen great chunks of the land below, and a tiny little river that seemed hardly worth the effort of one tenth the bridge. When Sam remarked on this, Esterhaszy grinned under his mask and shrugged. "They were *rich* back then, honey."

The trees grew close to the edge of the road at the far side of the bridge, growing together into a shadowy arch, and Keith and Esterhaszy looked wary as they passed under it. Not that that made any difference.

"Hold it right there, friends," a voice called from the gloom. "I have to ask just where you think you're going?"

Keith reined the mules to a halt, peered into the green darkness. "Spivey's Trading," he said. There was no response. "Unless we're not welcome. We'd like to deal some supplies."

"Davey." The voice was husky and sexless. "You just run down to Spivey's."

In a burst of rustling leaves, a boy exploded from the far end of the tunnel and was gone. "Kid ain't got no arms, but he can run *real* good," the voice remarked conversationally.

"I knew a boy like that round about these parts when I was a kid," Esterhaszy said. "Died when he was fourteen—marrow cancer. This wouldn't be his son by any chance?"

Silence. Sam stared into the leaves, watching the sparkle of radioisotopes within them, like tiny fairy lights in the gloom. There was a pale blob, a concentration of radiation back in the bushes, which was probably the guard. After some time she asked Keith, "What's Spivey's Trading?"

Unexpectedly, the voice answered for him. "Just what it sounds like—a place where you can barter your goods. Whatever you want, from lasers to long pork, Spivey's got it."

"Oh," Sam said.

"Cute girl. You planning to sell her?"

Keith casually laid a hand over his saddlebag. "No," he answered mildly enough. "The little guy's a medic. Thought we could sell his services."

Several pulses of the Reactor went by. Then there was another burst of noise in the greenery as the runner boy returned. A milky white shape emerged from the leaves. It was a pudgy albino woman, holding a shotgun in the crook of one arm. Her hair was orange and her skin was so pale that the nucleopore blended right into it. Her eyes were pink and watery. "Down the road." She gestured with the gun. "Can't miss it."

She stepped back into the trees.

The road was heavily traveled; there was a thin path down its center. They followed it up into a tributary valley, rounded a corner, and saw Spivey's Trading.

Keith pulled up the lead mule and laughed. Esterhaszy, who had been there before, did not.

The building had paint on it—that was the first thing you noticed—paint that must have come from Boston or Atlanta or the Canadian Maritime. It had vermillion pillars and hot pink dormers, electric green gutters and sunshine yellow shutters, and a length of clapboard siding diagonally striped magenta and chartreuse. There were sky-blue chimneys and flame-red doors.

Under the rioting colors, the building was a hodgepodge of styles, all piled atop and jumbled over one another—Greek

Revival columns against Federal stonework; a Victorian cupola atop the Georgian wing; an art deco façade beneath Tudor half timbering; and any number of doors and windows and architectural features that rightly had no specific style and were as often as not installed backwards or sideways.

"Jesus God," Keith said.

Esterhaszy said, "Spivey'll pay for anything, long's he doesn't pay much. If you care to work for food and a corner to sleep in, he'll send you out to locate intact housing and drag it in."

But Sam only saw the bright colors for a moment before the world darkened and they faded away. She saw the low, sway-roofed building (looking carefully, she could pick out the three original houses that had been swallowed up by the additions) and the fields and woods around it in gentle pastels then, under a smoky dark sky in which the sun was an angry red coal. Fairy tracings of radiation ran through the valley, separating out into tentacles that wound about and—sooner or later—converged upon the house, tracked in by the inhabitants of the valley. There were sections of land that were almost clean—the top inch of dirt was stripped from the fields yearly and dumped into the nearby river. But even there, the radioactive dust was creeping back, tracked in by farm workers, wafted over by gentle breezes, washed down from the trees by the rains. Invisible and pervasive, it returned.

The radiation was in the trees—she could see the thin veins shooting up through the bark like glowing fuses, bright needle-tracings of light. It was in the lesser plants too, drawn up from the soil and concentrated in the tissues.

As she watched, it all cycled through a full rotation. The trees sprouted from seeds and soared toward the sky, holding the sickness within and sucking up more from the soil, so that they grew and decayed at the same time, curling downward, stunted and malformed. They died and fell and returned to mulch and soil, and the radioisotopes were drawn into new plants. The gently glowing groundcover was eaten by brightly shining herbivores—crippled cattle and squirrels with running sores—and the concentrated radioisotopic dust within the plants was concentrated even more within their organs. They in turn were eaten by carnivores that burned like neon—twisty-legged coyotes, and flightless owls, and teratoid humans. The concentration of radiation was highest among these, and their pups and children were born malformed and mutated, sickly and treasuring cancerous growths within from the very start.

Sam shivered, and the vision was gone. Not so much as a single pulse of the Reactor had gone by while she was in the fugue state: neither Keith nor Bob had noticed. But she could read it all now, the colors and glowing lines of radiation all about her.

She understood what it meant.

Spivey himself finally appeared on the third day.

Sam was reading a girl with a blind eye and a cluster of tentacular growths on one cheek when he came growling up the halls. She could hear Spivey scattering those waiting in the narrow alcove outside. They cried out, startled, as he bulled through, but scurried aside for him.

The door slammed open and Spivey stood in the frame. Alarmed, the girl leaped to her feet, and snatched up her blouse. Awkwardly trying to button as she ran, she darted around the big man and was gone.

Spivey was a barrel-chested man with a full, black beard. His nucleopore hung loose around his neck, though there was a light breeze picking boneseekers off the hillside, and Sam had the windows open. He had the arrogant stance of a man who believed he could command the winds themselves. "Okay, what is this crap I've been hearing?" he demanded.

Esterhaszy had started forward when Spivey burst in. Now he cautiously returned to his seat by the medical bags. Uncrossing her legs, Sam sat up straighter on the crate of whetstones. One foot just barely grazed a sack filled with heavy chain. She looked the man in the eye and said, "I was told you didn't care what was sold in your house so long as you got your ten percent."

"I don't give a royal fuck what you were told," Spivey said. "Answer the question. When you arrived, you said the midget was going to set up as a doctor."

"I offer a free physical to all of Ms. Laing's clients," Esterhaszy said. "Unfortunately, not everyone takes advantage of the offer."

Spivey glanced down at the dwarf, as if seeing him for the first time. "You look like a sensible guy. Don't tell me you believe in this mumbo-jumbo."

"No," Esterhaszy said, "as a matter of fact I do not."

Oddly enough, Spivey looked reassured. He grunted. "So it's all a scam then, is what you're telling me?"

"It is *not*," Sam said indignantly. "I have the vision, and I can prove it."

"That so?" he asked dubiously.

She tightened her lips and nodded. "Take your shirt off."

Spivey crossed his arms. "I will do no such thing, little lady. You want to read my fortune, do it with my clothes on."

The radiation lines glowed on his forearms like Aztec carvings, and ran over his face and across his brow, crowding one upon the other. They were small and cluttered, the tracings of a complicated life, but she could read them. "Okay," Sam said. "To begin with, you're dying and you know it."

Spivey cocked his head slightly to one side, as if listening more carefully, and smiled.

"You're coughing up blood every night. You're a lot weaker than you used to be—that's why your skin is so pale. On a bad day you can't hide it, and the good days are getting scarcer. That's why nobody sees you around much anymore, why you stay hidden in your rooms. You don't want them to know that your body is failing." She followed a green line up and around one arm, wishing she could see where it lead, ascertain fully what it meant. "Right now the backs of your hands have no sensation whatsoever. You're having some trouble with your spine that you're able to control, and a periodic tremble in your cheeks that you can't. Your liver is losing function. It's going fast, but you're not going to have the time to die of it.

"Because you're going to die of pseudopneumonia within six months."

Spivey uncrossed his arms. "Is that all?" he asked ironically.

"No," she said. "You haven't been able to get it up for a year."

• • •

The mule train slowly climbed the valley, following the pre-Meltdown road up in a long curve. Keith, who had been called suddenly from his provisioning, was in the lead.

"You sure made Spivey mad," Esterhaszy said. He chuckled. "I thought he was going to burst an artery right there on the spot."

"No," Sam said. "He's going to die of pseudopneumonia."

Ahead, where the road curved around a stand of creeping willows, there was a pale figure standing calmly in the middle of the way, pack on back, leaning against a Drift-made rifle. Sam noticed that Keith let one hand rest on his saddlebag as they approached.

"Howdy." Keith reined in the lead mule. Bob had faded back, to cover the rear.

"Howdy." The boy was thin and lanky, about eighteen years old, and an albino. His hair was a fierce white thatch. "Name's Flinch. Used to live down at Spivey's Trading." They had seen him there the day before; Sam had given him a reading.

After a brief pause, Keith said, "Yes?"

The kid stared out into the woods, as if he were about to say something profoundly unimportant. "Heard you're going to Honkeytonk. Wondered if you minded people joining your party. Got my own food, and I can shoot. Can carry my own weight."

Keith shook his head, but before he could speak Esterhaszy called up, "Hold on a minute. It wouldn't hurt us and it might even help. The size of your party matters in the Drift. Some yahoo with a gun might want to have a go at us."

Still shaking his head, Keith said, "It doesn't matter what you . . ."

"He'll come," Sam said suddenly. They turned to look at her. "It's written on his forehead like a crown of fire. He's coming with us."

Flinch nodded and shouldered his gun. "Okay, Davey," he called up into the wood. "Lady says all right."

Leaves rustled, and a young boy ran out into the road. He had two short flippers where his arms should have been, like rudimentary, useless wings, and they flapped slightly as he ran.

By the time they made camp that night—in a clearing that

Sam declared free of boneseekers—they had an additional entourage of ten, all dropouts from Spivey's Trading.

On Esterhaszy's advice (though she would have done the same without it), Sam was careful to hide her vampirism from the Drifters. Bob slipped her a canteen of blood he had drained earlier and treated with oxylate. She drank it privately in her tent; it tasted of the anticoagulant, but was still good.

When she emerged, they were waiting for her. They formed a half circle a respectful distance from the tent, and fell silent at her emergence. Their eyes stared hungrily at her, and for an instant she quailed. But almost instantly, she rallied.

"I'll do one reading tonight," she said. "No more. They tire me out too much."

The Drifters consulted among themselves, murmuring, then let a dark-haired woman of about thirty come forward. She had the same blobbish blue tattoo on her forehead as did Sam.

"You've been in the Drift how long—about three years?" The woman nodded quickly. "Well, first of all take off that mask." The woman obeyed. She did not wear a nucleopore, but a homemade mask. It consisted of two linen squares sewn together with cotton batting in between, and two pairs of draw strings. Not terribly effective, but better than nothing. "Take a good, deep breath. The air's clean here; it's safe. Feels pretty good, eh?"

The woman nodded, flashed a shy grin.

Sam read her slowly. When she read the chest, she had the woman unbutton her blouse and open it, keeping her back to the others. Distantly, remotely, she noted how the woman's breathing quickened as she traced a radiation line across one nipple, and down past the navel. "Liver's in pretty good shape," she noted. "Lungs are clean. You're pretty lucky, you know that?"

The woman dipped her head, blushing.

Finally she had all the data and let it wash around in her head before pronouncing judgment. "Fifteen years," she said. "That's pretty good for the Drift, too."

As she retreated to her tent, she noticed Bob and Keith off at the outskirts of the group, watching her intently. Alone among the group, they both wore masks.

• • •

Sam's followers grew in number as they progressed north. By ones and twos they trickled in, guided by rumors and chance encounters with those already in the entourage when they ranged outward, hunting or foraging. They came from settlements of ten to fifty people, places so small and hidden that half of them had no names, and most of them Esterhaszy had never heard of.

By week's end there were close to fifty, and they significantly slowed the group down. Keith was visibly upset at this, and annoyed as well, Sam could see, by the realization that control of events was slipping out of his hands.

Bob advised Sam to caution. "Drifters are a skittish lot to begin with, and you're picking up the superstitious fringe. I've seen a dog-faced boy torn to shreds because the rumor went out that he was a werewolf. These people are volatile."

"I can handle them," Sam said.

But what proved harder to handle were her feelings for Keith. It was almost unbearable, sometimes, being so close to him day in and day out, and yet being unable to do anything about it.

The problem was not so much the difference in ages as the difference in experience. There were too many areas, Sam realized, where she was naive, young and dull.

One night, after brooding on the problem for a long time, Sam crept from her tent unnoticed, and quietly slipped to the pallet she had seen Flinch build. His hair was a dull red in the light of a dying ember fire. She touched him lightly on the shoulder and he started up from sleep, immediately alert and calmly watchful.

When she told him what she wanted, he didn't ask any questions, but slung his blanket over one arm and, taking her hand in his, led her away from the camp, deep into the woods. "So we won't be interrupted," he explained.

He was a careful lover, and considerate, and if the experience wasn't exactly wonderful, it was at least . . . sort of comforting. Afterwards, he held her in his arms, and she liked that.

For the longest time she lay there simply thinking. About the experience, about Keith, about how rapidly her life was changing. It hadn't been as profound and moving as she'd expected, giving up her virginity, and she thought about that too.

"Flinch?" she said.

"Mmmmm."

She hesitated because she didn't want to appear ignorant. But it was something she really wanted to know. "Why did you pull out all of a sudden right there at the end?"

"So you wouldn't have a baby." If he was surprised by the question, he didn't let it show.

"Oh." Sam filed away the information for future reference.

But Keith still remained aloof, distant, untouchable. The trouble was that she didn't have the slightest idea of how to approach him, how to let him know she was available.

The procession grew. There were over a hundred in the following by the end of the second week, and they formed a straggling tail a mile long in passage. Some few had motorized transit, Detroit three-wheelers or Cambridge steamers, and these would leap-frog ahead many miles and then set up their stills to brew fuel for the next day's trek. Others had horses or mules, or even wagons, and most simply walked.

Evenings, they pitched tents and built lean-tos, forming a camp with a certain carnival atmosphere to it, full of chatter and laughter and even games. Many fast romances formed around the campfires. There were liaisons made and broken, enmities that came out of nowhere, and even a knife duel that ended badly. The hill people lived at a fast pace.

Sam was required to give several readings nightly, the demand was so great, and the questions were taking a trend that she did not feel entirely comfortable with, away from the medical and toward the personal.

A boy with one shoulder much lower than the other and barely into his adolescence did not look grateful when she told him he would die at age thirty-six. "But it *hurts*," he said. "My insides hurt *all the time*. Every night I ask God to make it stop hurting, but every morning it hurts all the same. You got to make it stop."

And when she told him that she could do nothing, he spat

at her feet. Glaring at her accusingly, he called his pregnant wife to his side, and the two angrily left the camp.

Halfway through the next reading, a gaunt-looking woman stopped Sam as she started to unbutton her blouse. She seized one arm, digging her gnarled old nails in deep. "No," she said. "I don't want to know about my death. I want to know how I can have a healthy child."

The woman's ovaries were so tightly packed with radioisotopes that Sam could *feel* them, through flesh and skin and clothing. "You can't have a child," Sam said.

"I've had five children," the woman said in a monotone. "Three died coming out, one was killed by the hex doctor, and the last was crippled up real bad and died. I want to have a baby that'll live."

"I'm sorry, I can't do anything for you."

The woman would not let go. Hard, blunt fingernails dug deep into her arm. "I'm starting to lose my hair." Tears were rolling down her cheeks, but still her voice sounded dead. "There's only the time for this one more. It don't got to look pretty or anything. Just so long as it lives."

Sam was tugging at her arm now, trying to free it. Esterhaszy and Keith were away off by their campfire, arguing over something on the map. They could not see that she needed their help, and the Drifters sitting nearby simply leaned forward intently, watching. They did not move to help.

"What do you want from me?" the woman demanded. "I do what you want. I kill for you, if you ask."

Frantic, almost panicked, Sam glanced down to where the woman's gnarled hands held her, and froze in horror. She saw the lines glowing on her own forearm and read their gnostic message.

Death.

She burst into tears and, shocked, the woman let go. Leaping to her feet, Sam ran, crying, into her tent.

When Keith came in to find out what was the matter, she just dug her face deeper into the blankets and shook it helplessly back and forth. Until finally he had to go away.

She cried for several hours that night.

•   •   •

The next morning was spent crossing a brown valley, a place where the Meltdown rains had supersaturated the soil with radioactive dust. Very little grew there, and what did grow soon died. The grass crunched underfoot, and little puffs of dust flew up at every step. Sam kept her nucleopore firmly on, and the entire procession bunched together to cross the valley as quickly as could be done.

The clouds of dust blinded Sam. It was like passing through flames.

In midafternoon the crew passed a reasonably clean spot, and—after warning them all not to take off their masks—Sam declared a stopping place. When Keith heard this, he came back to angrily remonstrate with her. "We're moving at no speed at all! These clowns are only holding us back. By the time we reach Honkeytonk the whole fucking war will be over."

"There are more important things than your war," Sam said. It hurt her to see how hard he took those words. But they were true. It was her procession and she didn't have to take it to Honkeytonk if she didn't want to.

Esterhaszy had joined them. "There's a lot of talk going up and down the line about building 'the New Jerusalem,'" he said. "You wouldn't happen to know anything about it, would you?"

"I've heard," Sam said. "I haven't made up my mind yet, though." She turned, and left them behind.

She managed to slip away from camp unnoticed by the simple expedient of pitching her tent by the verge of the woods. She walked in through the front flap, and a moment later crawled out under the back wall. Half a mile back along the road they had come up was her reason for calling an early halt—an old church.

The church was a great old Gothic monstrosity from two centuries before, and the town it had stood in was almost gone, its buildings collapsed into piles of rubble overgrown with mutant thorn vines and small scrub. Only the church walls remained. The roof had fallen to the ground, and the stained glass that had filled the arched windows had long ago been picked up and taken away by scavengers.

Sam stood in the center of the church, listening for the

presence of God. It was a hot place. The air was blue with floating radioisotopes. She glanced up at the clouds and they staggered by as if the walls were falling in on her. She looked away quickly. The air flowed around her, calm and peaceful and blue. But there was no divine presence.

From the narthex, with gaping holes where the great wooden doors had once been, there came a crunching sound—footsteps. Sam whirled, and saw a man step carefully into the sanctuary, picking his way over the fallen slate and stone, and coming straight at her. His shirt was bright red, and it was the only thing in all the universe whose color remained unchanged by the radioactive blue.

There was something frightening and purposeful about the way he lumbered forward, advancing on her. Sam stumbled back a step. Her throat felt dry.

Then the man's head shifted slightly to the side, and the light hit him a bit differently, and he resolved into Keith.

"Keith." Sam felt weak with relief. She ran to him, wanting but not daring to hug him. "I thought you were—thought . . ." He took her hand, and started to remove his mask.

The boneseekers swirled and danced about him. "Don't!" Sam gasped. The air was as bad as she'd ever seen it.

Keith took a small device from his shirt pocket. It had a semicircular dial with needle gauge, and the initials SM&B on the top. "This is a scintillation meter," he said. "Look." He touched a button and the needle quivered, but stayed within the green part of the dial. "It's clean here. Nothing to be afraid of." He reached for his mask again.

"Oh, *please* don't," Sam wailed. He hesitated, then let his hand fall away, leaving the mask in place. She hugged him in relief, and he returned her embrace.

The blue light all around her was dazzling. It bewildered and entranced her. Keith said something, and then led her to the end of the church, where the altar had once been. There was a patch of grass there now. They sat, and Keith chucked a rock or two away, clearing it off.

It was amazing how quiet the world had become. There was an old radiation logo sign nearby, with dead and withered flowers at its foot. When Keith heaved it far away it fell without any noise. Then he began gently to remove her clothing, until she was wearing nothing but her mask. And then he did the same for himself.

She was too amazed and frightened and happy to do anything for herself. It was like watching events from a distance. But still, she was surprised how differently he held her than Flinch had. His lovemaking was so unlike Flinch's that the two could not even be directly compared.

It was an odd experience, and only slightly better than it had been with Flinch, but it would improve, she could tell, and having Keith as her lover made her happier than she thought she could bear.

Afterwards, Keith pulled away from her, so they could talk.

"You're in a very dangerous situation," he told her. "You make a single false move and those devotees of yours will tear you apart."

"They wouldn't hurt me," she insisted. "They practically worship me."

"That's what makes them dangerous." Keith sounded extremely serious. "I think it's about time for you to start healing them."

"But that's what I keep *telling* them," she cried in frustration. "I *can't* heal them. I just see the sickness; I can't do anything about it."

"Let me explain about faith healing," Keith began.

Sam listened to what he was saying, but only barely. She knew she would do whatever he told her to; she was his now, and his explanations didn't matter. She let his voice become a buzz of words, and stared at the side of his face, soft-lit and craggy in the dying light. She contemplated the revelation that had driven her here to the church in the first place. She thought of what she had read on her own arms the night before.

Looking down at her forearms, she saw the glowing lines again. Death was gathering under the skin, and she knew the date it would arrive. She had a little over a year. It was a bitter pill to swallow. But now, with Keith by her, she had the strength to accept it.

Idly, not really caring, she wondered why Keith hadn't pulled out at the end, the way Flinch had.

• • •

Esterhaszy was angry at something. Sam could tell by
the way he banged the pots and pans about as he cleaned them.
Ordinarily, he treated all made things with great care and attention, all tasks with near reverence. Sam ignored him, carefully opened the copy of Gray's *Botany* he had loaned her.

Sam's devotees had brought her flowers, great armloads of
them. She was sorting through them, placing the more interesting ones in the lap of her dress (it felt good to wear a dress
again; she had thrown her NIGH purples onto the campfire the
first night after leaving Spivey's). These she carefully compared with the old black-and-white engravings in Gray's, trying
to determine which might be mutations.

"Look," she said, holding up a small white flower. "I think
it's an albino buttercup. What do you think?"

Esterhaszy grunted.

Then Keith went hurrying by, off to arrange for the evening
healing ceremonies. He threw Sam a wink and was gone. Esterhaszy threw his pots to the ground in a great angry clatter.

"Look," Sam said in exasperation, "just what is the matter
with you?"

"Matter?" Esterhaszy said. He began quietly picking up the
cookware. "Nothing's the matter."

"Oh, come off it! You've been moping around for the last
three days." Ever since Keith and the church, she realized,
though she did not say anything. "What is it?"

"You don't want to hear—" he began, and then stopped.
After a moment's consideration, he said, "All right, it's foolish
and you're not going to listen, but I'm just mad enough to tell
you anyway. I'm concerned about you shacking up with Piotrowicz. And don't try to deny it—I can hear you two from
my tent."

Sam reddened. "You don't *have* to listen," she said with
some try at dignity.

"It's not the listening that bothers me! And it's not the
difference in ages, contrary to what you might think—you're
over thirteen; nobody's going to stop you. It's the fact that that
damned Mummer is using you. Anyone with half an eye could
tell. For the price of a little nightly wriggle-and-pant, Piotro-

wicz gets complete control of you—and you let him."

"What do *I* care?" she all but shrieked at him. "I'm just some drippy little kid with almost no hair at all, and no tits and this big ugly *blotch* on my forehead. *I* know that Keith would never give me a second look if I didn't have something he wanted. Well, so *what!*"

Tears running down her face, she fled back to her tent. Flowers scattered in her wake.

The healing ceremony that night consisted of a laying-on of hands. Keith gave Sam a quick rundown, in her tent, of how the ritual would go. "Keep your eyes closed a good five minutes on each one," he said. "Let your hands tremble a little. Throw back your head toward the end, and shudder. Make them think there's a lot going on."

Then Esterhaszy advised her. If he was still upset from earlier in the day, he didn't show it. His voice was all professional detachment. "Listen," he said. "It's not likely, but there's a one-in-a-million chance that you might do some good. How much do you know about faith healing?"

She shook her head.

"Well, almost all of it is bunco, but not quite all. Sometimes there's a spontaneous cure. Belief seems to figure in this somehow—sometimes the person who's cured believes, sometimes the person curing, sometimes both. But sometimes—and this is the interesting part—neither person believes in the cure, but it happens anyway."

"How?" Sam asked.

"It's an absolute bloody mystery. But as long as there's that one shot, let's give it your best, hey? When you lay on your hands I want you to seriously imagine, as hard as you can, that your hands have turned into vaccination guns, and that you're shooting chelating agents right through the skin and into the bloodstream. Got that?"

"Yeah, except—"

"Hush. I'm explaining as fast as I can. Now, a chelating agent is a very special chemical. Taken internally, it can flush out the boneseekers and other radioisotopes that cause a lot of these sicknesses. The radioisotopes are in combination with chemical components of the body—that's how they migrated to the different organs. The chelate migrates to the same place, then combines with the radioisotopes—are you following me?—freeing them from the body chemicals. Then the chelate is flushed out of the body by normal processes, taking the mutagen with it. I want you to imagine this process all the way through with each person you read."

"Chelating agents sound like pretty good stuff."

"Yeah, well, treating someone with them is pretty hit or miss. Still, they're better than nothing, and if we could get them in the Drift, they'd be nice to have." He sighed. "Look, time to get this fiasco on the road."

Sam paused at the tent flap, feeling butterflies in her stomach. Behind her, Bob said softly, "If things get rough out there, just remember—maybe it will work. You don't know."

She stepped out of the tent.

They were waiting for her, the devotees were, and all she could see of them were hundreds of pained, hungry eyes. The distorted, often repulsive bodies didn't matter. Not compared to the wet, caustic need of those eyes. They reached for her and drew her toward them, with all the magnetic tidal force of raw pain.

With a shiver, Sam broke free of the eyes, of their power, and opened her mouth to speak. But before she could say a word, a woman stretched out a bony arm and cried, "Give me children!"

"My arm!" the man beside her shouted. There were tears in his eyes, and his withered arm jerked spasmodically. "I want to be able to use my God damn arm!"

Then they were all reaching for her and making demands, their voices merging into a single dreadful moan. A man stepped forward, a halting, involuntary step, as if he were at the end of a string that had been tugged. Keith leaped in front of him, gun drawn, and when the man did not back down, struck him to the ground with a slashing blow of the pistol butt. The man howled as he fell, and blood welled up from the side of his head.

"Anyone else?" Keith shouted. The Drifters were suddenly still. "Either you control yourselves, or you won't have the chance to be healed! Think about that now!" Silence. Keith strode up and down the line of hill people; none would meet his eye. "All right, sit down—all of you!—right where you are. I'll send you up one at a time."

Slowly, awkwardly, they obeyed.

The first one sent up looked to be seventy years old—though looks and age were deceptive in the Drift—and her face was slightly lopsided. She knelt before Sam, staring up with huge, fearful eyes. Her nucleopore hung loose, and what few teeth remained to her were yellow and thin. Her breath stank. "They laugh at me," she said. "They pull down my dress and they kick me and they laugh."

Sam placed her hands on the woman's brow and closed her eyes. But the woman kept talking in a low, wheezing voice. "When I was little they take me in the back place and do dirty things. I tell my mama and she hit me and call me dirty slut."

Sam tried hard to blot out the woman's voice.

The woman was crying quietly. "I don't do bad things, I'm a good girl. You make me smart, okay? You make me happy."

Chelating agents, Sam thought as hard as she could. She felt sweat beading up on her forehead.

They came to a bridge that Keith had once crossed years ago. It had collapsed, and they had to decide whether to range upriver or down to find the next bridge. While Keith and Esterhaszy argued, Sam stared idly down into the river, picking out the fish, small concentrations of radioisotopes gleaming under silvery scales. A horsefly the size of a gnat settled on her arm and she swatted it, but not before it stung her.

Glancing up, annoyed, Sam was the first to see the soldiers across the river.

They were dark, almost free of boneseekers, and for this reason they stood out against the glowing vegetation. There were three or four of them among the trees, watching. One leaned casually on a rifle.

Keith looked up from his conversation when Sam gasped and pointed. He snapped his fingers, and a Drifter he had made his orderly fetched his Zeiss binoculars. They were vintage optics, over a century old, and worth a small fortune. The Drifter carried their case with exaggerated care.

Keith studied the opposite shore in silence. Finally he said,

"People's Militia. Looks like the Greenstate has finally located us."

"What are we going to do?" Sam asked.

He shrugged. "They were bound to find us sooner or later. We're getting close to Honkeytonk, is all. Be there within the week." He lowered the glasses and glared at the collapsed span as if it had betrayed him personally. "Three days if it weren't for that damned bridge."

They followed the river upstream with the soldiers pacing them on the far side. Sam didn't get any further glimpses of them, but several of her followers did. They seemed content simply to follow the procession.

The nights were merging one into another for Sam, and the days were fading into darkness. She was always tired. They could only safely pull so much blood from the mules, and if it was enough to feed her, it wasn't enough to satisfy her. She was continually hungry.

During the nightly healing ceremonies, she was prone to sudden flashes of hallucination in which the devotees—she had lost all track of their number by now—merged into one grotesque beast, with a hundred mouths and great clusters of mournful eyes. It stretched out its multiple necks toward the moon and moaned in pain, the millipede limbs thrashing about in agony. And every night she had to touch it here and there, everywhere, futilely trying to heal it, trying to still its cries, trying to keep it from turning on her.

The beast's skin was a riot of radiation lines, blue scars slashing across caustic pink, yellow burning an anguished track over green. They ran everywhere, forming a spasmodic tangle of arcane symbols, a pornographic encyclopedia of pain and cruelty. Often Sam would find herself flinching back from the beast's fangs as a great gaping mouth opened, revealing a tunnel of raw flesh for her to fall into.

She would draw back in horror and then—*snap*—find herself in the real world again, and a girl whose skin said she had three months to live would be on her knees before Sam, begging for a boyfriend and that her boils go away.

Esterhaszy noted her deteriorating condition, and the day they crossed the river—on a stone railroad bridge, which had a twisty up-and-down path between the gaps where the support beams had melted and the stones had fallen away—he took her aside and gave her a full physical.

"You're weak," he said finally. "We need to feed you a little more blood, but other than that you're okay. Hold still; this'll hurt a bit." He jabbed a lancet into her fingertip, drew out a drop of blood with a glass pipette. "Okay, now go aside and pee into this cup for me, and I'll have all I need to run a good spectrum of tests."

That night, shortly before the ceremonies, a member of the People's Militia walked into camp.

The man created a major stir. He marched in wearing combat greens, rifle slung over his shoulder, and asked for Keith by name. Drifters scurried out of his way, grabbed up their own weapons, came running back to gawk.

Keith came out to meet the man, waved all others back, and escorted him to his tent. Four Drifters—his personal guard— cordoned off the area. After a surprisingly brief time, the two men reemerged.

The soldier left, walking out the same way he had come.

"What did he want?" Sam demanded.

"Never mind." Keith glanced up into the hills, thoughtfully.

"Hey, look—I really want to know."

He looked at her then, and his expression was all business. "Who's in charge here, anyway?" he demanded. "This has nothing to do with you."

He turned on his heel and left.

Midway through the healing ceremony that night, Sam saw Keith gather together his four-man guard, and unobtrusively leave. He probably didn't even think she noticed. She waited until he was gone, then wound up the ceremony early, pleading tiredness. Then she retreated to her tent to think.

She organized her thoughts not so much in words as in moods—there were things she did not want to put into words. But she measured her feelings, listened to her emotions, stacking jealousy up against suspicion, frustration against resentment, until she knew what she had to do. Until she could decide on a plan of action, without actually having to admit that anything was wrong.

She strode out of the tent and searched up Flinch. He was

sitting by a campfire, talking with a young dwarf woman. He looked up at her approach. "Have you met Charlene?" he asked. "She's one of my wives."

The woman looked up at her with those too-familiar worshipful eyes. They had the same hurting kind of hope in them as did all the others, like a fly drowned in amber.

"Listen." She ignored the woman. "I want to find out where Keith has gone, what he's doing. And I don't want him to find out about it. Can you help me?"

"Sure." Flinch started to his feet. "Back soon, Charlene. Okay?"

The woman nodded.

At the outskirts of camp, they were stopped by a guard. It was Old Joe, a giant. He stood some seven feet tall, bent over, and leaned heavily on a cane. His eyes were weak, but he smiled warmly when he saw Sam, and touched his forehead. "West," he said in answer to Flinch's question. "There's a little town used to be up that way, and a few of the houses are still standing. Got to be where they were heading."

"Good stuff," Flinch said. He clapped Old Joe on the shoulder. "I'd appreciate it if you'd keep this quiet, okay? You'd do that for Samantha, wouldn't you?"

The giant straightened painfully. "I'd die for her," he said with quiet, chilling certainty.

They followed hill trails that had once been suburban streets up into the night. Even Sam had no trouble seeing which way Keith had gone—his party hadn't tried to disguise their passage.

After some time, to break the silence, Sam said, "I had no idea the camp was so organized. Guards and all."

"I guess you didn't," Flinch said. "The way you've kept away from everybody and all."

Sam made no response, afraid she would blurt out that she did not want to have more contact with her followers. She could not imagine their reaction if they discovered how they frightened and disgusted her.

Something small thrashed about in the underbrush, startlingly loud, and Sam clutched Flinch's arm in fear. He reassuringly patted her on the back and, embarrassed, she released him.

She concentrated then on not humiliating herself any further by showing alarm. Still, she almost jumped out of her skin when a voice from the darkness calmly said, "Password or die."

"Oh hell, Lem, I guess you know *me*," Flinch whispered back. Sam could make out the dark outline of the man now, atwinkle with bright radioisotopes. He nodded.

"Who's that with you?" he whispered back.

"Step forward and see."

When the man recognized Sam, he knelt in the earth before her. In a flurry of confusion, she touched his head lightly, and whispered, "Oh, get up out of the dirt."

"She wants to hear what's going on, without anybody finding her out," Flinch explained, quietly emphasizing the she. "Can you do?"

The man nodded again. "Follow me real quiet. Got to lead you around the Greenstate guards. They're not worth diddly-squat, but maybe you shouldn't do any talking."

He led them into darkness, up a slope, over a ruined wall. Sam noticed he had a kind of rolling walk, one knee half collapsing with each step.

A single window glowed orange with lanternlight in the back of an isolated brick building. Standing under it, they could hear a mumble of words, some few audible, but not enough to make any sense of the conversation. Flinch gestured to the guard, and they both joined hands to boost Sam up.

Clinging with both hands to the sill of the glassless window, and terrified almost to death, Sam peered within. The light came not from the room she was staring into but one adjacent to it. Through a doorway, she could see a table and two sets of hands on it. A lantern hung from the ceiling. Two men were sitting opposite each other at the table, but their hands were all she could see of them.

"—is not a well man," an unfamiliar voice said. "In his indisposition, I have been empowered to act as his agent."

There was a brief laugh, and a second voice—Keith's—said, "That's a very old ploy, you know. If you *had* the power you wouldn't be out here in the middle of nowhere, trying to trick me into giving it to you. Let's not kid each other."

"Well, it was worth a try," the stranger said urbanely. "Now explain to me once again why I shouldn't simply let my men round up your gang of rabble."

"There are over a hundred people in my encampment," Keith said in a patient voice. "Many of them are in reasonable health, some few have skills, and all of them are armed. You can come and take them, and I predict you'll lose a dozen of your Militia, and waste a good number of potential miners. Or you can let me walk them into Honkeytonk, and you'll have them all, with no violence at all."

"Interesting." The man mused for a while. "Still, I have to tell you, this improbable romance about Colonel Laing's daughter . . ."

"What's so improbable about it?" Keith snapped.

"Well . . . it seems so great a coincidence that just when you happen to need a bargaining chip, the daughter of the single most important man in the Drift should happen to wander into your arms."

"There are no coincidences," Keith said.

"Exactly my point."

After a moment's annoyed silence, Keith said, "Perhaps you've heard of a marvelous new invention called the telegraph. It operates by the principle of—"

"Oh, no need to explain the marvels of science to *me!*" the man said with exaggerated irony. "We are quite up to date in Boston, let me assure you."

"Then you understand how I could communicate with the capital in Atlanta, and even the authorities in Richmond, without having to actually travel to either place? You understand how I could ask the National Police to open their files on foreign nationals staying within the United States, and how I could then—"

"Enough," the stranger said. "Your point is taken."

Sam closed her eyes tight and tears did not come. She opened them again, and they were as dry as wood. She let go of the sill.

Flinch and his friend had to move fast to catch her, because she made no effort to break her fall. But catch her they did, and silently too. She let them lead her away, back to the guard's post, where Flinch asked, "Get what you wanted?"

She realized that neither of the others had heard a word of the exchange. She shook her head, no. "Let's go home," she said.

It was a long walk to the camp, and she walked it blind. Flinch made sure she didn't stumble into anything, but all Sam's attention was focused on the words she had overheard. Silently, she repeated them over and over, looking for some interpretation—*any* interpretation—of them other than the obvious one.

But there was no evading it. *Keith* had turned her over to the NIGH. Even before she had met him, he had betrayed her.

Back at the camp, she let Flinch lead her to Esterhaszy's tent, and then sent him away. She couldn't possibly go back to her own tent, alone. She needed somebody's sympathy.

"Bob?" she said. He was bent over his medical tests as she walked in, working over a low, makeshift table.

"Well," he said, not turning around, "you insisted on screwing around without taking any precautions, and now you've got to pay the price."

"What?" she said, bewildered.

"You're pregnant," he said sternly. He turned around and the disapproving expression on his face disappeared at the sight of her. His mouth fell open, and he hurried to her side to take her elbow. "Good lord, what's happened to you?"

"Pregnant?" she said wonderingly. She let him sit her down on a crate of books. She sat with her legs wide, forearms laid loosely across her knees. "Pregnant!" She began to laugh.

The laughter grew, slowly at first, but irresistably. She threw back her head and howled. The laughter filled her up and overflowed out her mouth. Gasps turned into sobs and wracked her body in wave after shuddering wave. Her lungs hurt with it. She rocked and convulsed with it.

Esterhaszy slapped her twice in the face, hard, but she didn't feel a thing. She waved her head back and forth, shrieking with laughter.

It went on and on, and at some point she stopped paying attention to it, and became aware of nothing at all until morning.

• • •

It was hot. Sam looked around and realized she was in a covered wagon. It was nowhere near as glamorous a vehicle as the history books made it out to be—just a wagon with wooden hoops and canvas stretched overtop. The air inside was still, almost breathless.

"I can't feel a thing," Sam said dully. It felt like she was hollow.

"I'm not surprised," Esterhaszy said from the buckboard. "After that laughing jag last night."

They were near the lead of the procession, a relatively dustless position. Keith was at the very front. "Did I make a fool of myself?" Sam asked.

"Well," Esterhaszy said. "Yeah. But what the hell—we all do sooner or later, right?" He clucked at the horses, twitching the team back to the road's center. "Care to tell me about it?"

So Sam told him, word for word, all she had overheard the night before. She recited it flatly, without intonation; she felt as though all emotion had died in her forever.

"Jesus," Esterhaszy muttered. He drove in silence for a time. "God damn." He slammed his fist into his knee, repeated the gesture several times. "You realize what he's planning on doing? He's going to send"—he waved an arm—"*all these people*— over a hundred of them!—into slavery!"

Sam shrugged. "I guess."

"You guess?" Esterhaszy swung around to face her. "What kind of cold, heartless—?" He broke off suddenly. "I'm sorry, kid. I guess you haven't been given much reason to feel altruistic toward anyone."

Sam shrugged again.

"So what do you want to do?" he asked at last. "Sit there and take it?"

"I—"

"Planning on being a victim all your life?" He was sneering now. "Going to pass it on to your child, let him be a victim all *his* life too?"

"Hey, now wait a minute!"

He turned again to speak directly at her in a low and earnest voice. The horses wandered to the side of the road, stopped to munch some stunted elm saplings. "Or are you going to do the socially responsible thing and break up this pilgrimage? Think about it. Scatter these people to the hills again and the People's Militia will never catch them. Take them and you away, and Piotrowicz doesn't have any bargaining chips for his Machiavellian little schemes. If you want revenge, you couldn't pick a better means. What do you say?"

"No," she mumbled.

"No what?" He began muscling the horses back into the procession.

"No, I'm not doing anything anymore. I hurt and I'm tired. Keith can do what he wants—I'm not going to get in the way."

"Still love him, eh?"

"No—yes, but what does that matter?" she said irritably. "I'm just tired."

But the thought of revenge would not go away. The long morning stretched on, and the sun grew hotter, and the thought kept returning and growing. Dust caked up on Sam's face; she clawed some of it from her forehead, and it felt heavy and clayish under her nails.

Hours passed, and the shadows did not shift. The morning was hot, breathless, eternal. The Drifters trudged along, heads down and eyes slitted. Their order did not change.

They were crossing a long valley, and however long they marched, they came no nearer to the hills. The sun hung two handsbreadths over the horizon and did not move.

Something was wrong, something was missing. Sam tried to track it down, for she needed something to distract her from the idea of revenge, which kept returning, burdensome and difficult and intimidating. Determinedly she puzzled over it and then finally—with a start—realized that the Reactor was no longer pulsing. Its steady, unvarying beat had been with her so long that she had forgotten its presence. Now . . . it was gone.

She could still feel the Reactor's presence, beyond the horizon, and still see the radiation lines on her own skin. She waited for the pulse—ten minutes went by. Fifteen. The Reactor did not pulse.

The people trudged forward in the same order they had

begun the morning in. Bob clucked at the horses as he had a hundred times that day. The sun floated motionless in the sky. They were caught, all of them, trudging through timeless waste, while the air grew hotter, and the hills remained distant.

And finally, just to get Time *started* again, Sam asked, "What did you have in mind?"

Esterhaszy turned around to face her. "Actually, I don't really have what you'd call an actual plan yet," he admitted. "Maybe a notion, is all. But the day is long; give me time to think."

The Reactor pulsed. They began to climb out of the long valley.

The Drifters were already beginning to gather around Sam's tent, keeping carefully back of the line Esterhaszy had drawn about it. The procession was within a day's march of Honkeytonk. Tonight's would be the last healing ceremony.

"I've used up half my medicines on this God damned trek," Bob grumbled. "They're supposed to be my pay too." He set his bags by the pile of bedding by the center of the tent. These and two camp stools were all the items in the tent—the others were already packed. "Sit down, rub your arm. Like I've just given you an injection. I can hear him coming."

The tent flap opened, and Keith walked in. "What's going on?" he asked.

"Sit down," Esterhaszy said. "You're next." He prepped a cotton alcohol swab.

"Sure." Keith rolled up one sleeve. "What's it for?"

Sam had felt confident that her expression would not give the scheme away; it seemed she had been hiding her emotions forever, and she was not sure she would ever return to expressing them openly. But watching Keith now, she was struck by the sudden insight that it didn't really matter, because unless Keith was looking for someone's reaction, he didn't see people at all.

"Sleeping sickness," Esterhaszy said, expertly sliding in the needle. "Yeah, stings a little, doesn't it? Now unclench your fist." He undid the band around Keith's arm. "Good stuff. Now just to be sure, I want you to count backwards from twenty."

"Twenty," Keith said. "Nineteen. Just what is this sleeping

sickness stuff anyway? Sixteen." He yawned. "Hey, maybe I've caught it."

"I'm sure of it." Esterhaszy caught the man as he slumped. "Give me a hand here, will you, Sam?"

They laid Keith down across the mound of blankets, head up and one arm thrown to the side. Bob undid his top three shirt buttons, examined the effect critically, and tilted the chin a bit higher. "There," he said. "The swooning victim."

He bent over Keith's neck with a scalpel.

"Oh, be careful!" Sam cried involuntarily.

The blade flashed, and Sam flinched away. Blood spurted. Esterhaszy rocked the head from side to side, spreading the bloodstain. He examined the wound.

"Won't lose much," he decided. He began staining Sam with mercurochrome: two thin lines from the corners of her mouth, a drop off-center on her chin. A large, dark splotch on the front of her dress, just over one breast. He hummed tunelessly as he worked.

Finally, he nodded. *"That'll* scatter them! Once they see their goddess incarnate revealed as a—forgive the expression—creature of the night, we'll have destroyed any reason they might have for hanging around."

Sam knelt by Keith. She felt dizzy. Esterhaszy came and went, removing the chairs and bags, emptying the tent. Sam half cradled Keith in her arms. She could have cried at how pale and vulnerable he looked.

"They're still gathering—almost all here." Esterhaszy patted her shoulder. "Watch out for the tent pole, okay? It should fall forward, but don't forget that it's heavy."

The Reactor pulsed twice while Sam waited. She stared at Keith's throat, at the red blood glistening on it. Daintily, she dabbed a finger into the blood, held the tip before her eyes. Slowly, deliberately, she stuck the finger in her mouth, and sucked on it. It was the first time in her life she had ever tasted human blood.

Her gorge rose at the taste, and she almost gagged. She wanted to vomit, but she did not. And at last she was able to remove her finger from her mouth, and calmly await what was to come.

An internal combustion engine snarled to life, grew to a

bass growl. That would be Flinch, who was not in on the plan but could be relied on to do what he was told.

West. Samantha oriented herself by the Reactor, which she could feel over the horizon, a little off south.

The engine sound changed as Flinch kicked the transport vehicle into gear and floored the accelerator. There was a whistling slash of air as the rope tautened, and the tent was suddenly jerked away. The canvas went *whomph* and was gone.

The semicircle of devotees gaped in horror. Some few were watching the tent fly away. But the others were staring at Sam and the tableau she formed with Keith. She raised her head from him and stared at them, frightened half to death. They in turn stood paralyzed by the trickle of mercurochrome from her lips.

Clumsily, Sam started to her feet, and ran due west. Esterhaszy was waiting for her just beyond the camp, with transportation and their belongings. He swore he could get them away safely.

She ran, but she was no longer sure she cared.

Honkeytonk was built up against the mountainside, where the old mine shafts opened to the surface. It was a bright Mecca of human accomplishment in the Drift. Not a tree or weed, not a shred of green grew within its boundaries. All was gleaming storage tank and soaring cracking towers. The roads between barracks were of packed slag, and the brick buildings were darkened by the fumes of industry.

Standing to the side and above, on the mountain slope, Sam said, "I'm afraid." She stared down at the town and the single track railroad that was being built from it, a brown gash north through the wilderness.

"Don't lose your nerve now, kid," Esterhaszy said. "We've been through the worst of it, you and me."

They walked down to the bare-earth security zone surrounding the city, moving slowly and with empty hands. There were guards patrolling everywhere, People's Militia in smart blues and pith helmets, their nucleopores a gleaming white.

At the perimeter, they were stopped and asked their business.

"I'm here to see my father," Sam began.

"Oh yes," the guard said. "We were told." He snapped his fingers, and two lower-ranking militia stood to attention. "Your escort."

"Who told—?" Sam started to ask, but thought better of it. They were guided into the town, over sparsely populated streets.

Then Keith breezed by in the open passenger seat of a Cambridge electric steamer. He waved cheerily as the driver took him by, a fistful of papers in one hand.

"What the hell?" Bob said. Sam stood motionless as the car dwindled down the road, into the Drift. She felt stricken and deserted. "Well," Bob said, "at least he's not holding any grudges, eh?"

They arrived at a restored Federal building near the town's center. There, after passing through an airlock and into a filtered set of rooms, their escort surrendered them to another military type, a tall, thin man with a small mustache. He smiled.

"So you are our beloved commander's daughter?" He offered his hand. "Of course you are. Take off your masks, make yourselves at home. Would you like to freshen up?"

"This young lady hasn't seen her father for some time," Esterhaszy said.

"This way then," the man said. "Colonel Laing's quarters are upstairs."

He led them to the second floor, and down a long, clean hallway. "I must caution you that Colonel Laing is not in the best of health. All these years stationed in the Drift . . . well, it catches up with you, no matter how many precautions you take."

He opened a door. "Call when you're ready."

Samantha's father was dying.

He lay in his bed, covered over with crisp white sheets and propped up by pillows. His proud aquiline features were seriously eroded by hollow cheeks and age lines, his hair whitened and thinned by time. At Sam's entry, he opened his eyes and stared blankly at her for some time. Then pain welled up silently as he saw through the shorn hair and indigo tattoo, the tattered clothing and the years of growth since he'd seen her last.

Sam stood dry-eyed, looking down at the old man, feeling

nothing. When he gestured her closer, she stepped forward and took his hand. It was weak and cold. She could have crushed its bones in her grip.

"Saman—" he began, and was convulsed by coughing. It was long and wet and went on forever. It sounded like he was coughing up all his lungs and was going to die on the spot.

Sam held onto his hand. It felt slimy.

Finally the old man was able to speak again. "Boneseekers," he apologized in a wheezing, pained voice. "They catch up to you." He turned his head to the side, trying to wipe a bit of drool onto the sheets.

Bob stepped forward and wiped the man's chin for him.

Colonel Laing stared at his daughter in horror. He seemed almost transfixed by her tattoo. "What have I done?" he moaned. Rheumy tears filled his pale eyes. "I have . . . enemies in Boston. I had to send you south. You should have been safe in the States. They couldn't reach you—" Again he was wracked by a fit of coughing.

Sam felt awful. "It's okay," she said meaninglessly. "It's okay."

"They can remove that tattoo in Boston," her father said. "They have lasers there—they can burn the ink away under the skin."

"Shush," Sam said.

"They can do it!" the old man insisted angrily. "By God, I have some influence yet! They owe me favors!" His eyes dulled. "Favors."

At last the old man fell asleep. Sam and Esterhaszy tiptoed from the room, and met with the slim military man who had shown them in. He sat them down around the kitchen table, and took out a tin of cigarettes. Sam declined and Esterhaszy accepted. The room grew close with the smell of Cuban marijuana.

"You must be hungry," the officer said to Sam. He took a thermos from the icebox and filled a tall glass with foaming red liquid. Sam looked at it, then up at the man.

"Hog's blood," he said. Then, "It's all right; your father has the same affliction. There's no superstition about short bowel syndrome *here*." When Sam began slowly to drink, he added, "It's very sad. For all your father's precautions, he could not guard against the boneseekers. They're in the food chain, and a hemophage feeds off the apex of the food chain, taking in the very greatest concentration of radioisotopes. It was inevitable that your father would die like this."

Surreptitiously, Esterhaszy shook his head. Sam noticed, and said, "No, it's okay. I've known what my chances are for a long time."

The officer smiled, as if recognizing something in her speech. "I have two pieces of bad news to impart," he said. "Best if we get them over with quickly.

"First . . . I know that as the Colonel's sole heir, you must be looking forward to inheriting his wealth. But you should know that there is no such thing as inherited wealth in the Greenstate Alliance. Our laws forbid it."

Esterhaszy snorted derisively. The officer raised an eyebrow and said, "At least your father is not wealthy enough to get around those laws."

"I never really expected money or anything from my father," Sam said. "Just—damn it, I expected to be able to feel something for him, and he's just this old man dying in an attic room. He's not at all like the father I remember, and it's hard to give a shit about him, one way or the other."

The officer looked away. "Yes, well . . ." he said. "The second bit of news is about your tattoo. I am afraid that the Colonel has just this morning signed a negotiated set of agreements with a representative of the United States government and the Philadelphia—"

"Keith Piotrowicz," Esterhaszy said. "We know all about him."

"Well, the framework calls for Honkeytonk and the resources of all the Drift to be operated for the joint profit of both national governments. The United States is to provide the, um, manpower."

"We understand that too," Sam said.

"Then you can understand that by virtue of a relatively minor provision, all colonists processed by the NIGH are recognized as such by the Greenstate Alliance?" He waited, saw by their blank expressions that they did not understand. "If you go into the Greenstate with that tattoo on your forehead, you'll be treated as a criminal."

"But . . . where will I go?" Sam wondered. It was a new question for her.

The officer shrugged. "Stay here. We can find a place for you." He leaned forward. "We can do that much for the Colonel's daughter."

"No," Esterhaszy said. "I have a homestead up in a pretty clean corner of the drift. There's a little community of like-minded people there; that's who I wanted medical supplies for. My wife and I will put you up."

"I didn't know you had a wife," Sam said.

"You'll like her. Her name is Helga."

Helga was a tall, rawboned woman with rough red hands. She had grown extremely fond of Samantha. Now she stroked Sam's upper leg, and said, "Yes, now breathe deeply—that's good. Now *push*. You're almost there."

Squeezing her eyes tight, Sam said, "It hurts, Helga. It really hurts." Esterhaszy took her hands in his and squeezed them. "Hang in there, kid."

Carefully, deftly, Helga reached inside Sam to guide the baby's head into position. "Just a little more, honey. *Push*. Yes, that's wonderful. A little more." A bit of dark hair showed, and she eased the head up and forward the slightest bit. "Keep breathing deep, sweetie, you're almost there. Now *push*. Yes. Again. Good baby, and ag—here it comes!"

And a tiny, outraged face suddenly peered out from between Samantha's legs. Its skin was still a light lavender shade. It opened its mouth to complain, and Helga hauled it out into the world.

The baby began to cry, and Sam opened her eyes in confusion. "What?" she cried. "Is it—"

"Look at your child, Sammy!" Helga placed the child on Sam's stomach. She reached down to touch it. So smooth. The umbilicus still trailed from its stomach back into Sam. She stared down at it through a blaze of glorious joy. Already it was turning pink.

But because she had never lost her gifts, she saw too, the

radiation lines running under the skin. Sam burst into tears. The tears poured from her, and she mourned for her baby. Not because it was a vampire like her, for she understood about dominant genes, and had been prepared. But for the destiny she read in her child's face.

The hill people did not know it yet, but they had a leader. Someone who would lead them out of subjugation. Who would make their enemies pay, and pay dearly, for all they had suffered.

Sam cried, because she knew what it meant to be a leader, and suspected what it meant to be a hero.

"It's a girl!" Bob announced happily. "A little baby girl!"

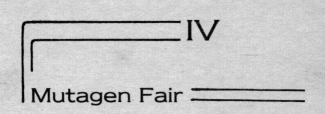

IV

Mutagen Fair

It was like a carnival, the gathering was, or like Thanksgiving come weeks early. The great yard before Morgan's stationhouse was filled with wagons and horses, and all-terrain vehicles. Bright tents of antique miracle fabrics sat beside new-woven canvas from North Jersey. There were people lifting bubbling beanpots from the cookfires, and setting up alcohol stills to brew fuel for the return trek, and arriving on fat-tired motortrikes.

All told there were some fifty people present, an incredible, even giddy number, from all over the Drift.

Vicky shrieked and ran excitedly between the tents. The stationhouse was in a green spot and her uncle had told her that so long as the wind didn't rise, she didn't have to wear her nucleopore. So she ran, filling her lungs with raw air, wild with freedom, seeing just how fast and how loud she could go and be.

Throwing her head back as she ran, Vicky looked beyond the thatched roof of the stationhouse, and saw a straight line of searing red trees running like a streak of fire through the motley autumn foliage. She recalled her uncle saying something about some trees preferring the iron-rich cindery soil of what had been the railbed, which she'd promptly forgotten. Now, suddenly she remembered, and saw how neatly it all fit together, and was dizzy with the wonder of it.

Distracted, she ran full tilt into an adult, and bounced back. Large, strong hands seized her shoulders and held her prisoner. She looked up into the face of one of the big people.

He was a large, pale man with a purple blotch on his forehead, like her mother had. He had a wide mouth and somber features, but he smiled anyway, an ingratiating, insincere smile. "What have we here?" he asked. He pinched her upper arm. "My, you're a chubby little thing, aren't you?"

Vicky's shoulders and arms tingled at his touch. A cold sensation ran up her spine. "Don't talk to him," Vicky's mother said sharply. "He's not a good man."

"Cat got your tongue?" The man looked amused; he studied her body with interest.

Vicky scowled and twisted her face to the side, so as not to look at him. But the man took her chin between thumb and forefinger and turned her back to him. His smile grew fonder, his eyes dreamy.

Then her uncle came up, and said, "Hello, Morgan, what's doing?"

"Victoria and I were just having a conversation," Morgan said, letting go of her at last. "Weren't we, sweetie?" He seemed incapable of speaking to her without asking a question. Then he said in an entirely different voice, "Well, Bob, we're about to accomplish great things."

"Depends on what you mean by great things," Uncle Bob said grudgingly. "But if we pull it off, it's a step in the right direction, I'll grant you that."

Morgan laughed, and slapped Uncle Bob's back. "Well said, little man." He walked off, not seeing how the dwarf glared after him.

"Uncle Bob," Vicky said. She liked him being a small person, because he always looked directly at her when he spoke. "My mother said that Mister Morgan is a bad man."

"Vicky, you're a big girl now, and you've got to learn to distinguish between imagination and—" Her uncle saw that she wasn't listening, and almost smiled. "Well, I suppose it can wait."

• • •

The meal was eaten indoors. At sundown the window shutters were closed and lanterns set in sconces on the wall, and a small fire built in the stone fireplace. All Morgan's things had been hung on the walls and from every rafter to make room for the tables and chairs. Within this cavern of objects, people ate, joked, and gossipped.

Early in the meal a skinny man, a smuggler from the New York Holdings border, brought as his contribution a platter piled high with smoked hams. Conversation faltered and died. "They're from South Jersey," the man said, reddening. "Look, I can show you the tins."

"Oh," said a woman. "Well. *Canned* meat. I suppose—" And the talk went on as before. But while several people tried the meat, only the smuggler and Morgan himself ate with any real gusto.

Vicky couldn't eat any of the food, of course, but she sipped from a mason jar of blood, and listened to the adults. They were certainly noisy. Uncle Bob had contributed a barrel of wine from his vineyard greenhouses, and it went quickly. The grownups grew ruddy-faced, and talked so loud it was hard to think.

"Uncle Bob." Vicky's voice was almost lost in the din. She tugged at his sleeve and held up the empty mason jar. "Can I have more?"

Morgan materialized behind her and took the jar from her hand. "Allow me," he said, running a hand lightly over her shoulder and squeezing. He stepped out the door, turning the opposite way from the wagon where the bloodbags were, and was gone for several minutes.

When he returned with the jar brimming red, he smiled at Vicky and pinched her arm again. "Ouch," Vicky said ostentatiously, but nobody noticed. She bent over her drink, sipped, then tugged at her uncle's sleeve again.

"Uncle Bob, this blood tastes funny."

"Funny in what way, honey?" her uncle said in the casual voice that meant he was concerned and didn't want her to know it.

She shrugged. "I don't know, it tastes funny."

"Does it taste bad?" he asked insistently. "Like it's tainted?"

"No, just funny."

Morgan had been listening carefully. Now he leaned forward and said, "It's chicken blood. I slaughtered some hens that weren't laying this morning. Maybe the little girl isn't used to it?"

"That's it, I'm sure," Uncle Bob said in a relieved voice. "Drink up, honey, it's okay."

Vicky waited a second, to see if her mother would add anything, and when she didn't, drank some more. Then a woman appeared at her side and said, "Is this Samantha Laing's daughter? Oh, I've heard so much about your mother." She knelt on the floor, so that her face was on the same level as Vicky's, and Vicky quickly licked up a drop of blood that lingered on the corner of her mouth.

The woman bent her head and said, "Bless me, in the name of your mother."

For an instant Vicky didn't know what to do. Silence and attention spread across the room. Then her mother provided her with the words, and she said, "From the boneseeker, mutagen, be thou free. Let the hot wind, marrow death, leave thee be," and dabbed a finger into the jar and touched a drop of blood onto the woman's forehead.

The woman looked up, eyes glowing, and said, "Amen."

"Get up off the floor, madam," Uncle Bob said coldly. Then, "We'll talk about this later, Vicky."

Soon the adults were talking again—it didn't seem possible to stop them from talking—and the room filled with noise. It was smoky too, for someone was passing around a tin of rolled Cuban marijuana. Vicky saw her uncle slip three cigars into a coat pocket when it went by him, and she was pretty sure she wasn't supposed to have noticed. She blushed, and stared down into her jar.

Morgan was telling a story. "—both of them real beauty work, all silver filigree and ivory grips. So I said damn me, George, but I wish I knew how you got a fine pistol like that. And he said, do you really want to know? Of course, I said, why not? He said, do you *really* want to know? I said yeah again. Tell me.

"So he hauled out his gun and shot Squirrel right between the eyes. Squirrel's body fell over and he reached into Squirrel's jacket and pulled out the gun, and dropped it in my lap.

"*That's* how, he said to me."

Uncle Bob frowned over his cigar. "That's exactly why we need a circuit judge," he said. "That's exactly the kind of event that—"

"Yes, but I think you're missing the humor of—"

It got even noisier. Vicky started to put her hands over her ears, and then her mother was by her side, and led her from the table. She unlatched the door and slipped out. Nobody saw her.

It was a lot cooler outside. Vicky took a deep breath. The air was clean too. Overhead, the sky was glittery with stars. Off to one side, the moon was full and bright and drowned handfuls of stars in its glare.

Still guided by her mother, Vicky went around to the back of the house. There, a little path led over the bump that used to be the railroad. It led to a storage shed, hammered together from antique lumber and nails yanked out of disintegrating houses. The front was a set of double doors with a padlock that somebody had forgotten to close.

Vicky's mother went away then, dissolving into air, and she was all alone. The woods were dark, and she shivered. But there had to be some reason her mother had led her here.

She undid the padlock and swung the doors wide. The hinges screeched as the doors opened. Inside was all dark and shadowy, but the full moon over her shoulder provided enough light to see by.

At least five human corpses were hung on butcher's hooks, slowly drying. The heads, hands, and feet had been cut off, but they were recognizable enough. They couldn't be anything else.

One of the corpses was fresh, and dripped blood slowly from its stumps. Beneath it was a galvanized tin bucket. As Vicky stood frozen, two slow drops fell into the bucket, making soft plunking noises, and a third was absorbed by the packed dirt floor.

All but one of the corpses were male. Vicky had never seen a naked adult before, but it wasn't hard to figure out. Somebody, she knew, was doing something very wrong.

Rough hands clutched Vicky's shoulders. She gasped, and

her legs half buckled under her. Then she was spun about, and a big woman with dull, pale features was peering down into her face.

"You're a little girl," the woman said accusingly. Tucked under one arm, as casually as walking sticks, was a pair of needle rifles, the kind that held hundreds of shots in one clip. "What you doing here?"

"Nothing," Vicky lied. She tried to break away, but the woman's grip was iron, unbreakable.

"I got to think," the woman said. "I got to think." Then, to Vicky's astonishment, she sat down right there in the dirt, and pulled the girl onto her lap. One arm stayed wrapped about Vicky's waist. "What am I to do?"

Belatedly, Vicky opened her mouth to yell for help. But before she could, the woman's free hand was clapped over her mouth. "None of that, now," the woman said slyly. "They can't hear you anyway. They making too much noise in there."

They sat in silence, Vicky breathing through her nose and frightened by the mute violence in the woman's hands, and in the strength of her arms. Then the woman began talking in a slow monotone, directed at no one in particular. "We come from South Jersey, my brother and me did. They didn't want us there, so we had to leave.

"But when we come here, they hurt us." Unconsciously she shifted an arm so she could stroke Vicky's hair as she talked. Vicky trembled. "Aw," the woman said, "are you cold, sweetie?" She hugged the child close, hooking her chin over Vicky's shoulder and murmuring into her ear. Her breath smelled bad, and though Vicky cringed from it, she could not evade it. "Me and my brother, we can't have no baby. Something's wrong with me, we can't have one. We tried."

Twigs snapped, off in the direction of the house. In an instant the woman swept up Vicky and darted into the shed, pulling the doors shut after her.

Footsteps approached. The woman cowered back, setting two of the corpses to swinging lightly. One of them touched Vicky. It was cold and clammy.

"Sally!" The voice sounded angry. "Sal—where the hell are you?"

A certain tension went out of the woman. But her grip tightened briefly, and she whispered, "Don't you move. That's my brother. If he sees you, he'll kill you. Don't you make a noise." Then she thrust Vicky down on the floor.

"I'm in here," she said, stepping outside.

"Now what were you doing in—well, never mind. Have you latched all the windows?"

Lying in the dirt, Vicky could see the pair through a crack between the doors. The woman, Sally, said, "I went around real quiet and latched them all up real good. Nobody heard me."

The man she was speaking to, her brother, shifted slightly from shadow to moonlight, and Vicky could see that it was Morgan. "We don't want any mistakes," he said. "You remember how hungry we got last winter."

"Ain't I reliable?" Sally sounded hurt. "You ever tell me do something and I didn't?"

Lying within the shed, with bodies overhead and dark all about, Vicky closed her eyes tight and tried not to cry. She shivered with cold—the dirt floor was chilly and hard.

Then her mother returned.

Vicky couldn't see Samantha, the way she used to when she was little. Only occasionally could she even hear her. But she could still sense her mother's presence. And she knew what her mother was saying, even when she couldn't hear the words.

Stand up, her mother told her, and Vicky obeyed. Moving very slowly, very quietly, she edged around the corpses to the back of the shed. It was hard not to bump her head into any of the bodies, but somehow she managed.

There were shelves in the back, invisible in the darkness. At her mother's direction, she reached up to one particular shelf, placing her hand *just so* and then on command closing it around something.

A butcher knife.

Now be patient, her mother told her.

Vicky slipped back in and onto her bench unnoticed. Her uncle hadn't even realized she had gone. When he finally looked her way, he said, "Oh Vicky, you've gotten foodstains on your nice dress." He dabbed at them with a dampened napkin, then sighed and said, "Your aunt will never forgive me."

Morgan rapped on his water glass for attention. "If I may," he said, and the tumult died. He smiled.

"Thank you. I have a little speech to make, and I hope you'll be patient with me." There was a smattering of polite applause. He held up a hand to quell it.

"Ten years ago, my sister and I came to the Drift. We had a wagon, two horses, and enough supplies to see us through. Men with guns came and took them away from us." He was standing at his place. Now he looked down bitterly at his whitened knuckles. "We barely managed to keep from starving that first year. But we got through. We found what we thought was an isolated location and homesteaded a farm.

"We just barely managed to make a going concern of it before men with guns came and burned our farm to the ground. They put chains on us and took us to Honkeytonk, to work the mines. These hands—" He held them up to show how rough and awkward they were. "These hands were almost crippled digging coal so that rich men in Boston might grow even richer.

"Some years later, I killed a man and escaped, taking my sister with me. We found a clean spot, and built here." He paused, looked down at his hands again, seemed to find strength. "Gentlemen—ladies—what you propose to do today is to bring civilization to a lawless corner of the world. I know that you claim more modest ambitions. But when the protection of law is extended to the innocent and weak, that is civilization. Now I hold that in the natural state, there are only two kinds of people in the world—the men with guns, and the victims. And the one kind feeds off the other.

"Good people, you are ten years too late. I am no longer a victim. I have my own guns."

As the group sat amazed and confused, he whirled around and stepped outside, slamming the door open wide. "Sally!" he called. "The rifles!" He stood with arm outstretched, waiting.

A few people began to rise from the table, chairs scraping back. Vicky's uncle took her arm and pulled her away from the door.

"Sally! Damn it, bring the guns!"

The room was full of people standing, eddying about, heading for the door. Uncertainly, the first few stepped outside.

Morgan darted first to one side, then the other, trying to locate his sister. "Come on, sweetie-pie, this is no time to be fooling around," he cried desperately.

People were boiling out of the stationhouse now. Some few headed for their wagons, to fetch the guns they had left behind. But most headed straight for Morgan.

"What I want to know is what about his sister?" a pretty-looking woman said. "Was that woman we found all cut up his sister? And if she was, why would he kill her?"

The meeting was breaking up. But still, everyone hung about the wagons, talking. They said they were laying the groundwork for next year's session, but Vicky had heard enough adults talk before to know they were just gossiping.

"Well, there's no doubt the man was crazy," Uncle Bob said. "I suspect it *was* his sister, because it had all the earmarks of a crime of passion. It looks to me like she was killed by having her throat slit. There was no rational motive for him to stab her in the heart, the way he did. None of the other corpses were marked like that."

"I wonder what he thought he was doing," the pretty woman said. She had one hand on Uncle Bob's knee, and was massaging gently. From her vantage point atop the wagon, Vicky watched with interest. This was almost certainly another of those things she wasn't supposed to see.

"We all know what made him crazy, don't we?" the smuggler from the New York Holdings border said. "It was eating human flesh. Feeding off the top of the food chain like that, all the radioisotopes get concentrated real bad. I'll bet you he'd've been down with leukemia in another year or two, tops."

But Uncle Bob cleared his throat noisily, and nodded his head toward Vicky, and the man shut up.

Later, Vicky was crawling under the wagon, playing a game with some dolls she had made out of dried grass, when she overheard her uncle talking about her. She snuck closer and listened. "Horrible thing to happen in her presence," he was saying. "She'll probably have nightmares about it for months."

Which was such a perfectly grownup thing to say that Vicky almost forgot she was eavesdropping and climbed out to set her uncle straight. Maybe it had been scary, a little, being grabbed by the woman, and certainly it had been no fun being stuck in the dark with all those corpses.

But when her mother had directed her to take the knife and wait for the woman to return . . . When she had leaped out and stabbed the woman exactly the way she'd been told to, and the woman fell down bleeding and dying. . . . That had been *fun*.

Her blood had been tasty too.

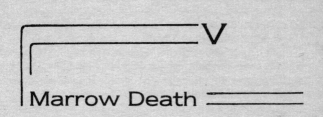

Marrow Death

Boston had an old world charm not to be found in the United States. The secret police, the curfews and shortages, the war hysteria, the constant presence of the mounted Militia—none of these could detract from the city's beauty.

Patrick Cruz O'Brien sat in an open-air cafe, the latest *People's Globe* spread open before him and a glass of foxwine by his left hand. His polesat transceiver—a clutch of instrument chips grafted into a portable typewriter with a whip antenna and independent power source—crouched at his feet like a faithful mongrel dog.

Throngs of workers in proletarian denim filled the street. They were returning to their homes and barracks, dinner buckets in hand. Not one in a hundred of them could have afforded the meal Patrick had just finished eating.

Briefly, Patrick felt the warm glow of being exactly where and what he *should* be: the war correspondent in exotic but civilized surroundings, waiting for the furtive contact that would lead him to the rebel strongholds in the mountains. He felt like Hemingway, or Ernie Pyle.

Then the information officer assigned to him said, "Maybe there's a story in that for you."

Children were selling bundles of driftwood by the side of the street. Draymen urged their wagons through the crowds, carting manure, ashes, and bone out of town to the alchemies, there to be transmuted into soil and eventually sold to outlying farms. There was a leavening of American, Canadian, and Québeois nationals in the crowd, bright and garish among the drab prole blues. An African strode by, his electrified arm bangles weirdly bright in the dimming light. "I'm sorry," Patrick said with forced politeness. "I wasn't listening."

"The recycling project," the information officer said. He leaned forward, and Patrick again noted how clean and unfaded the man's denims were. "Surely you could write about that." He pointed across Exeter to where the last of the city's Tall Buildings was being dismantled for its raw materials. Only the top third was gone, its demolition as slow and laborious as the construction of a medieval cathedral. Late afternoon sunlight flashed furiously as a gigantic pane of glass was wrestled in by antlike workers.

"One," Patrick said, "on the way north, my packet stopped in Manhattan, and I have already filed more stories on scrap metal, skyscraper mines, and unbuilding techniques than I hope to God I ever have to file again. And two, dismantling a building is not news. It's local color. Although I don't expect a civil hack like yourself to understand the distinction."

A Militiaman rode by on horseback, his leather harness creaking. The proles made way for him, faces averted. "Now if you want to talk about *news*, we could discuss those two Ethan Allen missiles that disappeared from Cambridge last week. Can I assume they were stolen by Drift insurgents?"

The man leaned back uncomfortably, looked away. His paunch strained open his jacket, pink flesh peeking from between two buttons. "The People's Militia are not missing any weapons."

Patrick formed a steeple with his fingertips. There was a fine breeze from the waterfront, and over the rooftops he could see the masts of ships at anchor, each—regardless of nation—tipped with an antenna for stealing weather data from the few remaining seasats. He wondered what would become of the shipping industry when the last of their orbits decayed and there were no more. "Ethan Allen is a tacnuke class, isn't it?"

The man sighed. "There were no thefts, I keep telling you. If any rocket batteries had been stolen—"

"Batteries?" Patrick asked with interest. "How many missiles are in a battery?"

The information officer leaned forward—Patrick grabbed his wineglass aside—and tapped the newspaper significantly. "Perhaps you could file a report on our local press."

One third of the *Globe*'s front page was taken up by a story about an exotic dancer in one of the cabarets who actually showed her naked stomach. There was a blurry photo of her face. The rest had obviously been assembled from government press releases. Back at the *Atlanta Federalist*, they called papers like this crapsheets.

"Let's just drop it, okay?" Patrick said disgustedly.

The sky was darkening and the crowds thinning. A waiter carried off the two tables nearest theirs. "The curfew will be in effect soon," the information officer said. And when Patrick did not respond: "It's easy enough for you to just sit there— your papers will protect you. But I'm in the civil service. The Militia won't even look at my papers."

Patrick smiled nastily. "I expect you'd better be running home then, hadn't you?"

Blandly the man said, "Well, maybe I'll stay."

"Please," Patrick said. "Don't bother pretending you're not a police spy. It's painful to watch you try." He stirred the dregs of his wine with a fingertip, and gave up all hope of making his contact that evening.

"Excuse me, gentlemen."

Someone slapped a handful of papers onto the table. Patrick glanced down, startled. A well-dressed old man—a dwarf, with huge head and shrewd eyes—stood before him, smiling. "Take a look," he urged.

Patrick glanced over the titles. "The Distribution of Radioisotopes in a Fresh Water System," said one. "Reproduction of the Sand Flea in Difficult Environments," read another. "Human Migration Patterns Within the Drift."

"Get out of here!" The information officer raised an arm, as if to take a swat at the old man. Perhaps he thought that dwarfism reflected badly on the People's Bureau of Health.

"This man is my guest," Patrick said firmly. He offered a chair, and the old-timer climbed up on it.

"Robert Esterhaszy," the dwarf said. "I've just submitted copies of these to the *New England Journal of Radioencology*. They charge an arm and a leg for publication, but they're not subsidized by the government, so it's worth paying extra for the credibility. Look at this." He separated out a piece of paper from the rest, slid it to Patrick.

It read: "I'm your contact. Can't you get rid of this jerk?"

Patrick looked up and shrugged almost imperceptibly. Esterhaszy nodded to himself, then removed a billfold from his pocket. He slid out three orange bills and laid them side by side in front of the information officer. "Take a hike," he said.

Without the slightest hesitation, the man took the money and left.

"Jesus," Patrick said.

Esterhaszy grinned. "Thought you were familiar with corruption, eh, kid? Come on, pay up and let's go. We have a carriage waiting."

As they stood, Patrick folded his copy of the *Globe* so that only the topmost quarter showed. CEASEFIRE IN DRIFT, the headline read. And in a smaller subcaption: *Truce To Be Signed Within Month*. "Have you seen this?" he asked.

Esterhaszy barely glanced at it. "Don't believe everything you see in the papers."

To go by appearance only, the carriage might have been built in Victorian times. It was new, though, manufactured in the Greenstate holding of Albany, and the suspension, axles, and tires were the product of late twentieth century technology. An automobile would have cost less, but internal combustion engines were banned from the city area, as part of the government's program to limit coal fuels to the reindustrialization effort.

After a glance through the curtain at the darkening street, Patrick asked, "How strong is you revolution here in the capital?"

Esterhaszy lit up a fat marijuana cigar. "I don't know what they've told you, kid," he said, "but there's no revolution *within* the Greenstate at all. It's simply Drifters trying to kick out the exploiters. We got no programs for dissatisfied Greenstaters at all. Let 'em launch their own war."

"Fair enough," Patrick said. "Tell me, from your own point of view—what is this revolution all about?"

"Coal."

When the man did not go on, Patrick said, "Could you elaborate?"

"Sure. The only thing the Drift has that anyone wants is the coal fields at Honkeytonk. Last surviving hunk of anthracite in North America. It's currently being operated by the Drift Corporation for the joint benefit of the United States and the Greenstate Alliance. They mine the coal, crack it, and ship half the coal oil north and the other half south. What we— the people of the Drift—want is to cut ourselves in on the profits."

The carriage was thick with smoke. Unobtrusively, Patrick cracked his window to let a little fresh air in. "That's a very cold reading of your own cause, Mr. Esterhaszy."

"I'm an old man," Esterhaszy said. "It's too late to kid myself. Obviously we think we're justified. But you'll have to talk to some of the younger folks to get the revolutionary jargon." He chuckled.

"What about this truce? Is it actually being considered? Will it be signed?"

Esterhaszy sobered. "Oh well, it's true there are negotiations going on between the Drift Corporation and us. In fact, that's the main reason we're here in Boston, to speak with some intermediaries. And it would be nice if we could settle it with words. But, no, I'm afraid there's a lot of blood and dying ahead of us before this one gets sorted out."

Secretly—unworthily—Patrick felt relieved. He'd sunk a lot of time into this junket, and had no desire for the war to fizzle out before he got to it. Covering wars was how a correspondent made a name for himself. This little revolution could do his career a lot of good.

"Still," Esterhaszy said wistfully, "at least we're talking. So there's always hope."

The carriage stopped. Through his window Patrick could

see old brick walls, and nothing else.

Then the door opened, and a woman stepped in. She was tall, and dressed in a red evening gown. Her hair was long and straight and white as albino flame. She kissed the dwarf on the cheek, then offered Patrick her hand. "Victoria Paine," she said. "I'm the figurehead of this particular revolution."

Patrick felt light-headed. He saw stars sparkling in Victoria's hair. Belatedly he realized that he had inhaled a lot of smoke from Esterhaszy's cigar. He hesitated, then said, "You're a very beautiful woman, Ms. Paine."

She threw her head back and laughed, exposing a long white neck, and a necklace made of small, oddly shaped lumps of silver. "No, no, I'm not. It's the height and the hair that fool you. If you look closely, you'll see that I'm actually rather plain."

The carriage lurched forward into the night. As she talked, Patrick studied the revolutionary closely: She was painfully young, perhaps nineteen, and her eyes were a blazing green. There was a thin pink triangle about her nose and mouth—the abrasion line from her nucleopore mask—but other than that her skin was pale and clear. And yes, if you ignored the life that shone through her face like clear, pure flame, she was not lovely.

"We could have the Corporation out of the Drift by spring, if we could only get our people off their asses," Victoria was saying. She spoke rapidly, urgently, as if she might not have the time to finish her next sentence if she dawdled. "But when you've got a life expectancy of—what is it, Uncle Bob?"

"Twenty-two point three years."

"Yeah, it's hard to get Drifters to give up a chunk of their lives—they've got so little of it. But by the same token, they're very emotional, very volatile. If we could find the right rallying point, we could *raise* them. Sometimes I think we need a martyr, like . . ." She hesitated.

"Horst Wessel?" Patrick suggested.

"Nathan Hale," she said coldly.

"What about those two batteries of Ethan Allen missiles you stole in Cambridge? What are your plans for them?"

Victoria grimaced and said, "That's Fitzgibbon's baby. You

can ask him about them when you meet him."

"One more question," Patrick said. "I understand that your mother was something of a legendary figure in her time—some kind of mystic or healer; I get varying stories. Has her memory been an influence on you? Was it a factor in your involvement with this revolution?"

"Why not ask her yourself? She's sitting right next to you."

The hairs on Patrick's neck crackled. He felt a strong sense of *presence* crowding against him on the seat, a hard certainty that someone was there beside him. His head whipped to the side, and he found himself staring into the cold, cold eyes of a pale-faced woman wrapped in a shawl. There was a dark blotch on her forehead.

Then everything resolved itself, and the woman was gone. The shawl became the window curtain, pulled back to afford a glimpse outside. The reflection of his own pale face stared back from the dark pane. And the forehead tattoo was only a finger smudge on the glass. Patrick twitched the curtain shut, feeling a small, involuntary thrill of horror.

"Gotcha!" Victoria crowed. For a fleeting moment her age showed, and she was young, painfully young.

But despite the laughter, her eyes were serious. She was watching Patrick, studying him, as if something very significant had just happened.

Twice they were stopped by the Militia, once as they crossed the isthmus that used to be the Back Bay landfill, before the harbor waters had reclaimed their own, and once at their destination. The first time they passed with a few muttered words from the driver. The second time, Esterhaszy handed out a white envelope with a red wax seal. "Real Arabian Nights stuff, eh?" he chuckled as they were waved up the drive. "Like something out of *The Count of Monte Cristo*."

"Damned poor security," Victoria observed. An automobile came up behind them, cut impatiently across the lawn to pass around them. At the end of the gravel drive, they alighted.

A string quartet could be heard, delicately mingling with party chatter. Patrick admired the tall dark oaks, the orange-lit windows of the mansion. "Electric lights," he said. "Must be outside the city limits, hey?" Then: "Tell me. Exactly where are we, and why are we here?"

Frowning, Esterhaszy said, "We're here to meet with some very influential people who will be attending this party. You, however, are only here because we'll be leaving immediately afterward for the Drift. I don't expect you'll suffer much discomfort waiting in the cab for a few hours."

Patrick glanced up at the luggage rack. His own bags were there, behind the driver. Who kept his face averted from them. "Listen, couldn't you get me in? Just for a peek?" Then, seeing their expressions: "Strictly off the record."

"Well . . ." Esterhaszy said. "We'll try. But the best we can hope for is to get you into the kitchen."

By standing to one side of the kitchen door, half crammed behind a serving table, Patrick could avoid the scurrying help, and get a glimpse down a long hallway into the party. The people looked rich and even glamorous from the distance, but he knew, having covered similar socials in Atlanta, that he wasn't missing much. Perhaps half the guests wore denim, but their suits were crisp and new, more an affectation of humility than a political statement.

There was a man standing just within the hallway, watching silently, hardly moving. After a time, Patrick snitched a glass of wine from a tray and took it to him. "Here," he said. "Must be tough, trying to guard a crowd like this."

The man turned slowly, studied Patrick with unblinking eyes. "Thanks," he said at last, and accepted the glass. He sipped delicately, then pursed his mouth in thought, all the while staring into the party. "Republic of California," he said at last. "Very good stuff."

Patrick followed the guard's gaze to a figure in red. Her hair stood out like a torch. "Quite a woman," he said noncommittally.

"That bloodsucker?" The guard spoke with quiet assurance. "I could kill her from here, you know that? Like *that*." He snapped his fingers.

"Why would you want to?"

The guard looked at him again. "If you don't know who

she is, you must be the only person here who doesn't." He handed back the glass. "Here. I can't drink on duty."

Patrick slugged down half the glass. The string quartet struck up, and half the party was given over to dancing, something slow and stately and old-fashioned. A gavotte or contra or something. "You seem to be the only one here who's upset," he observed.

"I believe in the revolution," the man said. "But by the same token, I'll obey its leaders. If I'm told to serve guard duty, it doesn't matter that the people I guard are fools or traitors."

"Your leaders don't seem to share your loyalty."

The guard didn't even glance his way. "A Southerner couldn't understand. But *seventy years* after the Meltdown that created the Drift, there were still active nuclear reactors in New England. I bet they don't teach that in your schools. And those suckers were only designed to last for thirty years. They were kept limping along by the capitalist oligarchs, and their running dogs in the government. It took a Socialist revolution to finally shut them down. We're here because of the revolution. Remember that."

"Uh . . . right." Patrick saw Esterhaszy coming his way, and faded back to the end of the hallway, by the kitchen. There, he bent over so the dwarf could speak into his ear. "Time for us to be moving on," Esterhaszy said sharply. "We've done all our business here."

Patrick hesitated. "I thought Victoria was coming with us."

Esterhaszy glared back at the party, and at the tall, elegant man dancing with Victoria. She nipped the man's earlobe with even white teeth, and he threw back his head and laughed. "She's old enough to bed down whoever and whatever she wants to. It's none of my business if she wants to fuck a pig."

Five days later, Patrick and Esterhaszy arrived in the Drift. There had been no trouble making rail connections for the border town in New York Holding, by the badly defined edge of the Drift. But once in Kingston, they'd waited for three days in a shabby old hotel bar before making contact with a gun smuggler. Over sour local beer, Esterhaszy had cut a deal for them to hitch a ride in on the smuggler's alcohol burner.

They had left that night, and been dropped off while it was still dark.

It was almost noon now. Patrick sneaked a finger under his nucleopore mask and scratched. The thing was hard to get used to. "Are you sure this is the right place?" he asked.

Esterhaszy was sitting in the shade of what might have been an apple tree; its fruits were rotting on the limb, brown and liquescent, whatever they were. Behind him a vast, semicollapsed brick factory building seemed to stretch on forever. Before him were the crumbled remains of an interstate. "Sure," he said. "I did some salvage work in this very building once— Empire State Gasket. Long as whoever's picking us up knows how to find it, we're all set."

"Terrific," Patrick muttered. But just then a muted whine rose from beyond the roadbed, and Esterhaszy was on his feet, clutching his Gladstone in both hands. Patrick hoisted his handgrip, looped the transceiver over one shoulder.

A battered old four-wheeler drove up the middle of the cracked and crumbling road. At the wheel was a tall dark man wearing a remarkable hat. The wind threatened to blow it off as he approached, and he set it down beside him, revealing a perfectly hairless head. He pulled to a halt before them.

"Old Esterhaszy! You surely do look like all fools in one, standing there." The man laughed.

"And you look like one fool in a Halloween hat," Esterhaszy snapped.

Patrick tried not to stare at the driver. The man wasn't wearing a mask; he seemed obscenely unprotected. Patrick could see his decaying teeth, the pink insides of the man's mouth.

"I don't need the whiteman mask," the driver said, as if in answer to Patrick's thought. "The spirit people, they protect me from the boneseekers, the marrow death, the hot sting of the radiation wind."

"Save that voodoo crap for somebody who'll be impressed by it. I want you to meet Patrick O'Brien. Patrick, this is Obadiah. He's a conjur man—kind of a quasi-religious con artist."

Obadiah stood up in the four-wheeler, slowly unfolding into

the tallest, most emaciated human being Patrick had ever seen. He was seven feet tall if an inch. A battered old frock coat opened to reveal loops of chains and amulets on his bare chest. His clear bright eyes transfixed Patrick. "I be your salvation in time of need, friend Patrick," he said. "I be your black Jesus. I crack your soul open and fill it with the *shock* of recognition!"

"Christ!" Esterhaszy muttered. "Let's just get the hell out of here, okay?"

The conjur man lifted a tall beaver hat with feather dangles and bits of mirror in the band, and seated it firmly on his head. With a good-humored wink, he said, "Old Esterhaszy has no appreciation of the power of vernacular speech."

The smell of burnt alcohol wafted up from the engine as Obadiah throttled it to life. Patrick held his transceiver cradled in his lap, and they drove off into the twisted wilderness of the Drift.

Hours passed. The vehicle slowly negotiated roads that had crumbled almost into nonexistence. Patrick was tired and bored, and he sweated like a pig in the midday heat. "Most native Drifters are vegetarians," Esterhaszy was saying. "They'd have to be quite literally starving to eat meat. That's because the boneseekers increase in concentration the higher up the food chain you go, until—"

"Hey," Patrick said. "No offense, but I've been writing about the food chain and radioisotopes and chelates and genetic drift since I came north, and frankly I'm sick to death of it. I came here to cover a revolution, not to become the damn science editor. When do I get to cover some real live news?"

Obadiah had been listening in silence; now he threw his head back and laughed, a chilling laugh and one that went on for far too long, irrational, eerily close to madness. Esterhaszy sulkily shifted in his seat and said, "You'll get your news." Then he lapsed into grim silence.

They were in the foothills now, the road steep and winding, broken to loose rock in places. Time and again, streams ran along the roadbed, occasionally undercutting a bend. Obadiah drove wildly, recklessly, plunging over ruts and clumps of brush that grew out onto the pavement. "Where are we, anyway?" Patrick asked.

"Just that way is the treaty town," Obadiah said with a careless flip of his hand. "Got a clearing coming up. You want to stop for a look?"

"If he doesn't, I do," Esterhaszy said. When they reached the mountainside clearing, Esterhaszy lifted the binoculars and stared downslope for a long time. Then he handed the glasses to Patrick.

The town was rankly overgrown with trees; Patrick couldn't even spot it at first. His vision shifted from forest to city to forest and back. Gangs of Drifter laborers, white rags over their mouths and noses, were at work clearing the town, under the supervision of a few armed Corporation Mummers. They were chopping down the trees and piling them into heaps in the center of town to be burned.

"It looks okay," Esterhaszy said. "But you can't trust that bastard Piotrowicz. I wouldn't put it past him to be planning some kind of trap." He sighed, signaled to Obadiah to start up the engine again. "Well, Fitzgibbon is in charge of tactics. Nothing we can do about it."

"I thought this treaty wasn't going to come off," Patrick said.

Again Esterhaszy shrugged. "Hell, I don't suppose it will hurt us to listen, eh?"

The road narrowed and became a dark tunnel as trees interlaced overhead. The four-wheeler left deep ruts in the loamy litter of leaves that buried the pavement. Obadiah drove slowly here, and with his head tilted to one side, as if listening to unseen voices.

Patrick, watching him surreptitiously, saw that Obadiah had a small earphone in one ear, disguised by feathers and bits of fur. He wondered briefly if it was possible the man had unearthed a functioning hearing aid from some abandoned house, then decided it was more likely just part of his costume.

Then Obadiah brought the jeep to a sudden halt, and leaped out. With an insane laugh he bounded up into the woods and disappeared.

"Hey!" Esterhaszy stared after him in disbelief, then clambered down. "You wait here," he told Patrick. "You'd only get lost."

Awkwardly, he jumped a ravine at the road's edge, and hurried upslope after the fugitive conjur man.

Left alone in the still, hot summer air, Patrick felt half drowsy, vaguely petulant. So far his performance as a war correspondent hadn't been exactly stellar. Well, grow up, he told himself. Boredom is a part of life.

Then he heard a distant growling, soft and almost subliminal at first, but growing swiftly. Motor vehicles approaching.

Patrick snatched up his transceiver and jumped down to the road. He had no idea who might be coming, but anyone he encountered on a lonely road in the Drift had potential for news.

Ahead, a four-wheeler rounded a corner, followed swiftly by a dozen more of its kind. At the sight of him they pulled to a confused halt, the foremost not a hundred feet away.

The jeeps were loaded down with Corporation Mummers in black uniforms and berets, their white masks dazzling in contrast. An old man in civilian clothing stood up in the lead car and querulously called out, "Who the hell are you?"

With a small electric thrill, Patrick recognized the man from old morgue photos. It was Keith Piotrowicz, head of the Drift Corporation and possibly the one man Patrick wanted most in the world to interview. "Mr. Piotrowicz, sir!" he cried out. "I'm Patrick Cruz O'Brien from the *Atlanta Federalist.*"

He started forward, hand extended, in the best tradition of war reportage. A meeting like this was golden. It was almost too good to be true.

A shot sounded—a flat *crack* like two boards being slammed together—and Piotrowicz bent slightly forward. His hands flew up to his chest, and his eyes opened wide in astonishment. He stumbled over backwards, falling into the rear of his vehicle. The two Mummers in his car grabbed for him. Patrick stood petrified with shock.

In one of the rear cars, though, a Mummer had recovered swiftly, and he snapped off a hip shot. A bullet whizzed by Patrick's ear and the side of his face tingled coldly in reaction fear. He heard the gun go off. The red dot of an aiming laser touched his sleeve, danced toward his heart.

Terrified, Patrick threw up his hands in surrender, turned, and tried to run. He lurched to the side as another bullet flew by, stumbled on the edge of the road, and fell clumsily into the ravine.

Three more rifle shots snarled, and bullets slapped into the earth overhead. In blind panic, Patrick scrabbled at the edge of the ravine, trying to climb out. Loose, moist soil crumbled under his hands, gave way, let him fall again.

The Mummers were holding their fire now, advancing on him. Patrick could hear them running forward. He thrashed through brambles and fallen tree limbs, deeper into the ravine.

The transceiver was gone, dropped in his haste. A cool part of his mind registered the fact and, insanely calm, said that he must go back to retrieve it. But his body was not under his conscious control. Twigs lashed across his face, leaving stinging red welts. His boots splashed in a trickle of muddy water underfoot.

Glancing back over his shoulder, he saw a Mummer loom into sight, head and chest rising above the branches, and lift a rifle to his shoulder. Patrick froze. The man paused with his stock halfway up, jerked suddenly, and fell.

Patrick gawked at the place the man had been. Then his mind focused on what his ears had heard an instant before— a sudden surge of cries and shouts and gunfire.

The noise doubled as the Mummers returned fire. Everything became a confusion of meaningless sound, of explosions and screams.

"Up here!" a voice shouted. He looked up to see Esterhaszy standing above him, offering a hand. He seized the hand and was almost thrown out of the ravine, he was hoisted up so fast.

"Upslope! Come on!" They ran through the trees. Patrick's stride was longer and he took the lead, but whenever he wavered to one side, Esterhaszy was there to urge him upward.

Over his shoulder Patrick saw flickering shapes on the roadway below, a mass of horses and men, and among them a slim, active figure with shocking white hair flying like a banner. The Mummers had regrouped about their four-wheelers, and were trying to turn them on the narrow road.

Patrick slowed, hesitated, feeling the loss of his transceiver for the first time. "I ought to be covering this for my paper," he said uncertainly. Esterhaszy gave him a hard shove in the back, sending him stumbling forward.

"Don't be a God damned hero. There's a nice grassy meadow ahead, and you can watch the show from there."

They broke into a clearing that was bright with flowering weeds, and fell to the ground. Patrick snatched up Esterhaszy's binoculars, rose and quickly scanned the land below. "God *damn*," he swore.

The Mummers were gone. Three disabled jeeps were canted across the road, and a handful of corpses dotted the ground. Horses milled about as the bodies were swiftly looted, and smoldering rags were stuffed into the vehicles' fueltanks. Then the attackers whirled their horses and retreated back into the woods. The road was empty.

Patrick stood, white and trembling with adrenalin reaction. Something big had just happened, he could feel it. It was more than just an assassination, it was a declaration of open warfare. And—"I blew it," he said in soft wonder. "I was right there, and I ran away."

"Took your time getting here, though," an amused voice said.

Patrick turned and saw Obadiah sitting crosslegged in the grass at the far end of the meadow. He had two horses and a pony hitched to a leafless sapling. "Got your transportation here," Obadiah said. "Somebody already taken care of the four-wheeler."

Lost in his own failure, Patrick said nothing. But Esterhaszy stormed up to the conjur man and lifted an angry fist. "Damn it, I worked *hard* to set up that treaty!" he raged. "And this little stunt smashes it flat into the ground."

Obadiah grinned complacently. "Ain't it a bitch?"

The first of the jeeps went up in a pillar of flame.

They reached the guerrilla encampment at sunset. It was sited in a small, deserted town, so overgrown with scrub and mutant creeper that it was invisible until they were upon it. The rebels had built their campfires and pitched their tents within roofless shells of buildings. They came and went between campfires, making it hard to gauge their numbers.

A rebel ran up to take their animals. He jerked his head toward one building. Faded paint barely legible on its windowless side read STEREO DISCOUNT. "In there," he said. The man's skin was piebald, all hand-sized patches of pink and brown, like a human quilt.

The building's first floor had collapsed into the basement long ago, and the rebels had lashed together a makeshift ladder to allow entrance. Patrick and Esterhaszy clambered down.

Two brightly colored tents were pitched at opposite sides of the cellar, with a campfire midway between. At their approach, Victoria whooped, and ran up to hug Obadiah. She thumped his back vigorously. "Nicely done, old fraud! We had the spirits riding with us this time, for sure."

Obadiah made a face. "Somebody cut it a little fine there at the start," he said. "Almost lost us a reporter."

Victoria dismissed this with a shrug. "They weren't expecting us, is the thing," she said. "It wasn't just the truce—they weren't expecting a daytime raid. We really caught them with their pants down." Then she turned to Patrick, as if noticing him for the first time. "Stand right there."

She darted into a tent, emerged holding his transceiver by the strap, and dumped it at his feet. "You're no use to anyone without this," she said. Then she whooped and slapped his back. "Welcome to the *war*, boy!"

Esterhaszy, ignored through all of this, glared angrily at her retreating back.

The moon had risen, and the rebels were clustered about their campfires, talking excitedly. Patrick moved quietly between fires, as they bragged to one another of the day's exploits, of each Mummer killed, of how the bodies had jumped as the bullets struck them. He listened silently, reconstructing the events, discounting the braggadocio. And he studied the pecking order.

Both Esterhaszy and Obadiah ranked high in this assemblage, that much was clear, possibly through their connection with Victoria. They in turn deferred to Fitzgibbon, a bearded, bearlike man with one useless arm. He walked with a slight limp, and his eyes were bitter and filled with hatred. Still, there was a sense of raw, animistic power about him, and his rumbled orders were carried out immediately.

Patrick could tell that Fitzgibbon outranked even Victoria. She did not give orders in his presence. But by the same token, he was careful what orders he gave when she was about. And the common run of soldiers treated her with a kind of awed respect that was special.

Between campfires, Patrick saw a man holding a cup to the neck of a spavined-looking horse. Blood flowed black in the moonlight, stopped when the man touched the horse's neck again. The transition was too swift for him to have staunched the bleeding. The beast had probably been implanted with a tissue-inert catheter.

Patrick followed as the man gingerly climbed down the ladder to Victoria's encampment. He saw the man proffer Victoria the cup on bended knee. She accepted it graciously and raised it to her lips.

All conversation stopped as Victoria drank. Eyes watched intently. She finished the cup in one long draught, and this seemed to please her observers; they returned to their conversations.

As Victoria lowered the cup, she shivered and barely managed to suppress a smile. Her hair flamed in the moonlight.

Off alone in the dark, Patrick stared at the rebel leader, horrified and fascinated. Rubble crunched under approaching feet, and Patrick turned to see Esterhaszy at his side. "Short bowel syndrome," Esterhaszy said softly. Victoria was deep in conversation with a guerrilla; he had no nose and his skin was waxy. "It's a rare deformity, thank God. Just try keeping a child afflicted with it alive! And *these* superstitious louts try to see something special in it."

A shriek of hideous laughter split the darkness. Obadiah appeared in the doorway above the ladder. He danced, waving a small radio receiver in the air, and cried, "I been listening to Radio Boston! Piotrowicz been hospitalized!"

A cheer arose, but he waved it to silence. "There be more! The Drift Corporation, in conjunction with both American and Greenstate governments, has offered a reward of *five hundred*

Bank of Boston dollars for the apprehension or proof of demise of one Patrick Cruz O'Brien, for complicity in the assassination attempt on Keith Piotrowicz. Ain't that something?"

Again they cheered, but this time mockingly, jeeringly. Faces turned to stare at Patrick. Even Fitzgibbon's dark visage wrinkled sardonically. Victoria threw her head back and laughed.

As soon as he could, Patrick moved away from the fire, into the darker shadows between one tent and the wall. He could hear cheers and laughter rise from one part of the camp after another as the news was passed from fire to fire.

Esterhaszy laid a hand on his shoulder. "Listen," he said after a moment's silence. "Be sure to dry your socks by the fire before you turn in tonight."

Patrick stared at the man, surprised that he *could* be surprised by anything anymore. Esterhaszy looked uncomfortable. "It's an old campaigner's trick, something you ought to know. You'll go to bed cold and miserable if your feet are wet."

Later, when all but the outposts were asleep, Patrick was still up. Feeling bruised and humiliated, he crouched by the campfire and added a handful of twigs to the glowing embers. They smoldered, went up in a sudden blaze of light, faded again.

By Patrick's schedule, the polesat would pass overhead about an hour after midnight. And whatever else had happened, he still had a bulletin to file. He thought for a minute before composing the dateline, then typed out: IN HIDING.

Socks drying by the fire, he set to work on his story.

Breakfast the next morning consisted of sourdough wrapped around a stick and baked over coals. Patrick was just finishing as Victoria approached. He bolted the last mouthful, washed it down with the last of his beer, and slid the mask back over his mouth. "Come on," she said. "I'm taking you and Uncle Bob for a ride."

The three drove off in a four-wheeler. On the outskirts of the camp they passed an overgrown cemetery. A work crew was digging there, unearthing coffins and dumping their contents on the ground. One soldier collected wedding rings, while others broke teeth free of jawbones, smashing them in metal nutcrackers for the silver fillings.

Patrick looked at the necklace of oddly shaped silver lumps that Victoria still wore with her khaki fatigues, but said nothing. "We're going to pick up a delivery," Victoria explained. "Something a city-prospector has unearthed for Fitzgibbon." She turned to Patrick and said, "Well, aren't you going to interview me?"

"Uh, yeah," Patrick said. He still felt a little fuzzy from lack of sleep. "I've been talking with a lot of your people, and they seem to feel that you have some kind of supernatural powers. Do you?"

"They believe I do. Me, I'm a politician. I agree with the majority of whoever I happen to be with at the moment."

"Okay, but when you're among people who believe—what exactly do they believe you can do?"

"Well," she began almost reluctantly, "they believe I have a Destiny. And in pursuit of that destiny, I will get clairvoyant flashes, the occasional glimpse into the future—that sort of thing."

"Is that all?"

"No, I can see radioactivity too. A hot area looks like it's glowing—usually deep red or dark purple. Kind of pretty. A hot wind seems to sparkle; I think that's just low-level ionization I'm seeing. And as a side effect, I have an absolute sense of direction. Because the Meltdown site is a very strong presence to me. Wherever it is—even hundreds of miles over the horizon—I can feel it. Right now, for example, it's over in *that* direction." She pointed off to one side.

Patrick looked in the direction she pointed, and yearned for a compass and a good map. "Have you ever been tested for this? Under laboratory conditions?"

"No," Esterhaszy said. "What would be the point?"

"And probably most importantly, I get advice from my mother." Victoria paused. "She tells me . . . things I must do, and this counts a lot among my followers, because they believe that when she was alive, she was a very powerful witch."

"Sounds to me like you're a bit of a witch too," Patrick said.

"No. My mother could heal, and I can't."

• • •

"Our destination is right in the heart of the Beast," Esterhaszy said late that afternoon. "Small place just off of Honkeytonk, central to the little constellation of holdings the Corporation had put together."

The four-wheeler bounced heavily. Patrick's stomach felt miserable. "How much farther?"

"Almost there now—look, just through those trees."

Their destination turned out to be a Victorian house, in amazingly good repair, set in a clearing just above the Susquehanna. The roof tiles were green and the sides and trim were painted three shades of red. Dirt paths led up and down the river, into the woods. "There's practically a village here," Esterhaszy said. "Little shacks all over. You'd be surprised how much business a whorehouse can generate."

The road twisted through a stand of leathery-leaved trees, and the house disappeared. A log thrust across the road at waist height, and Victoria had to slam on the brakes to keep from piling into it.

A giant stepped out of a guardhouse hidden among the trees. A shotgun held casually in one hand looked ridiculously small and out of scale. He squinted at them through a pair of amateurishly twisted wirerims. "We're here to see the Mermaid," Victoria said.

"Long time no see, Sid," Esterhaszy said. Smile lines appeared around the giant's mask. Tucking the gun under one arm, he made a series of quick signs at them, his hands swooping and soaring like birds.

Esterhaszy grinned ruefully. "Maybe so, maybe so. Listen—any Corporation types up at the house?" The hands flew and were silent. "Well, because if there are, we'd want to postpone our visit, is all."

Sid signed something else, then ambled back into the trees, to draw back the log. They passed down the lane and parked before the house.

Hex signs were mounted on either side of the main door—to ward off radiation, Victoria explained. She touched the center of one, and then her forehead. Esterhaszy scowled and muttered, "People will believe in just about any kind of superstitious crap nowadays."

Patrick hitched up his transceiver, adjusted its weight. "I'd think you'd be rather tolerant of superstition, considering the use your movement makes of it."

"Those suckers won't stop the boneseekers from passing through whenever there's a strong breeze. What they ought to do is cover the whole thing over with a geodesic with nucleopore skin and an airlock. Then they could decontaminate the interior, and it'd be as safe as Atlanta."

"Where would they get that much filter?" Victoria asked, amused.

Then the door opened, and the madam appeared in it. At the sight of Victoria, the smile crinkles about her eyes disappeared. "We don't want any trouble," she said. Behind her, several prostitutes peered out, bony young things with wary eyes. Patrick was appalled to see how unhealthy-looking they were. Some of them had to be seriously ill.

Victoria said nothing. One of the whores reached around the fat woman to touch Victoria's sleeve lightly. Still she did not react.

"We want to see Rebecca Schechtman," Esterhaszy said. It would have taken a blind man to miss the relief on the woman's face.

"Around back by the dock," she snapped, and slammed the door in their faces.

A dirt path led around the house and down to a small houseboat moored to a river dock. A wide wooden ramp bridged the gap between houseboat and dock, and at the far side of it sat a woman in a wheelchair, taking in the sun. When they hailed her, she hastily drew a blanket over her lap. But Patrick had already gotten a good look at her legs. They were fused together, misshapen, with no separate feet.

"Sirenomelus," Esterhaszy explained quietly. "It's a birth defect. Swims like a fish, though." He ran ahead of the others to greet her, bounding on deck and affectionately putting a hand on her shoulder, massaging it gently. "The Susquehanna's no place for you, Becky," he said. "When are you going to find a cleaner river?"

The mermaid shrugged. "Suits my business," she said. Then she put an arm around Esterhaszy's waist and squeezed. "It's good to see you, you old goat."

She led them to a storage room just off the whorehouse

kitchen. There, some twenty metallic suits lay carefully lined up on the floor. Astronaut suits, Patrick thought, and for a giddy instant marveled at their age, and their impossible survival.

Then—just as small differences were adding up, and Patrick could see his error—Esterhaszy said, "Where in the world did you ever find seven radiation suits?" And they weren't for outer space after all, but mere lead worksuits, protective covering for men who worked with beta- and gamma-emitters.

Victoria touched the first almost reverently, and shivered. Then Esterhaszy took out a scintillation meter and began running it over the suit, passing its pickup carefully over every square centimeter of surface.

"How much?" Victoria asked. She removed her necklace of silver nuggets, carefully untangling its several strands.

While negotiations dragged on, Patrick wandered to the kitchen door and peered in. A clutch of hookers were ladling out their suppers from a kettle. He stared at one, a weak and anemic-looking blonde, almost boyish in figure, with short-cropped hair. There was something odd about her, though he couldn't exactly place what.

The whore looked up and, seeing him in the doorway, smiled. She flashed open her gown, revealing small, sweet breasts and a set of tiny male genitalia dangling over her female parts.

Patrick blushed and looked away. The women laughed uproariously.

Then the others emerged from the storeroom. "Listen up," Victoria said. "R&R if you want it. But get some sleep afterwards. I've paid for rooms for us on the top floor—any company, you pay for yourself. We leave at dawn."

"Want me to give you the fee schedule?" Esterhaszy asked.

Patrick looked at the whores. He was horny enough, God knew. But they had laughed at him, and he doubted he'd be able to forget that. Then too, Victoria was listening. "No thanks; I've got some writing to do."

In the evening, Drift Corporation workers from the nearby alcohol farms filled the common room. Most of them could expect to spend their week's earnings on a quick half hour here. They lingered before spending, stretching their money as much as possible. Laughter and piano music strained into Patrick's room.

Patrick pulled a pillow over his head, squeezed his eyes tight. Footsteps hurried along the hall, and a door slammed. Leather bedstraps began creaking in the room next door. Patrick tried to ignore it. A few minutes later the noises stopped, and the door banged open again. Beds began to creak in other rooms. There were small human noises as well.

He had to jerk off three times before he could get to sleep.

A hand touched Patrick's shoulder and he awoke with a start. Victoria was leaning over him. She put a finger to his lips, and said quietly, "Let's get a move on. The Corporation is on our tails."

Patrick dressed quickly under the blankets. "How do you know?" he asked.

"I just *know*," she whispered urgently. She led him out into the hall and down the back stairs. From the yard, Patrick got a glimpse into the common room, where the hookers mingled with their customers. The women had bright makeup marks in the middle of their foreheads and—like some of their clients—didn't wear masks.

At the four-wheeler, Esterhaszy was struggling to load the newly crated radiation suits. When Victoria and Patrick pitched in, he grumbled, "Don't know why I bother. Just because you had one of your dreams."

"Look," Victoria said exasperatedly. "Have I ever been wrong? Have I ever once been wrong?"

"How could they know, though?" Esterhaszy said. "Mama Rosa runs a tight ship. She might not like us, but she'd never . . . Say!" He looked at Patrick. "What did you put into that story you filed tonight? You didn't mention visiting a joyhouse, did you?"

"Well, I figured—"

"Jesus! How many whorehouses do you think there *are* in this neck of the woods? How the—"

"Never mind that," Victoria said. "Can we slip past them?"

Esterhaszy threw up his hands. "We don't even know they're coming."

"Look there," Victoria said. Way off in the darkness, there

was a small, pale, almost invisible light. It moved forward, disappeared. "Idiot waited a frazz too long to turn off his lights." There was the faint humming noise of distant vehicles approaching.

"So I'm wrong," Esterhaszy said. The four-wheeler was loaded. Victoria hopped in, handed Patrick a rifle. "There's only the one road," she said. "If we move fast enough, we might just be able to blast through them."

There was a gleeful note in her voice, and Patrick realized that she was enjoying this, actually looking forward to the confrontation, with a kind of blood lust that was beyond his comprehension.

Patrick handed back the rifle. "I can't fire this thing. I'm a neutral."

"Then die!" Victoria laughed. The piano was tinkling gently in the background. Voices combined to sing *Yellow Submarine*. She handed the rifle to Esterhaszy, who expertly broke out the clip, snapped it back in.

"There's got to be another road out," Patrick said.

"Nope." Victoria started the engine.

Thinking as quickly as he ever had in his life, Patrick said, "Wait." There was another chance.

Somehow the four-wheeler wallowed down the dirt bank and onto the dock without tipping over. They were unloading the suits onto the houseboat before Schechtman wheeled out to see what they were doing. She emerged from the cabin livid with rage.

"Just don't give us any sass," Victoria said in a friendly voice. She gently brushed the muzzle of her rifle against Rebecca's lips. The mermaid shut up.

"All done." Esterhaszy unslipped the lines. Patrick grabbed a pole and helped push off.

Slowly, silently, the houseboat separated from the dock. The river current slapped lightly on the hull, lulled it downriver. Again they leaned on their poles, putting their backs into it. With agonizing slowness the houseboat eased into deeper water.

Back on shore there was motion in among the dark trees. At first Patrick thought it nothing but the firing of rods and cones within his eyes. But no—up there above the house, that was a four-wheeler for sure. And that swarm of midges that flowed silently along the bank—Mummers.

Victoria had dived into the interior of the houseboat as they had shoved off. Now she emerged again, lugging something that looked like a knapsack with an attached length of garden hose. It was a Lakes Federation make laser pistol with battle harness power source and connecting fiber optics cable. A real antique.

A dark figure crested the bank and halted at the sight of the boat out on the water. The soldier raised rifle to shoulder, and aimed.

Dropping the backpack and raising the pistol unit simultaneously, Victoria braced herself and fired. A needle of ruby light, so brief as to be almost not there at all, lanced through the man's heart. Silently, he fell.

"A scout," Esterhaszy said. "I don't think anybody else has noticed us."

Patrick opened his mouth, but said nothing. The houseboat continued sliding downriver, and the whorehouse grew smaller.

"Burned out the cable," Victoria said in disgust. She nudged the power pack with her foot. "Lucky we're not all dead."

Rebecca Schechtman was looking on with a curious expression. "How did you know where I had that hidden?" she asked. "Nobody knew about that."

"How did I know you were bluffing when you said you wouldn't take my final offer for the suits?" Victoria said. She boosted the apparatus into the river. It made a noisy splash, then vanished.

There were two rooms in the houseboat. Victoria commandeered the larger for herself, sent the mermaid to the other, and ordered Esterhaszy to stand guard on deck. Then she led Patrick inside.

The cabin was softly lit by an an alcohol lamp. Outside, the Susquehanna chuckled and whispered as it floated them downstream. "Do you know what the first principle of leadership is?" Victoria asked. "It's don't fuck the troops. It destroys discipline." She paused.

Patrick had been automatically scribbling down her words, rephrasing them into euphemisms acceptable to the *Federalist*'s readers. But when she paused, he looked up with sudden surmise.

Victoria fiddled with the top button of her shirt. It came undone. Absently, she played with the next, and it too loosened. "It can be a real problem," she said. "Because after combat, you're really wired. Just hopping with all this nervous energy, and sex is an awfully good way of dealing with it."

She looked directly into his eyes, waiting for his next move.

Victoria made love hard, and she left bruises. If Patrick had been any less aroused than she, he could not possibly have enjoyed it. But with all the pent-up desire and excitement of the past week, he found himself responding in kind, energetically and with an intensity that was almost frightening. Lost in the feel of flesh against flesh, he could no longer tell where his body ended and hers began.

Afterward, she held him tightly, and cried into his shoulder. But when he asked her why, she simply shut her eyes tight and shook her head. He could feel the fear within her, but he could not read it.

In the morning, Patrick awoke before Victoria. He dressed quietly and went on deck. He walked out slowly, trying to undo small cricks in his legs, and found that the boat had beached on a bend of the river. Esterhaszy was leaning on the rail, staring out into the water. Patrick joined him, saw that Schechtman was swimming gaily in the brown river water.

With a flash of white breasts, she surged forward and swept her arm across the surface of the river, spraying them both with water. Laughing, they retreated, and she swam off some distance.

"Jesus," Esterhaszy said wonderingly, "to be young again! *There's* a primordial experience, eh?"

But Patrick only smiled. He had his vampire lover in the cabin, and could watch mermaids with cool detachment.

By noon, Esterhaszy and Victoria had gone foraging and

returned with a horse and wagon. As Patrick helped load it, he asked, "Where did you get this rig, anyway?"

"The owner gave them to us because he liked our looks," Victoria snapped. "Any more stupid questions?"

Leaving the mermaid to shift for herself, they went on to rendezvous with Fitzgibbon. To Patrick's surprise, they curved around Honkeytonk and rejoined the rebels in a covert camp within quick striking distance of the coalfields. "We could never pull this sort of operation if Piotrowicz were still in charge," Fitzgibbon said in a pre-attack interview. "But his subordinates are all political appointees—mediocrities. They'll be dazzled by the obvious."

They attacked in late afternoon, as the shifts were changing and miners filing wearily out of the mountain. Patrick watched from the mountainside above Honkeytonk as the rebels attacked from two sides. He had wanted to be among them, but Fitzgibbon had refused to risk him. Indeed, the rebel captain had ordered him guarded and kept from the action, forcibly if necessary.

What he saw was a confusion of people running and yelling. Some of the people were shooting weapons. He could make out little pattern to the scurrying about.

There did not seem to be many Corporation Mummers in the fight, which confirmed what Fitzgibbon had said, that the main forces had been led away for a vengeance raid on what their leaders had been made to think was the rebel encampment. Honkeytonk was left all but undefended.

As Fitzgibbon had explained it, "They know we can't hold Honkeytonk. They know we won't destroy it. And they know it's not worth the loss of soldiers to steal what little we can carry off."

"Then why are you going to attack?" Patrick asked.

And then Fitzgibbon's face had twisted up in a snarl, and his withered, curled arm grasped spasmodically at his shoulder. "To make the bastards *pay*," he said in a chilling whisper. "To make them suffer, as I have!" Then, catching himself, "No, that was off the record. We're doing it for psychological purposes. To show the miners that we can, that we're not without strength, and that we don't ultimately intend to hurt them."

Off the record, my ass, Patrick thought. He smiled politely.

The conquerors formed a parade through the center of town. Townspeople flooded out of the crumbling brick buildings, to watch and cheer. They all wore white masks, almost all of cloth and only a few of nucleopore filter.

An aged woman kissed Victoria's boot as she rode imperiously by, and the rebel leader didn't even look down.

Following after, pushing his way through the jubilant crowds—either the Corporation was not very popular here or its advocates wisely stayed inside—Patrick noted with horror that most of the children were visibly malformed. They had twisted arms and legs, oversized and lopsided skulls, club feet and cataracts, wens and cysts and toothless jaws. The adults were not so ravaged by birth defects, and most spoke in Southern, Midwestern, or Philadelphia accents. But they were riddled by disease, marked with newpox scars, missing fingers or hands from accidents in the mines.

This was the first close look Patrick had had at Drift society. The rebels were a comparatively healthy lot; few of these people could have kept up with them.

He found Obadiah painting radiation hexes on the doorsill of what had been a Corporation Mummer bunkhouse, and paused to talk. "This be my work," the conjur man said. "Esterhaszy sets up a medical station for the grown, and I set up a conjur hut for the tiny. Between us, we handle life and death." And when Patrick asked, he explained, "Parents bring in their newborn for me to pass judgment on. I decide whether the mutations are functional or not, judge whether the child can survive. If it passes, I hand it back to the parents."

"And if not?"

Obadiah stared down at his large, knobby hands. "Hey, man. You can't expect parents to do it to their child themselves."

Patrick backed away, went looking for Victoria. She was busy directing her people in various tasks, but paused to give him a squeeze and a kiss. When he said something about the children, she nodded. "They break your heart, don't they? But think of their parents. Imagine knowing that your child could have been healthy if you'd had the money to buy a new mask whenever the old one wore out, for water purifiers, and gnotobiotic greenhouses...." Her voice trailed off. "Hell, I'm beginning to sound like Uncle Bob."

When Patrick went back into the crowds, a fourteen-year-old albino girl snagged his arm. "Hey, mister. You with the rebels?"

"No," he said. "Well, yes. Sort of. Why do you ask?"

"I want—" She choked, and went into a coughing fit. Finally, she hawked up a load of phlegm. "I want to join them." She was slight and breastless, with long, thin hair.

"It's not an easy life."

"Just so long as they give me a *gun.*" The girl spoke so fiercely that she began coughing again. She bent over almost double before she could control it. "Just so long as I get to kill Mummers."

"What's your name?" Patrick asked.

"Heron. They killed my parents. There was a strike. The food didn't come from the farms, and some of the miners took over the shafts. They wanted the Corporation to open up the storehouse and feed everyone. So the Corporation said sure, all right, and when they came out from the mines, the Mummers grabbed them all and took them outside of town and fucking shot them. And left them there."

"Go on," Patrick said quietly.

"So I—when I came out of the mines today and saw what happened, I went out to where the bodies were so I could bury them. You know? But the bones were all mixed together, so I didn't know which ones were right. So I was going to bury them all together. In one—in one hole, right? Only I didn't have a fucking shovel."

The child stopped. "How long have you been working in the mines?" Patrick asked.

"Five years."

At sunset a chair was set up for Victoria in the center square of Honkeytonk. Small fires were built to either side, for dramatic effect, making the chair appear a throne. The prisoners—the handful of Mummers that remained, and the

Corporate management—were lined up behind her, and those who dared could lodge complaints.

Watching from the sidelines as the first few townspeople came hesitantly forward, Patrick felt his vision blurring. He rubbed his eyes and his sight recovered for a moment, then grew fuzzy again. Victoria was listening to the complaints. She swiveled to question one of the prisoners. Patrick closed his eyes again. Colors swam on the back of his eyelids, coalesced into shapes, then images, and became suddenly crisp.

He was looking out onto the square but from a different perspective, from someplace close to its center. The square was transformed, too, overlaid with dark, intense colors. The shadows were shot full of light, and the smoke from the fires to either side of him drifted up, their depths lit with deep, purple foxfire.

He did not accept all complaints. He listened carefully, and judged solemnly. Then he pointed out three of the prisoners, and they were taken aside and shot.

The pillars of darker-than-blue smoke drifted up overhead, their somber fires thinning as the smoke spread in the windless air. The dark sparkling was the radioactive particles that had been sucked up from the soil by the trees they were now burning. As the smoke fanned out, the particles swirled and looped like snowflakes. Then, infinitely slowly, they rained down over the people of Honkeytonk.

The radiation was everywhere, in the soil and on the sides of the buildings as well as in the air, and Patrick itched to see how the crowds stood unnoticing as it swirled slowly about them. The remaining prisoners were stripped of their masks and clothing, shaved bald (amid much laughter), and marched off, to be shoved outside the city limits.

The warehouse had been broken into, and those supplies the rebels could not use themselves were tossed into the waiting hands of the crowd. Looking around at the excited throng, hands out and grasping as tins of food, tools, bolts of cloth were thrown this way and that, Patrick suddenly saw himself, standing alone at the edge of the square, white-faced and unsteady, eyes closed tight.

Startled, he opened his eyes, and the hallucination was gone.

He stood in his own body, and no flickering radioactive fires lightened the dark square.

Victoria was looking directly at him. There was an amused smile on her face.

At that moment Obadiah ran out of the warehouse, and with a bloodcurdling scream, leaped into the air. People edged away from him. He whirled his long staff three times over his head, and pointed it into the open warehouse doors.

From inside came a great explosion of flame. The crowd gasped and stepped back. Obadiah laughed, ran to the shadows crouching like an ape, then reappeared, swinging a stool wildly. He ran frantically to one side, then to the other. Then he slammed the stool down before Victoria, and sat motionless as a statue at her knee.

"I will now accept new soldiers," Victoria said. Behind her, the warehouse burned merrily.

After a moment's stunned silence, there was a stirring in the crowd, and a man stepped forward. Another followed after him, and then a woman. In short order there was a line of some thirty-five people. Fitzgibbon strode quickly before them, pushed three away. One of the three was Heron. Angrily, she stepped back into line.

This time, with a small smile, Fitzgibbon let her stay.

Patrick noted how Victoria looked at the young albino and shivered almost imperceptibly. She's reminded of herself, he thought, then rejected the idea as wild and sourceless.

Flames in the background, the recruits were brought forward one at a time to Victoria's chair. Each swore allegiance to the cause, placing a hand on the tip of the conjur man's fetish staff. He opened a vein in the arm of each and collected a few drops of blood apiece in a goblet. When they had all sworn, he presented the cup to Victoria.

She drained it.

Now Obadiah opened a small cut on Victoria's shoulder. Again the recruits were called forward, one by one, to taste a drop of her blood.

They approached more reluctantly this time, and touched lips to shoulder. Except for Heron, their contact was swift and fleeting. She, however, closed her eyes as she kissed Victoria's shoulder, and her throat worked, sucking in blood. When she straightened, her eyes were slightly glazed. She backed away slowly.

"You are mine now," Victoria declaimed, "and I am yours. I would die for you." She glared about her. "Do you doubt me? But you must be willing to die for me as well."

It was night by now, and there was a full moon. The rebels, slightly larger in number, rode out. Patrick was among them, and for him the moon doubled, joined, redoubled, time and again, through the night.

The party dwindled by tens and twenties as detachments were sent away. "The Corporation is still hunting us," Fitzgibbon explained. "And I don't have any immediate use for a large force."

By dawn only forty or so rebels remained. Most rode horseback, but there were three four-wheelers among them. "The hell of it," Esterhaszy was explaining to a bleary-eyed Patrick as the sun came up, "is that the money's there. Enough for masks and chelates and greenhouses and hospitals for everyone. But it all goes to rich bastards in Boston and Philadelphia."

They were topping a rise just then, and Victoria cantered up and said, "Heads up, Uncle Bob!"

Esterhaszy looked startled, then rose in his seat and cried, "Utopia!"

In the valley below, still wrapped in the shadows of night, was what looked like an antique version of the future. Utopia was a settlement of tidy walks and geodesic domes. There was a rustic-looking watermill by the small river, and a homebuilt windmill by one of the complexes of greenhouses. It looked like nothing Patrick had seen in the Drift, because there was not a single rehabbed pre-Meltdown building. It had all been built new.

"This is the wave of things to come," Esterhaszy said happily. "The valley is a natural green spot, hardly any radioisotopes in the soil at all. The rains bypassed it. But we work to cleanse it of what does seep in, too. Over there, that's our waste treatment plant. And by the forge there is the water filtration system. Bit by bit, we're removing the boneseekers and radioactive traces from the soil, taking it out of the food cycle."

"This is where you normally live, I take it," Patrick said.

"Along with a few friends. We're a pretty technology-minded batch, and what's wrong with that? By God, you *need* technology if you want to have any kind of life in the Drift. A century ago they were making plans to live on Mars, Venus, the Moon—why not apply the same principles to the Drift?"

At Utopia, the inhabitants warily came out to greet the rebels. Victoria slipped away by herself, and Esterhaszy took Patrick to meet his wife, Helga, who turned out to be a tall blond woman. Her face was worn and weathered, and there were vicious scars across both her cheeks. As they all three talked, Patrick leaned back in his chair, and wearily let his eyes fall shut.

Instantly, he felt wind on his face. He found himself standing in a grassy green field, before a small white tombstone. Uncle Bob's geodesic was to his back. He carried a few wildflowers, picked along the way, and now he let them fall before the stone. An incredible sorrow weighed down on his heart, and a huge, gnawing fear.

"Oh, Momma," he said—only this time he realized from the start that he was imagining himself in Victoria's place. "I wish you'd come talk to me."

There was only silence.

"It's been too many years. I need to hear from you again. If you'd only give me a few words, I'd feel a lot better."

Victoria waited, but she heard nothing. She glanced sideways at the dark presence that loomed over the horizon, the heavy feeling of menace that she could never entirely ignore.

Victoria? Patrick thought, trying to reach her even though he knew it was only another hallucination.

Startled, Victoria whirled around and saw no one. Back in Esterhaszy's home, Patrick opened his eyes and found the dwarf anxiously hovering over him.

That evening Obadiah performed a radiation ceremony. While the celebrants knelt and waited for the herbs and chelates that would protect them from radiation sickness and marrow death, he danced something solemn and ceremonial, rod in one hand and an active geiger counter in the other.

Standing in the doorway of his dome, Esterhaszy watched with a disdainful smile. But then several Utopians, his friends and neighbors, joined in the ceremony, taking the sacrament of chelates and herbs. Esterhaszy turned red. "Just what the bloody hell is going on?" he demanded of Victoria.

She didn't look up from the piece of needlepoint she was working on. Helga had told Patrick that it was begun when Victoria was fifteen, and that whenever she came home, she put a touch more work into it. "Fitzgibbon's been recruiting," Victoria answered carelessly.

Esterhaszy turned back to the door. "That's Jeremiah Peltz! And Rabbit! He's taking both my engineers!"

"You know what we need them for."

"That's supposed to be a *threat*!" he shouted. "You don't need my people when you're only bluffing."

Victoria started to say something, then stopped. She stood up slowly, and stretched. "It's awfully claustrophobic in here," she said, and left.

Patrick caught up to Victoria in the middle of the field behind her foster parents' dome. The grass and weeds were waist-high there, a dark, shadowy mass in the night. They swayed gently about her as she stared off into the sky. When he put an arm around her, she shuddered but did not move away.

"I really do love them both," Victoria said at last. "But my God, they can be insufferable." She giggled. "Did you see the look on Uncle Bob's face when I walked out on him?"

"Maybe you should—"

"Oh, don't give me advice." Victoria reached behind her head and unsnapped her mask. It fell free and she took a deep breath. Then, seeing Patrick's expression, she said, "It's okay; we're in a clean area. Look—not a sparkle, not a glint, not the merest firefly hint of boneseekers, poisons, dark and venomous vapors. . . ."

"Are you stoned?"

"What?" Victoria stared at him blankly. Then a smile broke

through, turned into an almost goofy grin. "Just a little giggle I got from Obadiah." Then, as he continued to stare at her, "Well? Take your mask off. Come on. Planning to be a prig *all* your life?"

Patrick glanced back at Utopia, at the tidy curves of domes and the atavistic fire in its center. Small figures, dark in silhouette, were being led in worship by the conjur man. He directed them with sweeps of his rod; from the distance he looked like Moses. Slowly, Patrick removed his mask, filled his lungs with sweet air.

When he turned back to Victoria, she had already thrown aside her shirt, and was hopping on one leg to pull free of her pants. He moved to help her, and they tumbled to the ground together, flattening the tall grass, rolling over and over in it, suddenly happy and carefree.

At the instant of Victoria's climax, Patrick's mind was flooded with sensation, her pleasure crashing through him, not at all like his own orgasm or what he would have imagined hers to feel like, but different, unexpected. And in the midst of his confusion and excitement, he became aware of someone standing over them, a woman whose features he could not see. "When you need me, I'll be with you," she said.

"What?" Patrick lifted his head and looked about. But no one was there, no more than there had been a second woman in the carriage back in Boston. He looked at Victoria and asked, "Did something just happen?"

But she only smiled happily and shook her head. Eyes gleaming, she reached out a hand to brush fingertips against a nearby white stone.

Somehow, Patrick was not surprised to find that they had been fucking on her mother's grave.

When the rebels next made camp, Esterhaszy was not among them. He had stayed behind in Utopia.

They were forced to pitch their tents in the middle of a brown-out, a valley where the Meltdown rains had heavily saturated the soil with radioisotopes. The vegetation was sparse and stunted; what little grew died out quickly. Dust puffed up underfoot. Only Obadiah did not wear a mask.

That night they held another radioprotective ceremony. The

lead suits were lashed to a string of X-shaped pole frames, looking for all the world like a line of bulky scarecrows. With shrieks and leaps and arcane ceremony lifted from Catholic and Native American rituals, the conjur man daubed them all with red and yellow paint in strange, cabalistic sigils.

Victoria tapped Patrick's shoulder. She looked tense. "Press conference." She jerked her chin toward Fitzgibbon's tent, and Patrick followed her in.

Fitzgibbon was seated on a camp stool, slowly rubbing some balm on the chapped skin of his withered hand. He nodded somberly at Patrick's entrance. "We're losing the war," he said.

"Are you?" Patrick flipped his notebook open, jotted a quick note. "From here you look like you're doing pretty well."

"This is a war of attrition." Fitzgibbon stood, a massive, threatening man. "It's not enough to survive—we must prevail." He glared at Patrick over his mask. "Autumn is coming. We live off the land and its people—off their surplus. Come winter, we'll have to go dormant. In the spring we can reform, but we won't be in shape to fight again until summer.

"Meanwhile, the Corporation is supplied from outside. They aren't hampered by winter. They can afford to laugh at us!"

He stalked back and forth in the small tent like a caged panther. As he walked, his crippled arm curled up in a spasmodic clench, relaxed, then clenched and relaxed again, over and over.

"What do you plan to do?" Patrick asked.

"We have a weapon," Fitzgibbon said. "Something big and dirty enough to force both the Greenstate and American governments out of the Drift forever. We have something evil!" He paused, and Patrick could see that he was grinning painfully beneath his mask.

"Something evil," Patrick echoed politely.

Fitzgibbon whirled, and his great dark bulk crouched over Patrick menacingly. His heavily muscled healthy arm reached out, hesitated, withdrew. "By God," he said. "If I thought you were mocking me, boy, I'd—"

"All I want," Patrick said quickly, "is a clear statement of whatever you're trying to tell me." He held his ground, hoping desperately that his fear did not show.

To one side Victoria watched intently, her face pale.

Exhaling slowly, letting the anger ease away in one long, protracted breath, Fitzgibbon sat back down. "All right. All right, I'll— Listen. Back before the Meltdown, every nuclear reactor produced tons of radioactive waste material each year. A lot of it was low-level stuff, and we're not interested in that. But there were tons of plutonium in the used fuel rods. They were placed in canisters about so high, so broad, and stored away. In the more sophisticated dumps, they'd bulldoze a hole in the dirt, drop the canisters in, and bury them. But at most reactors, they were stored on-site in temporary facilities— warehouses—while they waited to make arrangements for final burial. Sometimes these arrangements took years, and sometimes they were never actually made. Are you listening to this?"

"Every word." Patrick made a meaningless mark on his pad.

"We're going right into the heart of the Drift and pick us up some of that plutonium." He chuckled. "We're going right up to the Meltdown reactor itself."

Patrick's skin crawled. He managed to keep a poker face, though. "Radioactive materials degrade," he pointed out. "Even if it were weapons-grade stuff a century ago, you'd need a fair-sized industrial base to refine it now."

"To make bombs, yeah. But we don't need an explosion— we have the people who can process it into a fine powdery dust. That's simple enough when you have the know-how. And we have the missiles to deliver the dust with. I don't believe we need any more than that."

Horrified, Patrick blurted, "You wouldn't dare—"

Fitzgibbon exploded up out of his chair, his withered arm clenched and curled almost into a knot. "*Yes!* By God, I would dare!" He leaned over a low table with maps spread atop it, and slammed his fist down on it. "One burst upwind of Boston, and the dust will flow over the entire town. It will filter through the streets and houses. People will breathe it in without realizing a thing—not until they sicken, and start to die."

Fitzgibbon was staring off into the night now. He spoke with the calm fervor of a visionary. "It won't begin for a day or two. Then they'll fall down in the streets and be unable to get up, they'll rot in their beds, and keel over while they're squatting over their chamber pots. Fires will start, and there'll be nobody to put them out. Those who stay alive longest will kill one another for what canned and bottled food exists, and nobody from outside will dare go in to help them."

"There must be a hundred thousand people in Boston," Patrick said in a sick voice. "Two hundred thousand."

"It won't be anything new," Fitzgibbon said. "It all happened before. Right here."

"It does not have to happen," Victoria said. "The missiles and powders won't be ready until next spring, next summer at the earliest. If we can get the Drift Corporation out before then. . . ." Her voice trailed off uncertainly; she looked to Fitzgibbon for confirmation.

Reluctantly, he nodded. "Yes. We are not interested in destruction for its own sake. If there were no need, we would not use the missiles." Then his voice brightened a bit. "However, you saw what happened at Honkeytonk. We won a major battle, and only got thirty recruits out of it. It'll take some kind of miracle to win our fight before then."

Away from the tent, Victoria clenched her hands and said bitterly, "I did not join up to become famous as the woman who killed two hundred thousand civilians."

"Why, then?"

She gave him a tight little smile. "To be a *hero*, that's why. I'm not going to live long, I want my life to burn bright in the night, like—like some kind of beacon, either urging people on or warning them away, I don't care which. But it's got to be good and whole and pure. I want those bastards to admire me when I'm gone! And it's got to be under my own control, not that of Fitzgibbon or blind necessity or . . ." She hesitated. "Or anyone else!"

Patrick reached out to touch her, and she jerked away, then strode angrily off into the night. He went back to his tent to write up the interview.

Patrick threw in a few purple additions of his own, largely in the description of the dusting of Boston, which he played up heavily. He realized that this was what Fitzgibbon wanted him to do, that he was effectively serving as the propaganda

arm of the revolution, but he didn't care. It was important that
the outside world know.

When he was done, he walked the copy over to Obadiah's
tent. The conjur man scanned the text quickly, then said, "I'm
afraid most of this will have to be cut, old son. I can maybe
transmit the first five paragraphs with only a word or two
changed here and there, and then all this background stuff
toward the end. But that's all."

"Why?"

"For the same God damn reason we took your transceiver
away in the first place. How many places do you think there
are we can pick up radwaste in the Drift? Any of this shit gets
out, we have every fucking soldier in the world waiting for us
at the Meltdown."

"No thanks," Patrick said. "All or nothing." He took hold
of the story.

Obadiah refused to let go, and for a brief, ludicrous time
they acted out a small tug-of-war over the manuscript. "Tell
you what," the conjur man said. "I'll start it out 'Censored by
the People's Provisional Government of the Drift.' See? That
way they know they's parts of the story don't go through. Then
you get the hard copy back and you can send it uncensored
after we gone and pick up the plutonium. How 'bout that?"

Patrick hesitated, then let go.

The deeper they traveled into the Drift, the drearier the
land became. The green, relatively clean lands became rarer,
the brown spots closer together. By day they were plagued by
swarms of insects, none of which Patrick could identify. Obadiah chuckled. "Old Esterhaszy could tell you their names,
most of 'em. But some—no. They new. There be genuine
mutations in the insect kingdom, a lot of 'em, because their
generations be so short, and because there's so many. In the
animal kingdom, not so many, and most probably don't breed
true."

Something iridescent blue landed on Patrick's hand. Its thorax
throbbed twice, and it stung him.

"God damn!" Patrick whipped his hand away, and the insect
flew off. The sting was beginning to swell already; it hurt

fiercely. "I'll be glad as hell when I finally leave this godfor-
saken wilderness!"

"Oh?" Obadiah said innocently. "They's nobody you mind
leaving behind, then?"

For a second, Patrick didn't get it. Then he ripped off his
mask, and spat at the conjur man's feet. He stalked off angrily.

Victoria looked haggard that evening. They had traveled
hard and fast, and it showed. When she tried to pull Patrick
atop her, he held back.

"Why are you doing this to yourself?" he asked. "You need
a good night's sleep, not a roll in the sack—why are you
running yourself into the ground?"

"Oh Jesus." With a groan Victoria sat up. She eyed Patrick
silently for a moment, then said, "I keep telling you, I don't
have your lifespan. When I was born, they gave me twenty
years at best. If I reach thirty, it'll be a medical miracle. And
I don't expect to reach thirty. Nights like this, I'm amazed I'm
still alive."

"But that's exactly what I'm saying. If you took care
of—"

"I'm a vampire," she said in exasperation. "I don't get any
nutrition out of normal food. I can only digest whole blood or
egg whites—which means there's no way I can avoid the
radioisotopes. Every meal is another dose of death, another
step closer to dying of leukemia, like my mother did. So if I
want what little time I have left to count for shit, I've got to
live fast and glorious. Get it? I don't have the time for deferred
gratification."

"Listen, I'm sorry if—" Patrick began. But she rolled atop
him, effectively stopping him from saying more.

Some time later, in the midst of their passion, she muttered,
"The worst of it is," and then something else.

Patrick stopped, lifted her slightly away from him. *"What*
did you say?"

There were angry tears in Victoria's eyes. "I said the worst
of it is that I think maybe I love you."

It was as if a pain that was so slow in growing and so all-
embracing that he hadn't even noticed it was there had suddenly

gone away. Patrick threw his head back and laughed. "That's wonderful! That's the best news I've heard all—"

"It is not!" Crying, she hit him in the chest, hard. "It is not. Oh God, this is absolutely the most horrible thing that's ever happened to me in my entire life."

A week passed. They were in the most heavily polluted regions of the Drift, where few travelers went and nobody lived. They passed through a dark stand of rotting trees, phosphorescent fungi glowing on their boles. The ground was damp underfoot.

"Old Esterhaszy'd give his eyeteeth to be here," Obadiah observed. "It'd be his big chance to name something squishy after himself."

Beyond the wood the land was half barren, great expanses of baked mud cut through by erosion gulleys. Outlying scouts twice reported spotting small Corporation Mummer patrols at a distance. Once a helicopter passed within earshot. It was clear that they were being hunted.

"Thank God we took out Piotrowicz," Victoria observed after the copter had faded away. "We couldn't've jerked *him* around like this."

Radiation discipline grew stricter. At the nightly ceremonies, Obadiah handed out a doubled sacrament of chelates, and a thick paste he claimed was a mixture of radioprotectives. He brought a bowl of it to where Patrick was finishing off his latest dispatch.

Patrick eyed the mixture dubiously. "Esterhaszy told me that radioprotectives are almost useless."

"That so," the conjur man said. "Almost. You'd know all this shit if you came to my rituals."

"Well, something always seems to—" Patrick stopped. Looking up at the man he noticed for the first time that there were small filter plugs in Obadiah's nostrils. "I thought you said the spirit people protected you."

Obadiah looked puzzled, then figured it out and laughed. "Maybe I help them out a little."

Victoria no longer siphoned off blood from the pack animals. She drank from bloodbags dosed with dioxylate to inhibit clotting. They were traveling fast and light, letting the horses forage for their food.

Every night, after they made love, Patrick dreamed that Victoria sat up for hours, straining for a vision that never came.

They arrived at a place called Highspire, and camped within the walls of what had once been a roadside restaurant. Scratching about, several rebels found old orange tiles and lined their fires with them. While the two leaders conferred over a handful of century-and-a-half-old government reports and lay-out charts, Obadiah explained to Patrick that they were just out of sight of the Meltdown reactor's cooling towers.

"So you're going through with it," Patrick said. "You're going to let that criminal kill hundreds of thousands of people."

"Hey, I done my best. I got a doctorate in mass-behavioral psychology from Harvard, you know that? And I put everything I learned into building up Victoria. In fact, I think I did a pretty good job, considering. But you saw the results—people just not willing to give up that big a chunk of their lives."

"There's still another alternative," Patrick said.

"Well, there's martyrdom." Obadiah shrugged. "Worked pretty well for Joan of Arc. But something like that be hard to arrange. Victoria might not want to volunteer for it."

"What I was thinking of—" Patrick began testily. He stopped, lowered his voice. "I was thinking of assassination."

Obadiah looked surprised. "You going to kill Fitzgibbon?" He squinted at Patrick, shook his head. "Naw, you just want somebody to do it for you. Has it occurred to you that an assassin would probably die too? Now just who you got in mind for the job?"

Just then Victoria and Fitzgibbon emerged from the tent, and Obadiah had to hurry off to assemble the nightly ghost shirt ceremony. I could kill him myself, Patrick thought. But listening to the words, he found he simply could not believe them. It was not just that he had never fired a gun in his life. It was that he was a neutral, an observer. His job was to bring back word of what occurred, not to interfere, not to shape the events himself.

"Just beyond those hills, just over that rise," Obadiah told his assembled congregation, "lies the Meltdown island!" He gestured with his rod, and the guerrillas stirred in collective unease. "Tomorrow we go there to walk among the atomic fires. We will walk among the broken buildings and the whole, and the killing gamma radiation will wash over us. The air be so full of boneseekers you choke on it, and the ground be so hot it blister the naked feet.

"But you will be protected."

The ragged band of rebels hung on Obadiah's every word, listening to what Patrick could only summarize as a cross between a science lecture and a pep talk. Beyond Obadiah, Victoria stood before her tent, pale and expressionless, hands by her sides. When the ceremony was over, she ducked under the flap and disappeared.

When Patrick joined her, Victoria was still and shivering. She smiled wanly and said, "Oh hi," in a small voice.

"Hey," Patrick said, alarmed. "What's wrong?"

"Oh, nothing. Just your basic panic reaction at going up to the Reactor, I guess. Any Drifter would feel it. I'll be okay."

But it was not the truth. Patrick could feel her evasiveness. "No, really." He hugged her shoulders, gently rocked her back and forth. "You can tell me, I'm okay."

Tears formed in her eyes and, when she blinked, ran quickly down her cheeks. She buried her face in his chest. "Oh God, Patrick, sometimes I worry that maybe I'm crazy."

Patrick said nothing, continued to rock her gently.

"Ever since I was a little girl, I've heard things and seen things that other people don't. Sometimes I get advice from . . . someone who's been dead for a long time. Sometimes she tells me things I don't want to do."

"Hush." Patrick kissed the top of her head, stroked her hair with one hand. He had been about to tell her that she wasn't crazy, that he had seen the world through her eyes, when she made that last statement. "What kind of things?"

"Dangerous things, sometimes. But she's always been right, so I've always done what she asked. But now . . . there's something she always told me I'd have to do, and I'm afraid. And

I've begun to wonder if, if it's just that I'm crazy and all these visions were only hallucinations. The only time I've seen my mother appear in *years*, I was stoned flat on my ass." Her face was hard and tight. "Damn it, I don't want to die from craziness, I . . ."

"There, there," Patrick said. "Hush, little baby."

They made love awkwardly that night, and when Patrick finally fell asleep, he dreamed that the world was flooded with light.

The light was deep and blue and profound, and it burned right through the canvas sides of the tent, turning the things within into blurry and indeterminate shadows. It was not static light, but full of shifting emphases of focus and lumination. It washed through the tent restlessly, ceaselessly, like ocean water coursing through a tidepool.

He stood and pulled on a pair of trousers, put on a shirt. Barefoot, he padded out onto the grass.

Outside the light was a universal flood, wiping the stars from the sky, fading the moon into near invisibility in its wash. It intensified to the southwest, at its source just beyond the hills, at the Meltdown site. The bright nuclear heart of the Reactor could be seen through the earth hills, piercing through rock and dirt.

The light was all a single living creature, and it gloried in its life. Dark and beautiful and menacing, it tugged at Patrick, pulling him toward the Reactor. The earth seemed to tilt up on its side, and it was hard to keep his feet, hard to keep from sliding away into the Reactor's maw.

A shadow passed before him then, cutting off the sensation of pull, and equilibrium was restored. It was a woman, but he couldn't make out her features, only that she was terribly, terribly sad. She was dark and fuzzy in the flood of light.

"Momma?" Victoria said in a small voice.

Patrick found himself back in the tent, blankets wrapped around him. The reassuring warmth of his love beside him was gone. Determinedly, he kept his eyes shut, maintaining the tenuous contact between himself and Victoria.

"Momma, I tried so hard to reach you. I don't know what to do."

The woman's face was an oval of pure light, glowing too brightly for the features within to be made out. Her shawl and dress *blazed* with colors like none Patrick had ever seen— glory reds and golds and sunshine yellows.

Then the Reactor's rays flared up, drowning the woman in cold, actinic blue light. Her clothes faded, bleaching away to sere dryness. The woman's bones shone through the cloth, and the light left her head.

She had no face. A dry white skull grinned down on her daughter.

Victoria cried out and stumbled back. But her mother stepped forward, a skeleton in rags, to seize her hands. Bone fingers closed about her, and then took on flesh. Then there was flesh on the skull as well, and a face—an ordinary enough face, but the expression was filled with love and remembered pain. "It's nothing to be afraid of," she said. She hugged Victoria close, and for the first time it was obvious that she was a small woman, not nearly so tall as her daughter. And then Patrick slept.

But some short while after, he heard Victoria slip into the blankets with him, wriggle into a comfortable position, and murmur, "I had such a *nice* dream."

The cooling towers of the defunct reactor loomed over the horizon as the rebels topped the first rise, and continued to grow as the band toiled forward, a frightening presence, unbroken and perfect. Higher the four towers rose into the sky, and higher. They were huge and impossibly out of scale. It was almost beyond belief that mere human beings had built such things.

The land was dead and barren from horizon to horizon. Gullies runneled the soil, leaving behind rocks and baked mud. In the rare puddle or stagnant pond there grew swaths of name- less scum, microorganisms too simple to be easily killed. An occasional clump of weeds poked out from the rubbled remains of a building, spread out, sickened, and died.

Overhead, the sky was a clear and heartbreakingly pure blue.

They set up a work camp on the river shore opposite the island. The river between camp and island was almost gone. Before the Meltdown, a dam had connected island and shore, and with the shifting of currents a sand bar had grown there, with one swift channel cutting through.

Fitzgibbon led the first party of workers across. They wore radiation suits and brought hand-trucks with them. Laboriously they hauled the half-ton canisters from the storage building to the island's edge. There, using ropes and donkey engines, the drums were pulled across the sand. At both sides, the canisters were checked with geiger counters for radiation leakage. Several were abandoned.

Midway through the process, three trucks arrived, jouncing down an almost obliterated roadway. They were driven by people Patrick had never seen before, and had QUAKER STATE INDUSTRIAL WASTE DISPOSAL painted on their sides. Patrick wondered where and how the rebels had gotten them.

Victoria was standing by the edge of the sand bar when Patrick approached her. She held the radiation suit's hood under one arm, and stared off at the dozens of buildings on the long, flat island. Many had been broken open by the steam explosion that had ruptured the reactor containment building. Others were relatively intact.

A light breeze lifted Victoria's hair and flew it behind her like white flame. "I hear you're leading the second crew across," Patrick said, and then in a familiar doubling of vision, he saw the world transformed through her eyes.

The sky over the island was a patchwork rainbow of soft pastels, yellows and roses swirling and merging slowly, one with the other, robin's-egg blues flowing into muted golds so beautiful they took his breath away. The island below was all bright mist, shot through with dark flashes of color running along the building edges like St. Elmo's fire.

"It'll be a piece of cake," she said, and reached out awkwardly to hug him, the lead suit making her motions broad and slow. She kissed him with her eyes open, watching the rainbow sky reflected in his pupils, dancing in the tips of his lashes.

Then Patrick had stepped back, dazzled, and Victoria raised her hood and fit it over her head, the thick lead glass visor cutting her vision down to a mere slit. Her crew was ready, and she led them silently across the sand bar.

It felt good to be alive. To feel her muscles working, to see the sand sparkle underfoot. The channel of water was invisible, and it almost undercut her balance when she stepped heavily into it. With a muffled laugh and a lurch, she righted herself, and kept on. The island ahead was a single, complex structure, though the details were lost in mist. For an instant the land, mist, and buildings pulled together into a great, sleeping beast.

Obadiah slapped a hand on Patrick's shoulder. "Well, boy, tomorrow you get to file all your old dispatches in-tact and un-censored, eh?"

She was almost to the island now. Patrick tuned out his own surroundings, concentrated on the glowing line of brightly colored rocks that marked the end of the sand bar. "Obadiah, I've had some strange premonitions lately," he said carefully. "Maybe I've even seen Victoria's mother. What do you think it means?" There were only three steps to go. Two.

"Probably means you've had too much to smoke." Victoria's foot touched the island and the beast awoke. The shining white fog shifted, like the sides of an immense white bear fretfully preparing to emerge from hibernation. Deep blue spears of light shot up into the sky, and a great, silent roar boomed and echoed in her skull. Random emotions bounced up underfoot, died down. Then a huge, unfriendly sense of awareness focused on her.

"You all right there, brother man?"

"Just a little dizzy. Listen, I'm serious. I think I'm picking up on Victoria's psychic influences or something."

The crew stepped Indian file along a roadway that no humans had trod on for over a century. Victoria led them into the beast, bypassing the worst of the radioactive rubble, stepping aside from the purple curtains of gamma radiation that sprayed from the broken containment buildings. All the while, she felt immersed in its cold, amused scrutiny.

"Psychic bushwah," Obadiah snorted. "Don't tell me you're becoming one of her believers?"

She was surrounded by buildings now. They loomed up on every side of her, and still they were overtopped by the cooling towers, hanging massive and oppressive over her head. Victoria led her crew along a long blank wall, then across a pile of rubble that had once been a building. The low rise that sparkled just beyond that had been an access road. Long tentacles of emerald green and cobalt blue light washed restlessly over them, and daintily brushed against Victoria's suit.

"But I've seen it," Patrick objected. "I've seen things I couldn't possibly explain otherwise. There's no question but she's got some kind of powers."

"Here we are," Victoria said, and then realized that she could not possibly be heard outside her suit. She signaled for a halt, then waved her gang into the empty-fronted warehouse. They scattered to their work, moving quickly and efficiently. Night after night, they had practiced for this chore, and they were ready.

Standing alone before the warehouse, Victoria trembled. The canisters were lost within their own glow; she might as well be blind for all the help she could give. Still, she wished she could be in with her crew. Waiting outside, there was nothing to do but listen to the whispering of the Reactor.

A dark glee emanated from the Reactor. It wanted her, and she stood at the very fringe of its physical being. Wrapping tendrils lovingly about her arms and legs, it whispered *Come*. Victoria shivered again, and stood firm, her legs braced wide.

Obadiah sighed. "Well, okay," he said. "When I started with Victoria, I did some work with hypnosis and psychotomimetic drugs, and there were some suggestive results. Nothing definite, mind you, but enough to indicate that she might indeed have some sort of telepathic ability. But I had to give up that line of inquiry real fast."

"Why?"

The Reactor tugged at Victoria. It drew back the shining mist from the road before her, so that she could see the ancient roadbed as bright as burnished brass. The land tilted up behind her and down ahead, so that it was easiest to simply put one foot before the other and walk, lightly, quickly.

Nobody noticed her leave. The warehouse lost itself in the clutter of buildings, and Victoria glided toward the reactor containment building. It was huge, almost a third as high as the cooling towers, and it was as dazzling as a palace made of neon tubes.

"Why?" the conjur man said. "Because your girlfriend is none too tightly wrapped, if you'll forgive me for saying so.

I don't think she's actually crazy, but—I been watching her a long time, and it is my considered opinion that she is none too clear on where the line between fantasy and reality should be drawn."

A length of wall had collapsed on the containment building, swallowing up a slice of roof and whatever doorway might have existed. Twisted, half-melted girders stuck out through the gap. Within, a superheated vapor coiled about crumbling machinery, delicately veiling it from her eyes. And far beyond, visible only as a fierce red light piercing the mist, lay the Reactor's sister, the broken, simmering pool of the original Meltdown.

Am I not beautiful? the Reactor murmured. The blue-lit interior writhed in a slow cascade of shifting intensity. It looked warm, too, warm as the fires of Hell.

"She gets advice from her mother's spirit," Patrick said.

"I'm not surprised. Not only was her mother a famous mystic and healer, but she died when Victoria was real young. She grew up with everyone expecting her to fill her mother's shoes. It'd be more surprising if she didn't see her mother now and then."

For all the lure of the Reactor, Victoria did not move. The building crouched anxiously over her, eager to wrap its hot touch about her body. The radioactive slurry within was hot, hotter than the surface of Venus. *Join me,* the Reactor said. She knew what it wanted, and what was expected of her, but still she resisted.

Victoria was afraid. She wanted a sign. It wasn't enough that her mother had told her time and again that she would come to this moment. Not when her last two visions had occurred in a drug delirium, and in a dream. She wanted proof that she was not mad.

Listening, waiting, straining for the least sign, Victoria thought she heard a voice, weak as a breath of wind on a still day, saying, "Go ahead."

Slowly, Victoria raised her hands to her hood and prepared to lift it up. The fires leaped up about her in anticipation, and her heart quailed. She could not make her hands move.

Victoria, don't! Patrick screamed mentally. He willed with all his might for the words to reach her.

Victoria stayed her hand, turned around, saw nothing. "Patrick?" she said. She reached out with her mind, felt him linked to her. "Patrick." And in that firm touch of minds she found corroboration that No, she was not mad at all, that her telepathic experiences—and hence also her spiritual ones—were real.

She took off her hood.

The fires roared up as she shrugged out of her lead suit. They lifted up her hair and sent it flying in the hot air. She kicked free of the leggings, let the suit drop to the ground. Hot needles lanced through her body, thousands of them, leaving long straight trails of ruptured cells. She advanced to the edge of the building.

Inside, the bubbling heat chuckled and gloated. It was time for their trade, time to consummate their bargain of life for power. For an instant Victoria looked upon the Reactor itself, gigantic masses of machinery that had slumped and crumbled over the decades, but still crouched protectively over a half-melted core of dying fuel rods, like a gigantic metal spider.

Looking in, Victoria felt the gamma radiation intensify, the invisible spears leaping up to pierce her again and again. And then the steam within the building shifted and the machinery faded away, and was replaced by a single enormous eye. It was lidded over by mist, but still the sullen red shone through, threatening and evil.

The eye opened and looked at her.

Patrick woke to find he had been laid across the supplies in the back of a four-wheeler. It was in motion. Crammed awkwardly in among the baggage, Obadiah crouched over him. "What happened?" Patrick asked.

"You had a seizure." Obadiah frowned. "Why didn't you warn me you were prone to fits?"

"I didn't know." Patrick sat up, looked around weakly. "Where's Victoria?"

"Lie back down. She's fine. She's at the head of the procession now. In charge of the whole damn thing."

"I thought..."

"About an hour ago, there was a small steam explosion on the island. Scared the holy shit out of everyone. Then Victoria come out. She was barefoot, not wearing her suit at all. Only had on a little white shift that she wore under the suit. No mask either. Come walking out as cool as you please, and she say the reactor done give her power. Then she ordered everybody saddle up and said we were going to take Honkeytonk again, and keep it this time. Nobody had the nerve to say boo to her."

"Jesus. They're really following her?"

Obadiah glanced around, lowered his voice. "Hell, if she don't die in the next day or two, *I'll* follow her. Back into the Meltdown reactor if she tell me to."

But just as the moon was rising over the naked hills, Victoria fell off her horse. The rebels milled about her uncertainly. She tried to stand up, lurched suddenly, and fell again. This time, several hands helped her up. Afoot again, she leaned her head against her horse's saddle for a moment before remounting.

They made camp late, and the next morning Victoria turned down the proffered goblet of blood. She quickly shook her head when it was brought to her, and there was a queasy look on her face. Then she yanked off her mask, and disappeared into a nearby ravine. When she reappeared, there were flecks of vomit on her blouse.

Then a rebel assigned to monitoring the airwaves suddenly yanked off her earphones and said, "Corporation activity." With a swift bustle and clatter, the group began packing and mounting.

As Victoria wearily prepared to swing up onto her horse, Fitzgibbon rode up to her and said, "Don't bother."

Victoria looked up at him. The others fell silent, listening.

"The Corporation is on our tails, and we can't carry any excess baggage," Fitzgibbon said. "Look at you! You can't even ride without falling off."

"We could lash her to the horse," Obadiah suggested.

Fitzgibbon ignored him. "You've failed," he said harshly. "Admit it. You've got radiation poisoning and you're dying. Nobody is going to buy your little charade anymore." He glared about him. No one would meet his eye. "Nobody."

"It was just bad luck," Victoria said softly. "With this kind of exposure, there's usually a few weeks after the initial nausea before the sickness sets in again. Odds were I should've been able to pull it off." She handed the reins over to Fitzgibbon, backed away slowly. "Nothing but bad luck."

Their possessions made a forlorn pile in the road—blood-bags, water, Patrick's transceiver, enough food for a week. They also had, if they wanted them, several collapsible cots and stools, cook sets and shovels, all items lightened from the fleeing rebels' load. Obadiah pressed an old medical text into Patrick's hands, along with a syringe and morphine kit. "I've underlined the passage about morphine overdose—be real careful about that. It's easy and painless, so I hear." He clapped Patrick's shoulder. "Wouldn't want you to have any unfortunate accidents."

Fitzgibbon's horse cantered up at the last minute, and he leaned down to say, "Don't be stupid, boy. She'll be dead in a week, with or without you. You're not doing her any favors."

Patrick shook his head. "I owe her—" But Fitzgibbon, disgust plain on his face, did not stay to listen.

As the troupe rode away, several looked back over their shoulders. Obadiah glanced back frequently, and with obvious regret, but he went anyway. Heron, in contrast, shouldered her rifle and rode off stiff-backed, without once glancing back.

"Well," Patrick said. "Any idea what we do now?"

Victoria was lying on her back, eyes closed. "I don't know. I don't care. I'm just tired as shit." She began to cry.

Patrick found a development of townhouses, with the roofs and upper floors all collapsed. One had half its ground floor miraculously preserved, and he moved Victoria in there. The land was cleaner here, sparsely covered with stunted scrub, but still heavily enough laced with radioisotopes that there were no rats or other vermin to disturb them.

While Victoria lay on a cot by the door, Patrick busied himself cleaning out the room, and creating makeshift shutters for the windows and doorframe. Even these simple tasks were difficult without the right tools, and consumed a great deal of time.

Despite the constant toil, the next three days passed slowly, a cold, lonely nightmare, as Victoria sank deeper into her disease. She was weak and feverish, and Patrick applied wet cloths to her forehead as she twisted on her cot. Several times a day he would try spoon-feeding her blood. She did not always manage to keep it down.

Sometimes Victoria suffered from delirium, and then there was little Patrick could do but try to keep her from injuring herself as she raved and thrashed about. Halfway into these episodes, the hallucinations would begin to leak into his own mind, and he had to run outside, fleeing her presence, as the world filled up with monsters and demons, and he lashed out blindly, trying to destroy them.

Other times she had bloody diarrhea, messing her clothing and cot, as well as herself. Cursing himself for the part he had played in reducing her to this, Patrick cleaned it all up.

Once he heard a helicopter pass through the night, and thus knew that the Corporation Mummers were still in the area. Victoria had awoken then, convinced that he was going to feed her to some gigantic mutant insect, and she had to be restrained or she would have fled out the door and into the Drift. "My mother lied," she cried when she finally calmed down. "I was supposed to become a hero, and instead she sent me to Hell."

When he found time, Patrick typed out a full dispatch covering the events at the Meltdown island and beyond. It was written crisply and emotionlessly, as a kind of penance for how deeply involved he had become. Because he was in a state of constant exhaustion, he missed the polesat passing overhead, and filed it a day late.

On the third day, Esterhaszy knocked on the door.

Patrick had been sitting over Victoria, half dozing, when the dwarf appeared in the doorway. He stumbled to his feet, walked stiffly outside. The sunlight made him blink, and tears formed in his eyes.

"Don't bother explaining," Esterhaszy said. "I've already spoken with Fitzgibbon. How is she?"

"Sleeping." Patrick led his friend away from the door, to avoid disturbing Victoria. "How'd you find us?"

"It wasn't difficult. I knew Fitzgibbon's planned route, so when I finally decided I was wrong to abandon Victoria, he was easy enough to intercept. But how is she *doing*?"

"I think the fever has broken. But—well, the way this thing goes, there's a temporary remission after the first onslaught, which might last a week or two. But after that there's a relapse, and I'm afraid there's not really much hope for her."

"I know the symptomology of marrow death," Esterhaszy snapped. "I was just hoping that Fitzgibbon had told me wrong."

"Well, you—" Patrick stopped. There was a small noise from within the house. Victoria.

Inside, they found her awake. "Uncle Bob?" She took his hands. Tears were in her eyes. "Uncle Bob, my mother lied to me," she said in a little-girl voice. "She told me to go to the Reactor and offer up my life to it. She said that when I did that it would give me the power to drive the Corporation out of the Drift forever." An angry edge crept into her bewilderment. "God damn her, why did she lie?"

"Show a little spunk, child!" Esterhaszy growled. "I let you get away with blaming things on your mother for too long when you were little; I'm not about to let you start again. Don't try to foist off responsibility on someone else—straighten your shoulders, and make me proud of you."

They glared at one another for a long minute. Then her eyes fell. "Yes, Daddy," she said weakly, obediently. She closed her eyes, and her head lolled over to the side. "I'm tired," she said, and fell asleep again.

Now Esterhaszy stood motionless, still holding her hands. He bowed his head and tears fell silently. Finally, Patrick led him outside.

"Aw, jeez," the old man said. He took out a handkerchief, dabbed at his eyes, blew his nose, slid his mask into place. At last he said. "It's my fault. I tried to get her off this obsession with occult crap. But I don't know. Maybe I was too strict. Maybe I wasn't strict enough."

"Maybe there was nothing you could have done."

"I should have been in control." Esterhaszy drew himself together. "She's going to die unless she gets bone marrow transplants. The odds aren't good, even with the transplants, but that's all the chance she has. And the only place she can possibly get that operation is in Boston."

Patrick shook his head at the hopelessness of the notion. But all he said was, "How do we get it for her?"

"We surrender to the Drift Corporation is what we do," Esterhaszy said, "and try to cut a deal."

"They'd want names—you'd be a traitor to your friends."

"What concern is it of yours? You God damned neutral! You just stick to reporting the news; you're not supposed to take sides."

At that instant, something happened within the townhouse. Patrick knew it. He could feel it happening, could sense it by some means he could not have defined. It was as if the world had skipped a beat to let someone in. "Something odd is happening," he said dreamily. Victoria's mother was not far away. She stood in Victoria's presence, close enough for the rebel leader to touch.

"What do you mean, odd?" Esterhaszy asked.

"She's in the house!" Patrick spun about and ran.

But when they burst into the townhouse, Victoria was alone. She was sitting up in her cot, eyes bright and glittery. And when Patrick demanded to know what had just happened, she shook her head. "Nothing," she said, and Patrick knew she was lying.

"We've decided on a course of action," Esterhaszy said. But when he tried to explain, she brushed it aside. "What are my chances, even if everything goes the way you want—slim, eh? Practically nonexistent, aren't they?"

Esterhaszy frowned. "I wouldn't go so far as to say—"

"For as long as I remember, I've known I'd die young. I'm not afraid of it anymore." She took Patrick's hand and squeezed it. "I'm afraid I'm shameless, Patrick. When I needed publicity, I let you become an outlaw, and when I needed a . . . friend, I kept my secrets from you. There's no reason in the world for you to forgive me anything. But I still have one more favor to ask. I need your help. Will you give it?"

Patrick looked down at her thin hand in his, so much weaker than a few days ago. The practical side of his mind knew he shouldn't make any blind promises. But the honest side knew that it didn't matter what she asked. "Anything," he said.

She told him what she wanted.

It took only minutes to vacate the townhouse. Patrick helped Victoria outside while Esterhaszy piled up flammables.

He built the fire quickly and competently, first tinder, then kindling, then planking, then wall. "Stand clear!" he yelled; then he lit a match and torched the building.

As the smoke billowed upward, Patrick pulled out the whip antenna on his transceiver. It was far too early for a polesat transmission, but the Corporation might be listening anyway. He began typing.

Esterhaszy brought around his motortrike, a converted Citicab with roll bar and balloon tires, and parked it with the motor running. He slapped a hand on Patrick's back in passing, and went to the ancient truncated lamppost, where Victoria sat huddled in a light blanket. "Well," he said.

"You have the envelope?"

"Right here." Esterhaszy slapped his shirt pocket. "Though I don't believe for an instant this fool scheme is going to work."

"Piotrowicz loves his city. It's all he's got left," Victoria said. "I guess—"

"Don't say anything. I don't think I could stand it; I'd start crying." Esterhaszy forced a smile. "And we don't want your old uncle to cry, do we now?"

Victoria shook her head. "No."

"All right then." He turned away.

But before he got halfway to his vehicle, Victoria was on her feet and running to him. She hugged him from behind, getting down on her knees to do so, and hooked her chin over his shoulder, buried the side of her face into his neck.

"Now don't," the old man said. He patted her arm, then began to stroke it. "Oh, hell."

An hour later a Mummer patrol showed up, three fast all-terrain vehicles with armed Corporation Mummers holding their weapons ready. They found two beaten figures huddled under a makeshift white flag of surrender.

The jail in Honkeytonk was nothing special—a rehabbed brick rowhouse with bars set across the windows, and padlocks and peepholes added to the interior doors. But it sufficed to hold the new prisoners. They had been in custody only an hour when a guard unlocked the door and Keith Piotrowicz walked in.

Even though Patrick had only seen Piotrowicz once, and

then briefly, it was still a shock how the man had aged. The flesh on his face was loose and sunken, and his motions abrupt and graceless. But he still retained an aura of power.

Piotrowicz slammed a handful of papers down on the table with a peremptory thump. Patrick recognized a fragment of prose on the top sheet. They were pirated hardcopies of his dispatches.

"Just in by packet boat," Piotrowicz said. He jerked a folded copy of the *Atlanta Federalist* from under his arm and thrust it at Patrick.

The paper contained one of Patrick's early dispatches. They'd put it on the front page, a full column in a sidebar running down the left-hand side, and continued within. A quick glance showed that the editing had been light; most of his prose had been let stand. Patrick put the paper down. Once it would have meant a great deal to him.

Piotrowicz took a chair, studied his two captives from under bushy eyebrows. "Well. Shall we talk?"

"Let's not waste time," Victoria said. "You're concerned about the fact that a fanatic like Fitzgibbon has a battery of missiles and enough radioactives to dust Boston four times over." Idly, she drew the top sheet from the pile of dispatches, and flipped it over.

Piotrowicz nodded slowly.

"You're not going to catch him. So you want to know, does he really have the radioactives? Can he really use them as a weapon? Will he?" Among the possessions the guards had let her keep was a charcoal stick. She drew it from her pocket now, and began doodling.

"Well?"

"You bet your ass he will." Victoria glanced up and flashed a quick grin. Her gums were bleeding a little. "You just bet your sweet little ass."

Keith glanced darkly at Patrick, then back at the rebel leader. "You will both be tried as war criminals," he said. "You are both accomplices to the act, and you will pay. Crimes committed against civilian populations are not acts of war, and need not be treated as such." He paused, rubbed his forehead wearily. "I knew your mother," he said to Victoria.

If his intention was to startle her, it failed. All of Victoria's attention was on the paper before her. Her brow furled slightly in concentration. The blanket slipped from her shoulder, and she drew it back without looking. "Oh, yes?" she said.

"She had a lot of grit," Keith said. "And people believed in her. We could have accomplished a lot together. But she fell prey to a kind of false sentimentality. You can't help people out of weakness. It's damned hard to help people at all, but you can't do it without strength. Even then, the best you can usually do is minimize the pain." He glared at Victoria. "What do you imagine your mother would say about this plan to kill everyone in Boston? How would you justify it to her? Do you think she'd approve?"

"Pull your troops out of the Drift," Victoria said.

Piotrowicz blinked. "What?"

Victoria bent over her paper again. "Pull your forces out. Move out all the Corporation Mummers, your spies and agents and informers, your overseers and executives and officers. Everyone. That's the only way you can stop Fitzgibbon."

Slowly, Piotrowicz began to laugh. The laughter built. He leaned forward and then back, rocking helplessly in his chair. "My dear, my dear," he said at last. "It's not as easy as you make it sound. I don't have that kind of power." He sobered a bit and went on. "There are things which must be done, you see. There are unpleasant decisions which someone has to make. Someone has to personally decide to start this war, order that execution, abandon that faithful ally to the wolves. And the man willing to make those decisions is given the power to see that they are carried out.

"But he only has the power to make those particular decisions—he can't decide contrary to the interests of those he represents. If he tries to avoid that war, that execution, the loss of that faithful ally, then the power goes to the next man willing to make those decisions.

"*I* can't pull the Corporation out of the Drift. Too much money is involved. Those who reap the benefit of the Corporation will simply refuse to believe that Fitzgibbon isn't bluffing. If I move against their interests, they'll simply replace me."

"Maybe so," Patrick said. "But you could still lose the war.

It wouldn't be at all hard for a man of your ability."

"I concede the point." Keith spread his hands wide. "I could—if I wanted—fight so bad a war as to leave your forces in a winning position. But why should I? Even if I were totally convinced that Fitzgibbon can actually deliver on his threat— Boston isn't my city. Let him destroy Boston, and then I'll negotiate. But only to save Philadelphia, not because I care diddly-squat about some jerkwater metropolis in the Greenstate."

"Ah," Victoria said. She looked down on her paper with satisfaction. She had to hold herself upright with one hand, but still the map she had drawn was neat and tidy. "Excuse me, I didn't mean to interrupt. Please go on." She began writing small numbers on the map, distributing them in a gridlike pattern.

Keith looked annoyed. "Tell me the location of the lab where the radioactives are to be processed. You can't bluff me, and you've got nothing to buy with. If you want to stop Fitzgibbon, the burden is on yourself."

"Fitzgibbon left me to die," Victoria said. "He knew that I might live long enough to talk with you, but he didn't bother to shoot me. I have not the faintest idea in hell where he plans to process the radioactives." She finished the numbers, drew a series of long, looping lines. "Here." She handed the map to Piotrowicz.

"What's this?" he asked suspiciously.

"It's a map. There's Philadelphia down in the corner; you see where the rivers come together? And the numbers are radiation counts, and if you connect them up, it ought to be fairly obvious to anyone that Philadelphia actually lies inside the Drift. Not outside, like almost everyone believes. Inside."

"Where did you get this?" Keith cried, horrified.

"What does it matter where I got it? Your question is, does anybody else know about it?"

"Yes." Keith almost whispered the word.

"An identical copy of this map is in the hands of my uncle. You may even know him—Robert Esterhaszy? He certainly remembers you."

"The dwarf," Piotrowicz said. Then: "What is it you want?"

But when she told him, he shook his head. "No. I won't do it." He stood and walked to the barred window. It was bright outside, and the street was empty. At last he said, "I've done a lot of dirt in my time, and gotten damned little for it in return. Why should I even bother?" When nobody answered, he said, "Damn it, what's in it for me?"

"Nothing." Already Victoria was tiring; the effort she put into holding herself upright made her tremble. "Remember what you said about power. There's only one decision you can make, isn't there? You have the power—and you have to make the decision."

It was noon. People had been gathering in Honkeytonk all day. They thronged the center square—every Drift Corporation employee and indentured colonist that Piotrowicz could order to attend, every Drifter laborer that his Corporation Mummers could march in to watch.

"Supposedly they're all here because I want to teach them an object lesson," Piotrowicz said sourly. He pushed his mask down and spat, working his mouth in a ugly way. "This is what my life comes to. My own people hate me already." He handed Patrick his transceiver. Battered and familiar, the leather scarred and cracking at the edges, it was an old and faithful friend refound. He ran a hand over its surface.

"Break their hearts," Piotrowicz said.

He started to walk away, then returned. "I must be getting senile—I forgot to give you this." He handed Patrick a folded document, then headed for the reviewing stand.

In the center of the square, stackwood had been piled high around a tall, upright pole. Mummers were soaking the pile with coal oil.

Opposite Patrick, almost in a line with the stake, Victoria stood straight and poised in a long white dress. She was held in an open wooden cage, and guards kept the crowd at a distance. No one could get close enough to see how she had been dosed with painkillers to preserve the illusion of cool, proud defiance.

Already a few scattered individuals were casting glances his way. Informing each other that *there* was the Southern traitor who had turned in Victoria Paine.

Patrick looked down at the pardon in his hand, thought back to what Victoria had told him—years ago, it seemed—in the townhouse. "They'll hate you for it. Your name will be a curse for centuries to come in this part of the world, if we work this right." She had smiled through her pain then, shrugged and said, "Still, every martyr needs her Judas."

There was an ironic resonance to that thought, and Patrick discovered Victoria's presence inside his head again. He looked up and saw her smiling blearily at him across the square. His joints ached in sympathetic pain. He felt the irons about her wrists. She was straining to reach him; he could feel the effort reflected in her body—the tension up the side of her neck, the involuntary tremble of a muscle in her cheek. Until finally, as if from a great distance he thought he heard what might have been the merest echo of her whispered voice. The words evaded him, but the meaning did not. It was a goodbye.

It hit him then—and not for the first time—that all might fail, their plans and schemes, everything. Would the people of the Drift actually rally to the memory of a dead martyr? Here and now, with the dirt hard and real underfoot, with the sun hot on his head and harsh to his eyes . . . he could not believe. They were about to burn Victoria alive, and all for an abstraction, something intangible and theoretical.

A hand balled itself into a fist, unclenched. There was nothing he could do.

The charges were being read. Treason, sedition, subversion—more abstracts. Something about vampirism. It seemed to go on forever. After a time, Victoria found her eyes drooping. There came a flash of vision then, from Patrick to her and back, and she saw herself in the dock. She was tall and proud and in his eyes she was beautiful, as beautiful as a flame. A light breeze whipped her hair up, twisting and soaring, as if she were burning already.

Victoria straightened, suppressing a smile. The breeze felt good on her skin.

The smell of coal oil was pungent. Patrick wanted to look away and never look back. He wanted to break the link between himself and Victoria, wanted to kneel in the dirt and vomit up all the poisonous memories from his body. Tears began streaming down his face, and he couldn't for the life of him imagine where they came from.

Piotrowicz mounted the reviewing stand. Even from the far fringes of the crowd, Patrick could see how the other officials edged away from the old man. A guard standing by Victoria, and seen by no other eyes, made the sign of the horns at Piotrowicz, to ward off evil. The old Mummer stood in the eye of the crowd's gathering hate, as if oblivious to it.

He flapped a hand impatiently for the show to begin.

Victoria's hands were uncuffed, and she was jerked roughly out from the dock. She stumbled, and recovered easily enough, but she stubbed a toe in doing so, and the pain was annoyingly distracting. There was old straw ground into the earth underfoot. She noticed a child with mask askew, and her fingers ached to straighten it.

A set of wooden steps ran up the stackwood. The guards—one to each arm—allowed her to mount the stairs slowly, with some dignity, though the one to the left seemed anxious to get it over with. He tugged at her lightly as they climbed. There was an awkward moment as the cuffs were relocked behind her, so that she was chained to the stake. Then the steps were removed, and she stood atop the pyre, alone.

The view was good from up there. The colors were bright and clear; she could pick out Patrick's brown eyes from among the thousands that stared up at her. Tears dimmed Patrick's vision, and she washed away, only to be replaced again by the view from her own eyes.

It was strange. Standing there, knowing how little time she had left, she loved them all, from Patrick on down. She would have been perfectly happy if this moment could be frozen so that she stood looking at them all forever.

A hooded man appeared from nowhere, brandishing a smoky torch. He whirled it three times about his head, and threw.

It arched toward the wood.

Esterhaszy should not have been present. Indeed, their entire scheme would fall apart if Piotrowicz were to spot him. But the dwarf was in among the crowd, and Patrick glimpsed him at the front, among the people who had to be held back by a line of Mummers. Victoria saw him, white-faced and taut, straining as close as he could get to the fire. And when the torch landed at her feet, touched the wood, he screamed before the flames could even reach her.

The first flame touched Victoria, licked the front of her dress. Patrick flinched but did not close his eyes.

The pain was liquid, and it ran right through Victoria, pushing aside the painkillers as if they did not exist, searing through to the marrow of her bones. But she did not forget her duty. Blood trickled down Patrick's throat; he had bitten through his tongue.

"Freedom!" Victoria screamed as the flames wrapped themselves about her. "Rise up!"

The air was hot. The fever of summer had reached a peak, and was about to break. Autumn was almost upon them.

It was nearly harvest time.

MORE SCIENCE FICTION ADVENTURE!